Struggle
to
Survive

Struggle
to
Survive

A story about
Operation Babylift

WILLIAM T. YALEY

STRUGGLE TO SURVIVE

Copyright © 2015 by William T. Yaley

10 9 8 7 6 5 4 3 2

ISBN: 978-0-9912451-8-5

Published by
CORBY BOOKS
A Division of Corby Publishing, LP
P.O. Box 93
Notre Dame, IN 46556

Manufactured in the United States of America

To Arlene, with all my love.

ACKNOWLEDGEMENTS

I am grateful to all the people who have encouraged me to write this book, especially my loving wife, Arlene. Without her constant positive motivation and help, this story would not have been told.

Also, a special thanks to my writers' group- Dr. Chuck Mosher, Carole Snee, Tjode Favier, Kathy Brady and Meg Keoppen-for your invaluable input and innumerable insights. Thanks also to Ruth Shane and Rich Keller and Professor Robert Garratt.

I want to give a special thanks to Sister Kateri Koverman for sharing her heartfelt experiences with me. Her courageous life motivated me to put this story into print.

To Jim Langford and Tim Carroll of Corby Books for believing in me, and to Kerry Temple and Jeff Hamilton for all of your help.

CHAPTER

1

Has a 50 caliber round hit me in the chest? Did shrapnel from an incoming mortar rip through me? Lying on the deck, I'm half-awake. My eyelids are two lead weights falling toward the ground. Is this a dream? I look up and see two people trying to talk to me. I hear myself yelling, "Get the children out! Help them!" My shirt is soaking wet. My head floats in space. Now I relax. A beautiful white dove flies past me into the azure blue sky. I'm weightless. Is this the final minute of my life? How did I get here? Scenes begin to reel out before me like a movie stream. My eyes are opening to my past life. Suddenly the frame freezes at 1975.

I'm checking myself in the bathroom mirror, and see a young man of twenty-nine years. Brand new tan slacks, a bright yellow button down shirt, a solid blue tie and penny loafers confirm my presence. As I finish putting some Brylcreem on my freshly cut hair, I walk into the kitchen and pour myself a cup of savoring Folgers. I'm enjoying this hot cup of coffee,

1

and begin to rehearse in my mind how I will handle my first day on the job at Christian Adoption Services in San Francisco.

My apartment in San Bruno, California is about 800 square feet with off-white walls, which haven't seen paint in many years. The dark green shag carpeting holds many months of hidden dust. There is one bedroom, a bathroom, a living room and a kitchen. The gas stove, oven, and white cupboards round out the typical décor of the 1970's. It's a palace compared to the way I lived in Vietnam five years ago as an Infantry Platoon Commander in "G" Company, Second Battalion, Third Marines. Back then, I had constant thoughts: "I never want to sleep on the ground again. Camping? No way! Will I make it through the day? Will this war ever end?"

Gazing through the kitchen window at the small backyard, I suddenly remember those striking children in South Vietnam.

> Wow! How they loved us Americans. I can still see their little soiled faces with the wide grins and their bare feet as they begged us for any type of food. They were so thankful for the can of peaches from my C-rations or the piece of candy from my backpack. These children were innocent victims of the war, but they were always smiling. I truly wished we could have saved them all.

These children are the reason I decided to go back to school and get my Masters Degree in Sociology from the University of Notre Dame. I want to return to Vietnam and work with these astonishing casualties of war. Children, especially orphaned ones, are typically the forgotten victims of all conflicts.

Jumping into my seventeen-year-old black and white Ford Fairlane convertible and pulling out of the driveway on Easton Avenue, I head for the 101 Freeway to San Francisco. I accelerate onto the freeway from San Bruno Avenue and merge onto the 65 mile per hour traffic listening to "Let It Be" by the Beatles. The cool January air blows through the car. The broken parts on the dashboard create many strange sounds. Vehicles buzz by on the left and cut in front of me. The beautiful San Francisco Bay on the right and the mountains above Brisbane soothe and comfort me. Jet airplanes from the San Francisco International Airport take off over the car. My mind again flashes back to Vietnam in 1970.

> The atmosphere around Danang was full of activity as the F-4 Phantoms, helicopters, and C-130 transport planes made repeated holes in the cloud-covered sky. The earth shook. Shells, launched from as far away as ten miles from Navy ships in the South China Sea, were lobbed near our foxholes.

> I again remembered all the children who suffered from the atrocities committed by the Viet Cong during this most dangerous war. I can still hear the screaming of the young Vietnamese mother as she tried to pick up the remains of her small child who just stepped on a land mind. *Why the children? They are innocent.*

Beads of sweat develop on my forehead, and the wind from the damp South San Francisco climate cools me down. A horn honks as I turn into the exit lane and arrive at 555 Folsom Street in San Francisco. I quickly realize I have to find the parking lot for my new office. The signage points to a wide-open arena of asphalt with white striping across the street from the office. My watch shows me I have about ten minutes to get to the fourth floor to report to my new boss, Mr. Robert Darcy.

Quickly walking to the elevator in the brightly lit lobby of the newly renovated, six story building, I find that a crowd of people, who all appear to be going to the same place, surrounds me. I act as if I have done this every day for the past ten years in order to blend into the mass. *This is like being in a can of sardines! I'm a marathoner in the middle of a pack in a race of 2000 people!* The elevator stops at the fourth floor, and I edge my way out as the door slowly opens. To the right is a sign over a glass door that points to "Christian Adoption Services".

Inside the office, the small lobby is decorated with 1950's flowery wallpaper and brown commercial carpeting with white specks. Two chairs, a small wooden table with lamp, and two nondescript paintings of rural farms on the wall complete the meager furnishings of this room. A motherly looking woman, who reminds me of my very proper grandmother, sits behind a grey metal desk. She is dressed in a light brown skirt with a light blue blouse. Her whitish grey hair is neatly combed and is cut just above her neck. She looks about fifty-five years old.

"May I help you, Sir?"

"Yes Ma'm. My name is John Ellis, and I'm checking in here as a new social worker to prepare for my assignment in Vietnam," sounding as if I'm in the Marine Corps and reporting for duty.

Softly she replies, "Nice to meet you John. I'm Sister Mary Grace. Please be seated. Mr. Darcy will be with you in a few minutes."

My right foot uncontrollably taps as I fidget with my college ring on my right hand and think about going back to Vietnam. The Vietnam War, like all previous wars, produced an abundance of orphaned children, many of them the products of native Vietnamese women and the foreign soldiers who are mostly American. In Vietnam, these "Amerasian" orphans are in severe danger since most of the American servicemen have been pulled out of the country by now. To the North Vietnam soldiers and the Viet Cong, the Amerasians are a sure sign of American Imperialism. These innocent children are at risk if the North Vietnamese Army overruns South Vietnam. Many of these children could be massacred or imprisoned for no other reason except they had an American father. Many of the Vietnamese mothers have left these children on the streets or dropped them off at orphanages or clinics throughout Vietnam.

"Mr. Ellis?"

"Yes sir," I respond and stand up at attention.

I'm face to face with a six-foot plus gentleman, dressed in khaki trousers and a rust colored short sleeve cotton shirt. He looks about forty and has a pleasant smile. His meticulous appearance is highlighted with brown loafers polished to a reflective sheen, trousers neatly pressed, and his blondish hair combed to perfection.

"Nice seeing you again, John. Please relax, and come into my office."

"Thank you, Mr. Darcy." I quickly respond. *Calm down John.*

"Just call me Bob," he casually replies as I follow him.

I walk into Mr. Darcy's office and my metabolism slows down. Relaxation starts to set in.

"Happy to have you aboard, John. We have such a great need for more social workers at our orphanages in Vietnam. After a few weeks of orientation in this office, you'll be assigned to work in the Binh Trieu Orphanage near Saigon. I would like you to start your classes tomorrow. Will that work for you?"

"That would be great, Bob."

My heart beats faster as I realize that I'm going back to Vietnam. Maybe I **can** make a difference in this world!

What that "difference" would be will even be a surprise to me.

On the drive back home, I'm humming "Sentimental Journey," my favorite calming song as I hear a newscaster discussing the merits of Gerald Ford being our new President after Richard Nixon's resignation this past summer. The trip back to Vietnam is only weeks away. How will I react when arriving back in the country in which I have fought a war? Will there be anger? Will I be frightened? Surely, I was scared the last time I was there. Will I be able to use my social service education? I can barely contain my excitement. Looking in the rear view mirror, I smile broadly.

The next four weeks of orientation in the San Francisco office of Christian Adoption Services are exciting and enlightening as I learn more about the history and customs of Vietnam. With five other social workers in the class, I'm able to practice some of the common language phrases. Wow, what a difficult language is spoken there! Some of the phrases come back from my days as a Marine in Vietnam. But, now I'll have to speak some Vietnamese on a daily basis. I never was very good at learning languages, but my determination to master as much as possible of the singsong Vietnamese dialect drives me on. Our instructors have spent time in some of the orphanages in Vietnam and the stories they share are overwhelming.

Many of the tasks facing me in the orphanages weren't taught in my Masters classes—care of babies, feeding and changing diapers, extensive first aid, and dealing with burn victims and mental problems. We see films about children brought to the orphanage with polio, burns, deformed and missing limbs and with broken bones. Doubts fill my mind in class. Can I handle working with disabled children and all of their needs? One of the instructors talks about the Black Amerasians (children of a Vietnamese mother and a Black American father). These children are the most at risk. He says we have to protect them, and find families anywhere in the world to adopt them.

The paperwork involved in foreign adoptions is voluminous. Adopting a child from Vietnam is a cumbersome procedure that sometimes takes up to a year to process. I study religiously, and spend most of my evenings eating McDonald's hamburgers and fries while I crack the books. My body and mind are exhausted, but excitement persists. After all, this is my new job, at least for the next few years.

After four intense weeks, orientation is over. I stuff my belongings into an old light brown leather suitcase I used in college. I'm allowed only one large piece of luggage for the trip since there is limited space in the orphanages. It's February 23, 1975. I've learned the bare minimum of how to handle children from infants to ten year olds in four weeks, and they tell me I'm ready to work in an orphanage in Vietnam. My hands are clammy when I close the safety lock on the suitcase.

A horn honks outside. My good friend, and former Marine buddy, Jerry McBride sits in his bright red Corvette waiting to drive me to the airport. Jerry went to work as a stockbroker after his stint in the Corps. He loved the stock market even when we were stationed together at Camp Pendleton after our tour in Vietnam. *Looks like he is doing okay in business.*

I pick up the suitcase, grab a small carry-on bag, and quickly walk out to greet Jerry.

"Hi Jerry. Thanks for picking me up."

"Well Johnny boy. Are you ready for this assignment?"

With pride in my voice, I respond: "Jerry, I was born ready for this!"

He laughs and knows how I feel. We were both Lieutenants in "G" Company. Jerry and I experienced the horrors of that war. He understands how I feel about those children in Vietnam.

After putting my belongings in the back seat of the Corvette, I hop into the passenger seat, and Jerry leaves a strip of rubber as we head off to the San Francisco International Airport. Jerry drives just like he lives—in the fast lane. Ten minutes later, after our high-speed ride, he pulls his red Corvette up to the passenger terminal at San Francisco International Airport. I breathe again.

"Good luck, buddy. Keep in touch. Semper Fi."

"Thanks, Jerry. Semper Fi." The "Always Faithful" Marine Corps greeting reflects our special bond.

I jump out of the car, pull my luggage from the back seat, and head to the ticket counter for my Pan American flight to Tan Son Nhat Airport in Saigon.

After an uneventful six-hour flight to Oahu, Hawaii, we take off, on the second leg of the trip, for Tokyo. We have a two-hour lay-over in Japan for refueling before proceeding to Vietnam. When the plane lifts off from Tokyo, my entire body is wide awake. The pilot of this Boeing 720 announces that we'll be arriving at Tan Son Nhat Airport in approximately seven hours. He indicates that the airplane will make a quick, steep, landing at the airport due to possible hostile small arms fire. It's ten o'clock in the morning.

Wow! That's all I need to hear. I thought the war was almost over!

My left foot nervously taps as I wait for the landing in Vietnam. Finally, after I down a cup of coffee, the airplane begins descending toward Tan Son Nhat Airport. The surrounding area is green with a criss-crossing of rice paddies and small villages. Various military vehicles, along with some C-130 transport planes and helicopters, rest on the airport tarmac.

My heart misses a beat as the airplane starts to dive, and then makes a sharp left turn before leveling off for the final approach. In what seems like thirty seconds, I hear the wheels touch down on the concrete surface. The aircraft barely slows down, and heads toward a Quonset hut, surrounded by U.S. Marines with their M-16's at the "ready" position. As we move toward them, the plane bounces in and out of potholes.

Finally, the stewardess' voice comes over the intercom after the Captain expertly leads the plane to the building. She professionally announces, "Ladies and gentlemen, please exit the airplane as quickly as possible and proceed to the hut on your right side as soon as we come to a full stop." This announcement triggers thoughts of jumping in and out of helicopters during the war in Vietnam.

> The H-34 Sikorsky helicopters in which we practiced our maneuvers at Camp Pendleton, California were nothing like the ones in the combat zones of Vietnam. The ones in the states were clean, had nice seats with seat belts, fully secured doors and bulletproof glass windows. Jumping into a "chopper" that was full of bullet holes, and had no seats, no windows, and no doors in Vietnam was a chilling reality. I remember climbing into one with fifteen Marines under my command and the co-pilot yells at me, "Two of you jump out. We can't get this fucking chopper off the ground." Without hesitation, I ordered two of my men to get out and wait for the next chopper. My palms were sweaty. *They told me at Camp Pendleton that these H-34s hold sixteen fully combat-loaded troops. I guess the heat and humidity doesn't allow a full load in Vietnam.* I held on for dear life as we took off for some far off landing zone shown on my outdated map. The chopper was shaking like a patient with malaria as we barely cleared the treetops of a canopied jungle. After about thirty minutes, we made a steep decent and the crew chief told me to get my troops ready to disembark.
>
> "When I say "out", you get out immediately," he yelled above the noise of the helicopter blades. "Do you understand, Lieutenant?" I acknowledged his statement by raising my hand, and readied my men

to get out of the chopper. A short twenty seconds later, the crew chief shouts, "Out."

We were still ten feet off the ground when he started screaming at my men to jump. At about six feet off the ground, we were jumping off the chopper into tall thick elephant grass, half falling and half running to a rendezvous point designated with a red smoke grenade. Small arms fire from hidden snipers was popping in front of us. We couldn't see anyone because of the blinding green elephant grass, which was at least seven feet high. The confusion overwhelmed me. Sweat poured off me, and my utility shirt stuck to my chest as I gathered my men and waited for the next chopper to bring the rest of my platoon to the landing zone. Finally, all of my men were off the choppers and the head count showed everyone was okay. We were ready to move out for another six day patrolling assignment. Enemy fire had ceased. My Marines froze as they waited for their orders from me.

Upon hearing the stewardess' voice as the airplane halts, I jump back to reality. We exit, and walk quickly toward the designated grey building. We pass the Marines and move into the barren Quonset hut, which has a few wooden folding chairs scattered haphazardly.

A young Marine Captain, in camouflaged jungle utilities, stands in front of us. He has a ruddy face with grains of dust in the creases of his eyes. He wears a steel helmet, and a holstered Colt 45 strapped to his waist. He tells us all to gather around him.

"Welcome to South Vietnam. I hope you had an enjoyable flight. Buses are waiting outside to take you into Saigon. Once you get to the Majestic Hotel in downtown

Saigon, your representatives will meet you. Your luggage will be unloaded for you and put in the buses parked behind this building. Any questions?"

I listen to some of the passengers mundane questions. Sweat dribbles down my face from the ninety percent humidity and one hundred plus degree temperature. *Where is that San Bruno fog and wind when you need it!*

After about three minutes of questions and answers, two Marines, fully armed with M-16s, hand grenades, and K-Bar knives in their belts, guide us to the buses. They are so young. They don't look much older than my sixteen-year-old nephew who is still in high school.

Although apprehensive, I enjoy the bus ride into Saigon. Our driver dodges hundreds of bicycles and motor bikes, which are weaving in and out like busy ants hurriedly trying to find their separate colonies. Looking at the streets of Saigon, it's hard to believe a war is still going on in this country. The smells of pho, cooking on open pots along the streets, permeate the heavy air. Pho is a staple in Vietnam. It's a spicy noodle soup dish with chicken or beef. I watch the beautiful young women in their traditional ao dai dresses and white conical hats riding bicycles and as passengers on the back of motor bikes. Street merchants bark at passers-bys to purchase their vegetables, fruit or various other foods. This is truly a contrast to the war, which is still going on throughout the country of Vietnam. These people seem unaware of this catastrophic situation in their country. I notice many South Vietnamese military personnel and vehicles on the road. A jeep carrying two United States Marines, with their M-16's at the "ready" position, passes us on the right. We pass some military personnel carriers, 4x4 trucks, and tanks parked on a side street.

Arriving at the Majestic Hotel, I feel as if I'm in downtown San Francisco. The hotel is located across the street from the Saigon River, host to a myriad of boats—some floating markets, some homes, and some fishing boats. These watercraft create their own city on the river. The Majestic is a beautiful structure, constructed in the 1920's and refurbished in the 1950's during the French occupation of this country.

A young, well-dressed Vietnamese man greets us and escorts us into a lavish lobby. The expensive red velvet chairs and couches highlight the brownish colored tile floor. The massive overhead chandeliers sparkle like a ballroom dance rotating light. The hotel is bustling with people. Many are in military uniforms from various countries. Ex-patriots and reporters, with cameras hanging around their necks, roam the lobby. Some of the men are dressed in suits with ties. It reminds me of a convention in the United States.

"John Ellis. Are you John Ellis?"

I turn toward the voice on my left. I see a modestly dressed lady about forty years old. She's wearing a white blouse and dark brown pants, topped off with an Australian-type backcountry hat. Sporting a pleasant smile, she sticks out her right hand to greet me.

"Hi John. I'm Sister Anne Marie from the Binh Trieu orphanage. I have a van outside for our drive to the orphanage. It'll take us about thirty minutes. Please grab your gear and follow me."

Sister Anne Marie and I walk around the side of the

hotel to a narrow street. She points out the Volkswagen bus we'll be taking to Binh Trieu. My eyes pop open an extra twenty degrees as I look at the ten-plus year old vehicle. It was white, but is now a dusty brown with nearly balding tires, enough dents to have been driven in a destruction derby, and at least three cracked windows.

I quickly throw my suitcase in the back of the bus, and jump into the "shotgun" seat. Sister Anne Marie is already starting up the engine, which sounds like nails bouncing around in a tin can. She backs the vehicle out of the parking space, puts it in gear, and we're on the road to Binh Trieu.

Sister Anne Marie drives like she's Richard Petty in a Winston Cup race at Darlington, South Carolina. She's dodging bicycles, motor bikes and pedestrians as she casually holds a conversation with me.

"John, I hope you're ready to go to work as soon as we get there."

CHAPTER

2

My armpits are soaking wet and the blood in my fingers stops flowing from squeezing the side of the van door.

"Wow that was quite a ride, Sister! How'd you learn to drive in and out of your lane, dodging all of those motorbikes and bicycles at that speed?"

"Just practice, John. There are no rules of the road in Vietnam. Everyone for themselves, or you don't survive."

I finally relax as the van slows down when we arrive in the little village of Binh Trieu around six-thirty in the evening. The setting sun peeks through the broken grey cloud cover. "Dirt poor" is hardly an adequate description of the village. The main street is "paved," with potholes about every three yards. The remainder of the town is dirt walkways and dusty side streets. Most of the stores along the street are little shanties consisting of wood or metal siding with canvas and metal roofs. These buildings look like the homemade forts my friends and

I used to build in vacant lots when I was a kid. Intermittently, an unpainted stucco one-story building appears. Landscaping is nonexistent. Trash is everywhere and the smell of sewage is dominant. Cows meander in the streets. Merchants, dressed in black pajama bottoms and various colored loose fitting shirts, squat in front of their stores selling vegetables. Many are wearing the traditional bamboo conical hats. They hawk a myriad of food items, including raw fish and freshly skinned chickens. Mothers hold partially naked children in one arm as they tend to their stores. Some bare footed children help their parents, while others play in the dirt. The fish sauce and cilantro smell of pho, cooking on open fires, is ever-present in the thick humid air.

Friendly waves come our way from the adults and children along the roadway as our Volkswagen bus slowly passes by. The womens' smiles show the black betel nut stains on their front teeth from years of chewing the mild stimulant, detracting from their pretty faces and beautiful jet-black eyes. The presence of war is visible. South Vietnamese soldiers and brown military vehicles roam the streets. While staring at these road scenes, my mind wanders back to 1970 and those villages, which were in the path of our guerilla operations near Le My.

> The women and children stared at us as we passed through their squalid village. The Viet Cong had ransacked it the previous night. Women cried as they carried the dead body of their village chief, who was murdered by the Viet Cong. Our medic diligently worked on the young children who were wounded because they happened to be in the path of the hand grenade explosions. The putrid air

smelled of burned flesh and drying blood, and the once bamboo shacks were nothing but ashes. We gave pieces of candy from our backpacks to the children, which caused small smiles across their dirty faces. *War is a mess! These kids didn't do anything to deserve this! Tears found their way over the dust on my cheekbones.*

I'm jolted back to the present as our van hits one of the big potholes in the road. We pull up to a plain brownish one-story stucco building, with toys scattered in front. Children play in the sand. After Sister Anne Marie parks the vehicle, children run toward her like a group of puppies racing to their feeding dishes. She greets them with her infectious smile as we walk to the front door.

"This is Binh Trieu Orphanage. Welcome to your new home," she casually tells me. I follow her into the building.

Heading down the hall, we stop at a closed door. When she opens it, my jaw drops, and my eyes open as wide as an owl at midnight. The room is no bigger than ten by ten, filled with at least a dozen children, from infants to six or seven year olds. The babies lie in little wooden cribs, two to a bed, and the older children sit on mats, which cover the floor. One little girl, about four years old, has burn scars on her arms and legs. A boy about the same age has a totally deformed leg, which appears to be damaged from polio. Some of the children whine and cry, but generally, the room is relatively quiet as I watch two adults helping the children. Most of the non-infants are skinny and dressed in black pajama bottoms and various colored cotton T-shirts. The clothes are clean, but meager. Whimpers turn to smiles as Sister Anne Marie weaves around the room greeting the children with hugs. It's evident the children love her.

An Oriental looking woman, about thirty years old and around five feet tall, dressed in a light green skirt, white blouse and white apron, walks over to me and introduces herself as Sister Elizabeth. She's beautiful, with smooth white skin, eloquent slanted eyes, and neatly cut short black hair. *She sure doesn't look like the nuns who taught me in grade school!*

"You must be John Ellis?" So nice to meet you. We surely can use your help. Please let me show you to your quarters."

"Nice meeting you, Sister."

I follow her to another small room. This room is barren except for an old canvas army cot, and a grey metal desk with a gooseneck lamp. The walls are an off-white color. The few nails showing are in definite need of some pictures to brighten up the space. There is one slightly opened window viewing a rice field bordered by an area which looks and smells like a refuse dump. The wooden floors are dust free and shine from the many layers of lacquer. A tiny bathroom adjoins the room.

"Make yourself comfortable. After you unpack your things, please join us in the kitchen for dinner," she says.

During a pleasant meal of pho, rice and some steamed vegetables, I'm introduced to a Vietnamese nurse, Sister Nguyen, who is not much older than I, and Sister Joan McKenny, a social worker from the United States who looks about forty. Sister Joan is the supervisor of this orphanage. Sister Nguyen is about five feet tall, wearing dark slacks and a light grey blouse. She's slender and her jet-black hair falls down to the middle of her back. Sister Joan looks to be near five feet ten, and towers over Sister Nguyen. She's dressed in tan slacks, a dark blue flowery shirt and the typical white apron worn by the staff. The black marks under her eyes indicate that she's overworked and tired. When speaking, her voice has a command presence like a colonel in the military.

She introduces me to two female Vietnamese volunteers. Jet lag starts to hit me, and I'm daydreaming as everyone at the table is discussing the day's activities.

After dinner Sister Joan shows me around the entire building which consists of three small bedrooms full of children, a kitchen, three bathrooms, and five additional tiny rooms for the staff. The total building can't be more than two thousand square feet, and there are at least thirty children and the staff living here. The children range in age from infancy to eight years old. Many of the children in the orphanage are Amerasians, some with very dark skin.

After my tour, Sister Joan says, "You'd better get a good night's sleep since we start our days at five o'clock in the morning."

"Good idea, Sister. I'm beat."

Heading back to my room, I think the idea of exhaustion is about to be redefined for me.

Morning comes in an instant. A tap on the door awakens me. The table clock reads 5:00 AM as I roll off my cot, go into the bathroom to shave and shower. Breakfast is earlier than I am used to at home.

Sounds of children crying and little voices chattering in Vietnamese fill the building. At breakfast, Sister Joan explains to me that I'll be working alongside Sister Elizabeth and Sister Nguyen.

"Just watch Sister Elizabeth and Sister Nguyen and they'll guide you. We have a lot to do. They'll assign you your working shifts. Also, you and I will be taking trips to some remote areas soon to pick up new children."

After breakfast Sister Elizabeth and I walk into one of the children's' rooms. She hands a baby to me and says, "Just hold him. That's all he needs. His name is Binh."

Her prediction rings true. Little Binh snuggles against my rib cage. He appears to be about five months old but I learn later that he's actually nine months. He's a victim of a condition known as "Failure to Thrive". My research explains that children who fail to thrive don't receive, or are unable to take in, retain, or utilize the calories needed to gain weight and grow as expected. After birth, a child's brain grows as much in the first year as it will grow during the rest of their life. Poor nutrition during this period can have permanent negative effects on mental and physical development. Since many of the children in this orphanage are found on the streets or abandoned by their mothers, their early nourishment is unclear. If the condition progresses, starving children may become disinterested in their surroundings or may not reach development milestones like sitting up, crawling, walking and talking at the usual age. Unfortunately, some of them may give up and die.

Binh has a light coat of black hair, smooth brown skin

and tiny fingers and toes. He feels so weightless to me. He isn't crying, but cuddles his little body into my arms. *Where did you come from, Binh? Who's your mom? Please don't die on me.*

I hear the slow beat of his heart as he closes his eyes and falls asleep. I walk over to a chair and sit down, contemplating my surroundings. The sounds of children crying and chattering bounce off the thin stucco walls of the orphanage. A mixture of English and Vietnamese languages fills the building. Sister Joan walks past holding a folder. She glances into the room and keeps moving to her office. Pots, pans and dishes clank in the kitchen as the older children help to clear the tables and clean up after breakfast. The sounds are similar to a nursery school starting the day.

Sister Elizabeth hastily walks into the room, gently takes Binh from me, and says, "Sister Nguyen needs your help in the front bedroom. Please hurry."

When I get to the room, Sister Nguyen is removing the bandages from the arm of a little girl with second-degree burns. The girl grits her teeth, but makes no sound. Her arm is a sea of blisters. I'm faint.

"John, would you hand me that salve on the counter, and take these wrappings and put them in the basket on your left?"

I take the bandages and throw them in the wastebasket. While handing her the salve, bile rises to my throat as I look at the badly burned arm.

"Please hold Chi's hand as I put on the cream. It'll help to calm her."

Chi moans from the intense pain as Sister Nguyen gently puts the salve on the wound. Ooze flows off the burned limb and the smell is overwhelming. Her arm looks like a twisted yellow and red rope. I'm light headed. *Hold your cool, John. This is your new job.* My whole body aches. After applying the ointment, Sister Nguyen gently wraps the arm with some gauze, and Chi relaxes. Sister then tells Chi to go to the other room and lie down.

"How'd she get burned, Sister?"

"Her village was overrun by the VC (Viet Cong) last month, and they set the whole place on fire. The Viet Cong killed her mother, and no other relatives survived the attack. One of the South Vietnamese soldiers brought Chi here. Her father's in the South Vietnamese army and is off fighting the war somewhere."

The activity continues like this all day. I hold babies, help polio victims walk, assist with first aid, and learn to deal with mental and physical disorders of the children. To top everything off, I hear some explosions far off in the distance. *Must be some more clashes with the North Vietnamese and the Viet Cong.* Those sounds keep reminding me of my military days in Vietnam when incoming mortar rounds and the sounds of artillery overhead made me as tense as a guitar string after tuning.

> I remember lying in a puddle of mud as incoming artillery shells sounded like low flying airplanes over my head. I hoped the artillery forward observer calculated his target correctly. Any mistake and we were in the hereafter! My head rested on a clump of grass and I could smell the water buffalo dung on the side of my face. My body was as low as it could possibly get to avoid the overhead

explosives bursting around us like popcorn in a popper. Concussions of rockets and large artillery rounds made the ground shake and bounce slightly as if stretched out on a trampoline. I hoped it was not going to be the end for me.

"John, are you alright?" says Sister Nguyen.

"Sorry Sister. I was just wondering how we're going to get these children to new homes in the states," I lie, since I don't want her to realize that the terror of a few years ago is still haunting me.

"Don't worry, John. Sister Joan is taking care of it."

After a long day, we settle the children in bed by eight o'clock in the evening, and have a staff meeting in the kitchen. Sister Joan reviews the day's activities and explains the paperwork needed for one of the children who we'll be sending to Saigon in the morning for her trip to the United States to meet her adoptive parents. She also briefs us on the condition of the war. She tells us that reports have been coming in from the United States Embassy that the North Vietnamese have gotten stronger and are planning a move to overtake various cities in South Vietnam. General Giap, the military commander of the North Vietnamese army, claims his forces are capable of controlling the entire Vietnamese nation. Since the United States military has withdrawn from the war two years ago, the South Vietnamese army has slowly been collapsing.

Sister's comments are somewhat upsetting to me.

"What'll we do if the North Vietnamese do overrun the country? What about all of the children who need to get to their adoptive parents in America?" I ask.

"We'll get them out of here. We're making progress every day," Sister Joan matter-of-factly says.

Our meeting adjourns at around nine o'clock and I head directly to my room. I fall on my cot like a worn out trout after a long fight with a fisherman. My body hits the bed like a ton of bricks. As I think about the day's activities, I wonder if I'm cut out for this type of work. *Too late to worry about that John. You're here and there's a job to do!*

I hear a knock on the door. Is it five in the morning already? I just fell asleep!

Sister Joan states in her best command voice, "Breakfast will be served in half an hour."

The five-in-the-morning to nine or ten o'clock at night routine prevails for the next two weeks. I learn more and more about taking care of children. Boy, would my mother be proud! Sister Elizabeth and Sister Nguyen are great instructors. I'm relaxing around the children and become more closely attached to many of them. I'm also doing much paperwork to accelerate the process of getting the children on their way to their adoptive parents in the States.

It is early March 1975 and we hear reports from the U.S. Embassy of massive North Vietnamese forces moving into South Vietnam. President Nguyen Van Thieu of South Vietnam orders the withdrawal of South Vietnamese troops from II Corps in the Central Highlands. II Corps is one of four Corps areas of South Vietnam designated by the Army of The Republic of Vietnam (ARVN). It is in the middle of South Vietnam, just north of Saigon. The major city of Ban Me Thuot falls to the North Vietnamese Army. There are reports of retreating refugees crushed by North Vietnamese tanks and fired upon by North Vietnamese artillery. Thousands of refugees move south toward Saigon.

During breakfast, Sister Joan discusses the two trips she took to the United States last month. "I pleaded with American families to consider adopting black Amerasians. I met with various adoption agencies and groups of potential adoptive parents, telling them that these children are in danger of being killed by the North Vietnamese since they are an obvious sign of American imperialism," she says.

She looks exhausted, but continues optimistically. "I did find some families who are willing to take black Amerasians," she proudly states. "Although many of the children in our orphanage are already assigned to adoptive parents in the United States, I'm working zealously to find parents for the mentally and physically disabled children. In the past few weeks, about ten children have been transported to the States. Another ten have arrived in the orphanage, mostly from refugees flowing into Saigon," she continues.

"John, tomorrow we'll be picking up some children in outlying areas. We need to increase our efforts to get the children out of Vietnam soon since more reports are coming in from the embassy and our main office that massive military movements by the North Vietnamese are overtaking more cities north of Saigon," she states.

"How far away are these children?" I ask

"It's just a few hours from here. I'll brief you about our trip in the morning," she answers.

I'm tense as I think about an "outlying area." I remember going on patrols with my Marines to these areas in front of our lines.

> Back then, I always wondered if it would be my last patrol. My senses were keen and butterflies roamed around in my stomach. Adrenalin pumped through my body from the time we left our battalion area until we safely returned from our patrol. It was "cat and mouse" guerilla warfare. We were looking for the Viet Cong and they were looking for us—each trying to eliminate the other. Our movements were very calculated. We prowled like wolves, always on the alert to our front, back and the sides, searching for the enemy. Would it be him or us? I kept my composure, but it was terrifying.

I walk to my room. I'm anxious. The familiar butterflies find their way into my system. I'm thinking about getting all of these children out of this country to safety and wondering where we'll be picking up additional ones.

Tomorrow should be interesting.

CHAPTER

3

"Hit the deck! Hug the ground!" I yelled to the squad leader, Private Lemon. The incoming mortars had us targeted at our outpost north of Danang. The familiar whistling of 81-millimeter rounds was terrifying. I felt like my blood was freezing. I was flat on my stomach, with my cheek pressed so hard against the damp leaves that they made imprints on my unshaven face. I listened for the impact of the mortars. Again, I wondered if today was going to be my last day on earth.

I wake up abruptly from this dream to the sounds of far off explosions. Quickly jumping out of bed and looking out the tiny window, bright lights flicker in the distance. The horizon lights up periodically like a bulb blinking on and off in a large room. This reminds me of those days during the war when the sounds of exploding artillery shells constantly racked my nerves. The fire in the sky appears to be miles away. It's obvious that the NVA (North Vietnamese Army) is getting closer to us. Glancing over at my alarm clock, I focus on 4:00 AM.

I have only a half an hour to try to sleep. Lying back on the pillow, I recall that night in 1970 when I was sitting cross-legged in a bunker on some unnamed mountain.

> I watched the fireworks near Danang that evening. The sky flickered on and off like a flash bulb on a camera. Sleep was out of the question. I wondered how many Viet Cong were out there waiting to attack. What are they feeling? *Do they have family and friends back home in North Vietnam? Do they want to be here anymore than I do?* These flashbacks haunted me all night. The night was misty on that mountaintop. Just like a well-trained motionless mime, I was not moving but was extremely alert to my surroundings. I continuously thought I saw things move---was it a person, animals, birds, bugs, snakes? Exhaustion set in from lack of sleep, but my eyes continued to focus into the darkness. I was ready to defend myself if attacked. It was like being in a scary movie waiting for a monster to jump out of the bushes. The combination of intermittent light rain, high humidity and pure nervousness turned my shirt into a wet washrag. My senses were as sharp as a razor blade. I sat there trying to concentrate on an area one hundred feet in front of me. I was wrought with fear, with my nerves stretched to the limit.

The knock on my bedroom door nudges me out of the daydream, and a soft voice calls out, "Time to get up. Breakfast will be served in half an hour."

At the kitchen table, Sister Joan discusses our plan for the day. "John, you and I will be driving this morning, for about three hours, to a small village to pick up some orphans. We'll stay there for a few days. After we meet the children, we'll be going to a landing strip, twice a day, to meet an airplane, which will be transporting the children to Saigon. From there, our workers will get them to Binh Trieu orphanage."

After a breakfast of eggs, rice, fruit and toast, and two cups of coffee, Sister Joan says, "We need to be out of here in twenty minutes. We'll meet out front. We're taking the van."

"What do I need to bring with me, Sister?"

"Just yourself and an extra jacket."

Sharply at six o'clock, we leave the orphanage for the village of Tan Ngai. Sister Joan drives like a native of Vietnam—no holds barred on the road. Although there are not many cars, bicycles or motor bikes on the two-lane road at this hour, she passes at will, toots the horn continuously, and drives in whatever lane she desires. *Man, she must have gotten her driver's license in Vietnam!* I try to relax, but I'm as tense as a choirboy walking on stage for his first solo performance. Finally, we're on a deserted two-lane road, heading south. The orange sun lazily shows its colors on our left.

When we arrive in Tan Ngai Village in the Province of Vinh Long, I open the window and breathe in the damp morning air. People squat in front of ramshackle buildings, cooking in open pots. The familiar aroma of pho fills the air. The muddy Mekong River slithers at will along the shores of the village. The mud flows beside sand banks littered with trash. Shacks built on wood stilts line the river. These residences have metal and thatched roofs, wood floors and no windows. A few small boats, guided by men shaded in conical hats, haul fruit and vegetables. These vessels appear to be on their way to a market. People wash clothes in the river and children run and play along the shore.

Near the end of the road, we drive up to the gate of a small Catholic church. The structure is a pinkish color and is of French architecture, with a beautiful wood door and colorful stained glass windows smiling at the drive-way. As we approach, a short Vietnamese priest quickly runs out of the front door of the church to open the gate for us. Sister slides the van into the gravel parking area in front, and the priest directs us to move the vehicle to the side of the building.

Sister Joan and I jump out of the van and walk toward the priest.

"John, I would like you to meet Father Tran, my favorite priest in all of Vietnam," she says with a wide, complimentary grin.

"Hello, Father. My pleasure. Sister has told me much about you."

"Very nice to meet you, John," he says as he offers his hand.

While shaking my hand, he says, "The children are in the vestibule waiting for you." What time are you meeting the plane?"

"We were told the plane will pick up the children around ten o'clock," Sister Joan replies.

"There are five children ready to go with you, Sister. One's an infant and the rest are toddlers. I picked them up at the clinic in the village. Mothers are dropping off more children at the clinic every day because they hear the NVA is closing in on this area. If that happens, they fear for the life of their child, especially if the child is Amerasian. The clinic is running out of room for the orphans."

We all walk into the church with a sense of urgency. The foyer has a musty smell from years of humidy and constant rain. Varnish on the oak floors is barely visible due to the constant wear and tear. A cardboard box lies on the table. An infant wrapped in a multi-colored blanket is tucked inside.

Sister Joan and I look at the baby, and Father Tran says, "She's only four weeks old. She was born at the Tan Ngai Clinic. Her mother gave birth to her there and left the next day. The mother was probably a young teen-age girl with no money, and had no means to take care of the baby. The volunteers named her 'Soon Yen', spelled XUAN YEN. She appears to be Amerasian—maybe black Amerasian."

The beautiful little girl in the cardboard box mesmerizes me. *Oh my God, only four weeks old. What's her future in this world?* She has a head of jet-black hair, round black eyes and soft brown skin. She's so tiny. I was about that size when I was adopted.

"Do these children have adoptive parents waiting for them in the States, Sister?" I ask.

"Yes, all of them will have approved parents waiting for them. This baby will be processed for a family in California. You'll be working on her paperwork when we return to the orphanage, but she won't go to the United States for a few months. She's too young. Also, getting all the papers approved by the South Vietnamese officials can be as slow as a tortoise walking ten miles in deep sand."

I look around the room at the other children and notice they're staring at me with eager eyes. One boy, who looks about three years old, leans on a crutch. He's missing the lower part of his left leg. His smile reaches across his happy face from ear to ear. I judge the other boy and two girls to be about four years old. All are dressed in black pajama bottoms and various colored T-shirts. Although the clothes are clean, little holes in their shirts suggest many months of use. They're all wearing flip-flop sandals. One of the boys and one of the girls are very dark skinned with black curly hair, and their eyes do not have the typical slant of the Vietnamese. *These also must be Amerasians.*

Father Tran interrupts my thoughts. "They're all ready to go. You'd better hurry so you don't miss the ride at the landing strip. After you get these children on the plane, and return here this afternoon, I'll have at least four more children from the clinic ready for you. Be careful. Things are heating up. The North Vietnamese are making life more difficult for us every day. We've got to get these children to Saigon for processing, and out of the country. Our time is limited."

We usher the children into the van. I take little Xuan Yen in the cardboard box and set her on the floor next to my feet. I'm going to make sure she has a safe ride to our pick-up point with the airplane.

The drive to the airstrip is on a dirt road right outside Tan Ngai Village. Although the road is bumpy and dust is coming through the windows, the children don't complain. Chattering in Vietnamese engulfs the back of the van. Explosions erupt in the distance. They are constant reminders that a war is still going on in this country.

After about twenty minutes, we're driving in the middle of nowhere. We pass checkerboards of rice paddies, thick clumps of trees, some shrubbery and a few shacks. The sun is fully awake, shining brightly through the dirty windshield of our van, causing the temperature to rise inside the vehicle.

"John, this is a new landing strip for the pick-up. The last time I was in this area, we met an airplane on the other side on Tan Ngai Village. Hopefully we'll find this airfield."

Sister Joan bounces the van to a stop every few minutes to look at a crumpled map to make sure we find the airstrip. The stop and go is like driving in rush hour traffic that is practically gridlocked.

"Looks like the strip is about another mile. Hold on. The road isn't getting any better," she says.

After about ten more minutes, we come out of a thicket of overhanging trees, and I see an open area about two hundred yards to our left. *That must be the landing strip. Where are we? Where's the plane?* The landing strip is nothing more than a dirt pad about two kilometers long and a hundred feet wide. The ground is uneven and poorly graded. It looks like a rough excavation performed by a D-8 bulldozer.

I hope a plane can land on this.

Sister Joan pulls the van alongside the dirt landing

strip and commands the children in Vietnamese to get out and sit next to the van. The children quickly exit the van and gather in a group on the ground. We look toward the horizon for an airplane. Little Xuan Yen stays at my feet in the front of the van. She is sound asleep.

I hope she's okay. She looks so content.

It's at least an hour before we hear the sound of a plane in the distance. Sister Joan looks through her binoculars, watching the aircraft begin its descent to the airstrip.

As the Cessna 206 is on final approach, my heart beat increases. I'm hoping these children will be flown safely to the orphanage. A dust storm rises as the plane touches down and makes its way down the runway. We all make a quick one eighty to avoid the brown canvas of dust engulfing us. The airplane comes to a stop at the end of the runway, and turns toward us. The aircraft moves slowly in our direction. I notice there are no markings indicating to whom the Cessna belongs. *Is it American or Vietnamese? Is it Air America?*

The airplane has a camouflage paint scheme—two tone brown coloring. Looking closely at the side of it, I notice some holes and large scratches. *Those look like bullet holes! Those are bullet holes!* The co-pilot's window has a large crack and one of the tires is partially flat. The plane looks like it's been in combat!

The pilot maneuvers the small aircraft to our location. It looks like a limping duck, waddling its way to the side of a pond. I worry about these children making it back to Saigon in this rattletrap.

The Cessna comes to a full stop next to us, and the pilot jumps out, takes off his helmet, and greets us. He looks American, has a blonde crew cut, and is about six feet tall and very handsome. He appears to be slightly older than I. His military utilities, with no markings regarding rank or country, are soiled and his boots lost their shine months ago. A Colt 45 is strapped around his waist. The co-pilot remains in the plane.

"Sister Joan. How are you? Sure glad we got here before the midday heat. Small arms fire hit our plane about fifteen minutes from here. We had to take an alternate route. Sorry we're late. The Cong are relentless, trying to keep us out of the air."

"We're so happy to see you, Captain Becket. I'm glad you made it in one piece. Will the plane be able to take off with that flat tire?"

"It should be okay Sister. I have a small hand pump to get some air in it for takeoff. The leak won't let enough air out before we reach Saigon. I don't have the gear or time to patch it."

"Should we get the children on the airplane now?" she asks anxiously.

"Yes. We need to hurry. The VC and the North Vietnamese now know we're here, and I want to take another route out of here to Saigon. Also, if the weather heats up too much, I won't be able to get this baby off the ground with a full load."

At that moment, the co-pilot jumps out of the plane, walks to the other side, and begins pumping air into the flat tire.

Sister Joan turns to me and says, "Let's put the children on the airplane. There's little time to waste."

I pick up Xuan Yen and carry her to the plane, as the

other children follow me. Captain Becket puts the little box holding Xuan Yen between him and the co-pilot's seat. Sister Joan and I lift the other children into the cabin of the plane. None of the children makes a sound. We strap all of the children in their seats and Captain Becket signals us to move away from the aircraft.

"How long will it take them to get to Saigon, Sister?" I ask.

"It depends upon their route back, but hopefully not more than half an hour or so."

The children wave as the engine revs up and the dust begins to form a brown cloud in front of us. The plane taxis to the end of the runway and stops for its pre-flight run-up to check all instruments, fuel and engine. Captain Becket gives a thumbs-up prior to accelerating down the runway. After using the entire dirt landing strip, the Cessna slowly lifts off the ground and becomes airborne. It makes a sharp left turn and heads toward Saigon. It's quickly a speck in the sky.

"Who are those pilots, Sister?"

"They're some of the most courageous men I know. They're former American pilots who have stayed in country, after they were discharged, to help get these orphans to safety. They work alongside South Vietnam pilots in saving as many children as possible before the North Vietnamese overrun this country. They know the danger involved with their job. Captain Becket has told me that he thinks we're only a couple of months away from the North Vietnamese Communists taking over the entire country of Vietnam."

"How much longer will the pilots stay in Vietnam?"

She replies, "As long as necessary to get these children out, I hope. Let's get out of here. We have another load of children to pick up at the church."

On the ride back to the church, Sister Joan and I are very quiet. I figure she's thinking about the children as much as I am. I silently pray for their safety. I can't stop thinking about the bravery of the pilots who are ferrying these children for us.

> I remembered how the pilots, who flew the O-1 reconnaissance airplanes called the "Bird Dog", would fly over our outposts in 1970 looking for Viet Cong and North Vietnamese positions. Those little airplanes were sitting ducks, but the pilots would bring the planes in low enough to locate enemy positions. They saved the lives of many American servicemen. Captain Bracket could very well have been one of those pilots. Those brave men paid a heavy price during the war. Many were shot down by small arms fire and SAMs (surface to air missiles). They would be so low and slow that the Viet Cong could hit them with fifty caliber machine guns. The SAMs were so quick that, if the enemy zeroed on them, there was no chance of survival for the "Bird Dog".

By the time we arrive back at the church, I'm tired and hungry. Sister Joan wears the freshness of a young rose. She pulls the van up to the side of the church and asks me to check with Father Tran to see if he's picked up the other children from the clinic.

Father Tran is in the small kitchen adjoining the church. Four children sit on benches at a table, each of them eating bowls of rice. They all stare at me as I walk over to the priest. One of the boys, about four years old, has a deep scar on his face—probably a bad burn. His mangled arm reminds me of a broken tree limb. A young girl has only one arm. The other two boys appear to be physically okay, but neither of them shows any emotion. When I come up to the table and grin at them, both the girl, and the boy with the badly damaged arm, smile as broadly as a full moon. The other two boys look away.

"Hi John. How was the trip? Did the children get off okay?"

"Yes, Father. It was quite an experience. That plane looks like it's been through a lot."

"Those pilots are the best," he replies. "They fly all-day, every day. I don't know how they do it. They're saints, and they understand how important it is to get these children out of here, especially the Amerasians. Those men know how close the NVA are to taking over this country."

"Well, they have my vote for bravery."

Sister Joan walks into the kitchen and sits next to the children. She gives each of them a hug. Her love permeates the room as she asks Father, "Will we be able to have something to eat before our next trip out?"

"Khanh will bring us some steamed vegetables and rice in a minute."

"Thanks, Father. I'm going to go freshen up."

After I take a seat at the table, a young Vietnamese woman brings a sweet smelling dish containing an array of vegetables beautifully covering a mound of white rice. She places the food on the table in front of me and, in broken English, tells me to help myself. At this moment, Father Tran returns to the table and takes a seat next to me.

"Go for it John. This is it until later this evening."

I didn't realize how famished I was. After filling the plate to the brim, I eat like an athlete at the training table after a long practice. During the meal, Sister Joan and Father Tran trade small talk. After finishing our lunch, Sister Joan reminds me that we'll be going back to the airstrip with the four children. Another airplane will be arriving to pick up these kids.

"We're leaving in about fifteen minutes, John. Can you start rounding up the children with Father Tran, and load them into the van? Be especially careful with the two boys. They have some serious emotional problems, and I don't want them to get apprehensive. Just treat them with kid gloves."

"I understand. We'll be ready to go," I state with as much enthusiasm as possible considering that I was hoping to get a short rest before our trip back to the airstrip.

Father Tran and I gather up the children and begin loading them into the van. They continue to chatter in Vietnamese amongst themselves, but respond in an orderly fashion as Father Tran gets them settled in their seats. He also slips each of them an orange, which they guard like a piece of gold.

At that moment, Sister Joan walks up to the van. She looks like she just got out of the shower, with her hair neatly combed and wearing a clean blue blouse.

Doesn't this woman ever get tired?

"Are we ready to rock and roll, John?"

"All present and accounted for Sister," I quickly respond in my best Marine Corps tone.

"Okay. Let's go. We need to be at the airstrip by three o'clock this afternoon. The pilots don't like flying after sundown. Aircraft flying at night in South Vietnam are considered absolute enemy targets for the VC and the North Vietnam soldiers. We want to be back to the church before dark since it's not a good idea to be out here at night. That's when the Cong like to come out."

She starts up the van, and we head to the airstrip. Being familiar with the bumpy roads by now, I start to relax. My head begins to bob as I fall in and out of short power naps. On this trip, Sister Joan doesn't have to stop and look at the map. She pilots the vehicle over the dirt road like a veteran traveler on vacation.

We arrive at the airstrip a little before three o'clock and wait for the airplane. Sister Joan tells the children to sit next to the bus. The afternoon temperature is at least one hundred degrees with extremely high humidity. The children don't complain, sensing that Sister Joan and I are guarding them from any danger.

After an hour wait, there's still no sign of an airplane.

"They're usually here within an hour of the scheduled time, John. I hope they're okay," she whispers with a faint smile.

"Who sets the schedules for their estimated time of arrival here Sister?"

"The orphanage at Binh Trieu takes care of this for

us. They give me the arrival times and let me know how many children they can take on each trip."

By five o'clock, the children are quite restless. They've all eaten their oranges. Sister Joan is showing signs of concern by her pacing around the van and quick looks to the sky at the slightest sound of a bird chirping or a branch of a tree blowing in the heated wind of the early evening. Also, the intermittent explosions in the distant make her head pop in that direction.

After about another hour, she exclaims, "I'm concerned. The plane should have been here by now. It's six and we have to be careful about driving in the dark around here. Let's put the children into the van and head back to the church."

We quickly load the children. They're very quiet and hungry by now. Sister Joan fires up the engine and we slowly begin our journey back to the church.

As the pink sun lethargically falls behind some forming clouds and into the earth, Sister Joan drives at a very slow speed. Suddenly, I hear the popping of rifle fire up ahead. Immediately, Sister Joan brings the van to a complete stop. Fortunately, we're in a thicket of trees.

"I need to move the van off the road into these bushes, John."

She slowly drives the van off the road into a little opening that is sheltered by some heavy trees and underbrush. There is dead silence in the van. The rifle fire intensifies in the distance. Drops of rain start to plummet on top of the van. Darkness sets in. The rain increases steadily to a heavy deluge.

Sister Joan softly tells the children to keep quiet. She hands each of them a candy bar from her travelling bag and lets them know that we'll be here for the night. She tells them to be still and that they will be sleeping in the van. They're amazingly relaxed, and respond to Sister Joan's request.

Wow, these children must be used to some nerve-racking situations!

"We can't take the chance of moving in the dark," she says. "There's too much danger of the VC taking these children from us. I think we'll be okay in this location. I can't see the road from here, so I don't think anyone can see us. Thank God, it's also pouring rain. We can take turns sleeping. I'll stay awake and watch for anyone for two hours and then you can do the same when I wake you up. So you'd better get some sleep."

With that, she pulls out a Colt 45 from under the seat, concealing it from the children, and sets it on her lap.

CHAPTER

4

I awake with a jolt when Sister Joan taps me on the shoulder and hands me the Colt 45. She casually whispers, "John, it's your turn to be our lookout. Wake me in two hours." I look at my watch and see it's midnight. Sister has let me sleep for four hours.

Before I can even respond to her comment, she turns away and leans her head on the side of the driver's door.

It's stopped raining but I can't see a thing due to the white blanket of fog, which envelops our van. I crack the right hand window. The silence is eerie. It's like the moment before someone touches you in the dark and yells "boo!" *What's out there? Are the Viet Cong or the North Vietnamese soldiers patrolling around us?* I pick up the pistol and check to see if it's loaded. The magazine is secure in the handle of the pistol. In order not to wake Sister Joan or the children, I slowly pull the barrel back and carefully move it forward to make sure a round is in the chamber. I think back to those nights I was on watch with my platoon on Monkey Mountain above Danang airfield.

> My radioman, Corporal Mathews, and I would take two-hour shifts in our foxhole, looking for Viet Cong who like to attack at night. Those were nerve-racking hours. Sounds came from in front of our position. Not knowing if it was a human or an animal, my adrenalin spun like a house fan in over-drive. Would I make it through the night? It was terrifying not knowing if one or one hundred of the enemy was out there in the black hole to our front. It was darker than an unlit coalmine. I remember the night that two of my Marines had a Viet Cong soldier jump into their foxhole with a knife. Fortunately, they were able to grab the enemy soldier and wrestled the weapon away from him. He was then taken to the company commander as a prisoner.

The soft crying of one of the children quickly brings me back to reality. I reach over the seat and put my arm on his shoulder, and he quietly returns to sleep.

The next two hours feel like two days. I look at my watch every five minutes, hoping that half an hour has passed.

A twig snaps outside the van. I tense up. *Oh, crap, what's that?* My body is as still as a mongoose ready to strike at a cobra. There's another movement. Time freezes. No more sounds. I wait. Finally, something making pitter-patter sounds skips away from our vehicle. I sigh deeply in relief. *It must have been an animal. I hope.*

Finally, at two o'clock, I realize it's time to wake up Sister Joan, but decide to hang in there for a while longer. *After all, she let me sleep for four hours.* By two forty-five, my eyelids droop periodically and my head bobs.

"Time to wake up Sister," I whisper. I nudge her on the shoulder and she snaps up and says, "Thanks, John. Go ahead and give me the gun, and you get some rest."

After handing her the pistol, I rest my head on the door. Sleep is impossible. My nerves are shot. *What am I doing in this situation? I sure didn't realize I would be out in the middle of nowhere in some van hiding out from an enemy who may try to kill me. That's what it was like during the war. Now I'm a social worker, just wanting to help the orphans. Trying to make a difference in this world is a challenge.*

My thoughts continue wondering. *What will Sister Joan's plan of action be in the morning? The children need to get to Saigon, but they'll also need to eat. What about the airplane that was supposed to pick up the children? What happened to it?* I pray that no harm comes to the pilots.

I doze off now and then for the next two hours, but don't get much sleep. Sister Joan nudges my arm.

"It's time for your watch, John."

"Okay. Got it," I respond as she hands me the pistol.

My wristwatch reads five minutes to five. I look out the van window. The fog or mist, or whatever it was, has lifted and the area is ink black. I see absolutely nothing through the window. *The sun should be coming up soon. I can wait this out. Be alert, John.*

An uneventful hour passes as light peeks through the thick brush to our van. There is dead silence all around. Full daylight begins to display itself. Sister Joan and the children start moving and, within a few minutes, everyone is awake. No one talks, as if a command was given to be silent.

"John, please give me the gun. I'm going outside and look around." Would you watch the children and make sure they stay quiet?"

"Sister, I'll go check the area. Why don't you stay with the children," I quickly respond.

"All right," she answers.

I quietly open the side door and walk slowly around the van. I scan the vicinity, holding the pistol in the ready position. After a few minutes, I determine the area is secure, and make my way back to the vehicle.

"Looks good," I softly tell Sister.

We both help the children out of the van. They sense that talking is not okay. Sister tells the children that we'll be going back to the church to eat soon. She then takes the girls into the bushes for their privacy. When they return, I take the boys in order for them to relieve themselves.

"Everyone back into the van," Sister instructs in her best Vietnamese.

After we settle in the van, she informs us that we're heading back to the church. "Father will be worried sick. I sure would like to know what happened to the plane."

"What about possible Viet Cong or North Vietnamese troops?" I respond.

"If any of them were out here, they would be gone by daylight. They typically operate at night in this area."

I hope she's right.

Sister slowly drives out of the thicket and onto the dirt road. We arrive back at the church around eight o'clock. Father Tran comes running out to greet us when we maneuver into the parking lot. He steps up to the van and, as Sister Joan rolls down the window, says, "I'm so happy to see you. What happened?"

"Let me park the van, and I'll tell you the whole story. The children need to have something to eat," Sister politely says.

During breakfast, Sister Joan tells Father Tran the story of our previous night's adventure. Father tells her that he had a communication from Binh Trieu Orphanage that the plane was hit by enemy ground fire on the way to the air strip and had to turn back to Saigon. Fortunately, neither the pilot nor the co-pilot was hurt and the plane landed safely.

"Thank God. When will the next flight come out for the children?" Sister queries.

"There'll be two flights today. One will arrive at noon and the other at three-thirty this afternoon," replies Father. "I was so worried when you didn't get back here yesterday afternoon. I sent two of our church workers out to look for you around five o'clock. But, they got frightened when they heard some gun shots, and turned around," Father continues.

"Thank you, Father. We were okay. The Lord looked after us."

"We have another five children arriving later this morning. The war situation seems to be getting worse. More children are showing up at the clinic daily. Also, more orphanages in the area want to get children to Saigon. I hope we can get all of them out of this area soon enough," Father says.

After breakfast, Sister Joan and I get the children organized for the trip back out to the airstrip. I grab some oranges and candy bars and put them into the van. For the next hour or so, I play games with the children and practice my Vietnamese with them. They're in great spirits and crave the attention.

"Time to go," says Sister. "Let's get the children in the van and get ourselves out to meet the airplane."

After loading everyone, we're on our way to the airstrip. It's very hot and humid. Even with the windows of the van fully open, it feels like we are in an oven with hot air blowing over us. Sister Joan and the children retain a light coat of perspiration on their faces.

We arrive at the airstrip around eleven thirty and anxiously search the sky for the airplane, which will take the children to Saigon. *I hope the plane makes it this time.* Time stands still. Each minute feels like ten. Our eyes strain to find that speck in the sky, and I think back to that morning of the ambush in which Corporal Watson was killed and Private Cohen and Private Sanchez were wounded.

> We were waiting for help. I needed a medical evacuation immediately. I made radio contact to the battalion headquarters, which was six thousand meters away. We used the PRC-10, a radio with a huge battery pack weighing nearly thirty pounds. I was unsure they received my garbled message. I waited for what seemed like an eternity for that chopper to arrive. My eyes were glued to the sky, probing for that speck in the horizon. *Please hurry. My wounded needed to get out of there.* Private Cohen had been shot in the leg and Private Sanchez was wounded in the face. My medic, Corpsman Abbot, was able to stop the bleeding on Cohen's leg. Abbot said Cohen was okay, but Sanchez was struck in the eye and needed immediate attention. My platoon

was set up in a defensive perimeter and we were prepared to fire off a flare when we saw the choppers. I was focused on the sky. Finally, I spotted two specks in the blue sky. The dots were getting bigger. I knew they were the helicopters to rescue my guys. We fired the flare and the choppers swooped down like geese heading into a pond. I almost cried I was so happy to see them.

"I see the plane," says Sister Joan as my mind snaps back to the present.

The spot in the sky above us becomes a real airplane on final approach. Sister and I shove the children behind the van to avoid the dust storm as the plane touches down.

The Cessna taxis over to us and stops a few feet from the van. It's the same plane that was here yesterday. The once flat tire appears to be fixed. As the pilot gets out, I notice it's not Captain Becket. This pilot is wearing the standard olive green flight suit with a pistol strapped to his waist. He's about five feet six, around forty years old and good looking. A neatly trimmed black mustache covers his upper lip.

"Good afternoon, Sister. How are you?" says the pilot.

"Major Danak. So good to see you. I expected Captain Becket. Is he okay?"

"He's fine. Just needed a break. He'll be on the next flight this afternoon. I needed a little extra flight time."

"Major, this is John Ellis."

"Hi, John. Nice meeting you," he says, extending his right hand.

"Nice meeting you too, Major. Thanks for picking up these children," I respond as we shake hands.

"It's my job. My pleasure," he casually replies.

"Are you ready for us to load the children?" Sister asks.

"Yes, let's get them in right away," Major Danak responds.

One by one, the children settle into the airplane. I close the door and the co-pilot revs up the engine. Major Danak gets into the plane, straps himself in, and gives us a thumbs-up. After its pre-flight run-up, we watch the airplane move lazily down the runway and lift off into the crisp indigo sky like a duck leaving a pond for the freedom of the wild blue yonder.

Sister and I get into the van and head back to the church. On the way, I think about my friends at home. I wonder what they're doing today. They're probably going to work at the investment banking office or to the classroom to teach or to the office at the telephone company. I'm in the middle of a foreign country helping children to get out of here and preventing them from losing their lives. I wonder if my buddies have a clue what I'm going through in this new job.

For the next two weeks, Sister Joan and I make one or two trips a day to the airstrip to get children ferried to Saigon to be processed for adoption in the United States and other countries. The flow of children to the clinic at Tan Ngai and the surrounding orphanages is unending. Their mothers bring children to the clinic because they have no way to feed or care for their child. Occasionally a woman will come to the clinic for childbirth. After delivery, the mother leaves the child for adoption.

"Our orphanage in Binh Trieu is also receiving

children who are abandoned in hamlets, found on the streets begging for food, or were given to anyone who had any compassion. Many arrive in poor health. They have ear infections, pneumonia, tuberculosis, lice, intestinal parasites, missing limbs, napalm burns and other physical, mental and emotional problems. As soon as the children get somewhat healthy, the orphanage tries to move them to the airport in Saigon for transport to the adoptive parents in the United States," Sister Joan tells me.

On Friday, March 28, 1975, Sister Joan and I head back to Saigon. We have helped get approximately seventy orphans to Saigon in the past two weeks. The airplanes came in every day within an hour of their estimated time of arrival and made the flights back to Saigon without any major problems. *Thank God!*

The three-hour drive back to Binh Trieu with Sister Joan is almost as frightening as the night spent in the van near the airstrip. She manages to move the vehicle in and around traffic like a bee flying to and from a hive. She's a driver with a mission to be in front of every car at all times. Her use of brakes is almost nonexistent. The gas pedal for her is the driving force. She accelerates up to within spitting distance of the vehicle or motorbike in front of her, quickly looks to her left, and shoots the van across the centerline to pass. Her turns back into the right lane are sharp, as the tires screech when we weave to avoid the oncoming traffic. Then it is on to the next car, or motorbike to our front. I feel like a passenger in Cale Yarborough's car at Darlington Speedway in South Carolina. *She is one aggressive driver!*

When we arrive back at the orphanage, Sister Nguyen

and Sister Elizabeth are there to greet us. Walking through the building, I'm surprised to see that the number of children has not increased much.

"Where are all of the children we sent to Saigon on the planes?" I ask.

Sister Elizabeth replies, "Most of them were sent to other orphanages in the area. We can only take children to replace those who have been sent to the United States. Our space here is limited."

"Did little Xuan Yen make it here?" I inquire.

"You mean the tiny baby with the gorgeous black round eyes and full head of hair?" she asks.

"Yes, we put her on the airplane about two weeks ago. I was hoping she made it here." Somehow, I felt this strange attachment to the little infant. Maybe it was her beautiful black eyes, so full of innocence.

"She's here. Did you know her name means "Bird in springtime"? Sister Elizabeth asks.

"Wow. That's very fitting for that child. May I see her?"

"Of course. Let me take you to her," she replies.

As we walk into the room, I immediately see Xuan Yen. She's sharing a wooden crib with two other tiny babies. I look at those big round eyes and wonder what will become of this little girl when she gets to her adoptive parents in the States. She stares at me as if she remembers me carrying her to the airplane a few weeks ago. *Of course, she doesn't remember. Or does she? How lucky is this little Amerasian girl to be able to get out of this war torn country. Who are her mom and dad? Who gave her that beautiful name? She'll never know.*

"How long will it be before these babies get sent to the U.S.?" I ask Sister Nguyen.

"They'll be here awhile. It takes at least six months to get the necessary paperwork completed through the South Vietnamese government to send the children out of country. There's a growing number of orphans in South Vietnam, and the government considers it an embarrassment that they can't take care of their own children. So, they don't make it easy for us to process these children for adoption in another country," says Sister Nguyen.

At that moment, Sister Joan walks in the room and reminds me it's time to eat. While at dinner, she tells us that things are heating up around Saigon. Refugees are pouring into the city from the north, since the North Vietnamese are continuing to take over more cities. Children, especially those who are handicapped and Amerasian, are being left on the streets.

"We need to help these particular children. If the North Vietnamese take over Saigon, these children are in grave danger," Sister Joan tells us.

"Can we take more children here?" I ask.

"We may have to. Things will have to tighten up in the rooms. We can't refuse these kids," she says. "Also, I've been told by the Unites States embassy people that some orphans in an area, about a twenty minute helicopter flight from here, need to be picked up. It's a half-way house, and they feel it's too close to the North Vietnamese forces moving into that area. They're asking us to help. I told them we would."

"How many children have to be picked up?" I ask.

"There are only about ten to twelve. Some are Amerasians. Would you like to come with me, John?"

"Absolutely, yes!" I reply.

"It looks like we'll be going out with two helicopters tomorrow. The pilots are South Vietnamese. The choppers belong to the South Vietnamese Air Force and have been directed by the government to help us evacuate orphans from these dangerous areas. They'll pick us up in an open field about two blocks from here. We should be ready to meet them at the site around seven o'clock tomorrow morning."

Although anxious and a bit nervous, I look forward to the journey.

After dinner, I help Sister Elizabeth tend to the children. We change bedding, clean wounds and bathe the infants. One young boy, about five years old, is missing his right foot. His name is Trung. He uses one crutch to get around the room to help Sister Elizabeth with the younger children. He's very good looking and always smiling. I take deep breaths, trying not to show my emotions, as I watch him. My eyes water as I see Trung bring a ray of sunshine to the room. *How lucky am I! How lucky are most American kids back home. I hope Trung gets a great home in U.S.* We finish around nine o'clock, and I head for my room and plop into bed. I'm suddenly thinking back to that day when our small infantry platoon had just crossed a rice paddy, and we heard a sharp explosion.

> A horrific scream followed the blast. I sprinted over to the area of the detonation and found a child lying on the ground and a woman holding an infant in her arms. As I walked up, the young boy on the ground was grabbing his mangled leg. He had stepped on a

mine in the middle of a path along the rice paddies. Corpsman Abbot went to the wounded child and carefully moved him off the path. The rest of the Marines formed a perimeter defense around us. I tried to console the woman who I assumed was the mother. Tears rolled down her sad weather beaten face. I felt helpless.

"How's the boy?" I asked Corpsman Abbot. "Not good, Lieutenant. I'm going to put a tourniquet on his leg, but he may lose part of it," he said. The leg looked like a piece of raw meat. I started to gag, and quickly turned my head away. "There's a village about five hundred clicks (kilometers) from here. Let's take him there," I said as I peeked over my shoulder. "Okay, Sir. But first I have to wrap this leg to keep out the dust and bugs."

I radioed the Company Commander and told him our situation. He okayed our detour to take care of the wounded boy. We took the young boy and the mother with her child to the small village. The wounded boy didn't make a sound. The look on his face was obvious that he was in intense pain, but he seemed so thankful that we were taking care of him. When we arrived in the village, I found a local Vietnamese doctor who was able to take the boy to his clinic.

I cease my daydreaming and stare at the ceiling. To this day, I wonder what happened to that young boy. *Did he survive the war? Did he lose his leg?* I conjecture about Trung losing his foot. I lie awake for an hour thinking about these unfortunate children of war.

I'm out of bed at five o'clock the next morning ready to take on another day in Vietnam. I'm anticipating an interesting time. A helicopter ride to pick up some more orphans sounds a bit scary in this unpredictable country of South Vietnam. Continuing reports of the North

Vietnamese moving nearer to Saigon are coming in over the radio. Having read General Giap's book *People's War People's Army,* I know the North Vietnamese will not quit until they take over the entire country of Vietnam. General Giap is one determined military commander.

I suddenly realize that getting all of these children to the United States is taking on an urgency that I didn't expect. Time appears to be getting critical.

After breakfast, Sister Joan and I walk over to the open field to wait for the helicopters. Around seven fifteen, I see two spots against the pinkish sky. The familiar "woosh-woosh" sound of helicopter blades heads our way. The planes begin their descent. Sister Joan and I turn our heads away from the wind and dust storm. When the choppers land, a shower of brown crud blankets us. The rotors flutter to a stop and one of the pilots jogs over to us.

He's dressed in a grey flight suit, and has a Colt 45 secured to his waist. At a little over five feet tall and maybe twenty-five years old, he looks like a high school student. His complexion is as smooth as a dark brown leather chair. He removes his helmet to greet us, revealing coal black hair.

In well-spoken English, he says, "Hello Sister Joan. How are you? Are you ready to pick up the kids?"

"Good morning Lieutenant Huy. So nice to see you. Yes, we're ready. Where exactly are we going?" she asks.

Does Sister Joan know everyone around here? She sure seems to be a prominent person in this part of the woods!

"There's an abandoned air strip about ten kilometers

from Vinh Long Province. Someone from the half-way house near there will meet us. There've been some VC guerilla attacks in that area, and the people at the half-way house want to get the Amerasian children and the abandoned newborns out. Should take us about an hour to get there," Lt. Huy says.

The crew chief helps us get into the H-34 helicopter. I wonder if this plane will get off the ground. The unmarked, camouflaged choppers not only look worse for wear, but also seem downright antiquated. They have the typical bullet holes of a combat airplane, with no doors and no windows. Our crew chief picks up his fifty caliber machine gun and signals for us to sit on a flak jacket and hold on to the framing bars inside.

I'm fretful. My armpits are soaked with sweat. My body is as tense as a rubber band ready to snap. *Are we in danger? You can't fool me. I know why I'm sitting on a flak jacket!*

Sister Joan looks calm, but she must be a little uneasy too as she scans the inside of the chopper with a critical eye. She stares at the crew chief's machine gun.

Lieutenant Huy settles in the cockpit and fires up his engine. The pilot of the other helicopter follows suit. A cloud of brown mist covers the ground below as the chopper begins to suck us upward.

I hang onto the post next to me and make sure the flak jacket is totally covering my butt. I focus on the crew chief. He scans the area, looking as if he is heading into a war zone. *Are we, I wonder?*

This could be a remarkable trip!

CHAPTER

5

The chopper shudders like the inside of a blender as the pilot gives the engine full power. After a slight hover, it jumps into the sky mimicking a dragonfly startled by a cat. With a sharp left turn into the wind, we are fully airborne.

The engine is so loud that yelling isn't an option. We're so close to the treetops that the branches bend to horizontal as the plane skims over them. Finally, I breathe a sigh of relief as the helicopter gains more altitude into the clear pink sky.

I try to get Sister Joan's attention with hand signals. Looking around, I worry about the children being secure on this helicopter. Everyone holds on tightly to the frame of the aircraft as it shakes like a bobble head. The crew chief, with a stern look on his face, sits next to the open door with his fifty-caliber machine gun and scrutinizes the area below.

The accompanying helicopter flies in formation off to

our right. Lieutenant Huy earlier told Sister Joan that the other chopper is coming along for support and protection since we are flying over some hot Viet Cong controlled areas. Also, this plane is needed to help pick up the precious cargo of children. The sister aircraft looks like it has been in some serious combat. Light permeates through the bullet holes in its fuselage.

South Vietnam's beauty is evident as we fly over cultivated lands, exhibiting various shades of green and yellow. The farmlands contrast with dark green areas of flooded rice patties surrounded with the criss-cross patterns of dikes. Jungle canopies, with a mix of yellows, browns and greens break up the scenery. The rice paddies and other vegetable crops form a multicolored checkerboard. Numerous small villages dot the countryside. Water buffalo roam like lost children in a park. The open agricultural lands and countryside remind me of the Central Valley in northern California.

After about fifteen minutes of soaring over this stunning terrain, we begin our descent. More rice paddies cover the open areas, and water buffalo herds scatter as the helicopter closes in on their terrain.

As the ground below flies by, a "ping-ping-ping" ricochets off the fuselage like someone is throwing rocks at us. The helicopter makes a sharp left turn and immediately gains altitude. My eyes open as wide as a child in a "Big Eyes" painting by Margaret Keene.

"Rat-tat-tat!"

The crew chief fires his machine gun in the direction of a thick tree-covered area below. I'm on edge, feeling like a boxer ready for round two. Looking out the window, I stare below with intense concentration.

"Hug the deck!" I scream to Sister Joan.

When no response is evident due to the noise, I reach over, tap her on the shoulder, and flap my hands in a downward direction. She lip syncs "OK,"and lies as close to the belly of the helicopter as possible. The children follow suit.

Both aircraft gain the altitude necessary to get out of small arms range. The crew chief leans back close to Sister Joan and shouts something in her ear. She looks over at me and puts her hand in the air with a "thumbs-up" signal, signifying that things are okay. She points her finger out the door toward the ground and moves it toward the back of the airplane, indicating to me that the pilot is going to attempt another landing.

Swell.

The chopper quickly drops toward the earth and banks sharply as we head for a landing area, reminiscent of an H-34 going in for a medical evacuation during the war. With nail biting tension, I hold on for dear life. Two vehicles are visible in an open area below. We head at a sharp angle toward a clearing on the ground. The pilot skillfully maneuvers the chopper close to the vehicles, and we are on the brown surface in what seems like an instant. The second chopper lands about one hundred yards away.

The engines are set to idle and the crew chief signals for us to disembark. Sister Joan and I jump off the plane and duck as we run over to the vans parked near us.

Lieutenant Huy quickly gets out of the chopper and joins us. He has a haggard look on his face.

"What happened up there?" I ask him.

He quickly replies, "It was a sniper position that got off a few rounds. Fortunately I was able to out maneuver him."

"Good job, Lieutenant," I tell him.

Nine children and two Vietnamese women get out of the vans, and Sister Joan quickly introduces me to the two adults. They take four of the children to the other helicopter.

"John, we need to get five children into our helicopter. Make sure they sit on the extra flak jackets stored in the back and that they hold on tight."

Two boys are sitting in the vehicle waiting for direction. One boy is holding crutches. He slowly gets out of the van. The other has both arms wrapped in gauze. The one with crutches, who looks about five years old, moves toward me dragging his motionless legs. The other boy remains seated and does not move. Both of them stare at me with their big round brown eyes. The deep black grooves under their eyes indicate a lack of sleep.

"I'll get the little one in the van? I don't know if he can walk. The boy on the crutches can follow me," I yell to Sister Joan.

"Okay," she shouts back as I pick up the boy and carry him toward the plane. He's weightless. Although he looks about six years old, he's so light that it feels like I'm carrying a three year old. He smiles at me. I'm half jogging to the chopper. I put him in the corner of the plane on top of a flak jacket and signal for him to hold on to the post. The boy with the crutches moves in next to him.

Sister Joan and I then help two little girls, ages around three to six, onto the helicopter. Another boy, maybe seven or eight years old, limps behind us to the plane. Scanning the area to make sure all of the children are sitting on flak jackets and holding on to the framing of the chopper, I jump in next to one of the boys in the corner of the plane. I pull the other two boys close to me and hold all three tightly. Lieutenant Huy, sitting in the pilot's seat, checks his instruments for takeoff.

"Hold on to them, John," Sister Joan pleads with me as she gathers her arms around the girls.

Lieutenant Huy turns toward us and gives a "thumbs-up" signal. His face is stern and determination floods his eyes.

Sister Joan returns the signal, and the engines begin to rev up. The plane shakes akin to a cement mixer as the rotors are set to full throttle.

Our lift off resembles a balloon being released by a child. The chopper makes a ninety degree turn into the wind and we are immediately gaining altitude.

Looking at the children, I realize that all of them have the round eyes characteristic of Amerasians. *Who are these children? Where were they born? How were they injured or crippled? Who are their mothers and fathers?* As the helicopter bounces through the air, memory of the war starts to move stealthily into my consciousness.

> I saw the maimed and injured prisoners of war, which we captured in that desolate area near Danang in 1970. I also remembered the pile of dead bodies of Viet Cong soldiers near our base camp. I wondered how many children were maimed when

they raided that village the night before. The dead bodies of children in the village, and the wounded adults and young boys and girls that my medic was helping made me want to vomit. Mangled bodies, bloody limbs, burned skin, crying babies and the desperate looks of mothers who had lost their children were everywhere. The Viet Cong had burned the village to the ground. It was just a pile of ashes. These people lost everything, including many of their loved ones. It was a reprehensible scene. Who said war is glamorous!

"Rat-tat-tat!" "Bam-bam!"

Our helicopter bounces sharply. *Oh my God. We've been hit!* The chopper quickly turns left and attempts to maintain altitude. The plane falters for a second, drops radically toward the earth, and finally starts to move upward. I look around to see if anyone is hurt or if there is any damage. Everything looks okay.

Sister Joan has terror in her eyes as if she has just seen a ghost. Two of the children are crying. Sister Joan pulls them in tighter. The children next to me are motionless, like statues. They make no sounds.

The helicopter is shaking more than it was before, but it seems to be holding altitude. Viewing out the glassless window, I notice black smoke waving at me. It's coming from the engine. Our chopper is listing first to the right and then to the left. *We're in trouble. This thing isn't stable.*

The chopper starts to descend. A pocket of open ground below stares up at me. *This is an unscheduled stop! He's putting this baby down!*

We're falling rapidly toward the earth below. The chopper skims some treetops, which appear to be a jungle canopy. The sound of the engine changes to a whirring. The helicopter is auto-rotating, meaning we have no power. The air coming up is turning the rotors as we go down. Although we seem to be descending in a reasonably constant manner, the chopper is shaking like the inside of a rattle and continues to move hurriedly toward the ground. *I hope Lieutenant Huy can get this cargo of children safely on the ground.*

The co-pilot, with serious concern in his eyes, turns back to us and shouts, "Hold on!"

I close my eyes and embrace the three boys. Silently praying, I wait for the crash.

Finally, the chopper plops to the ground like orange falling out of someone's hand. The landing feels like we are moving in slow motion. As the plane bounces once on ground, there is a loud cracking sound as if a large tree branch just snapped. On the second bounce, the chopper settles in complete silence, and tips slightly to the left side. Nobody moves. I look around and everyone seems to be waiting for a command from someone. *Lt. Huy maneuvered this chopper to a miraculously soft landing!*

The other helicopter lands to our right. I'm uneasy. All of the children and Sister Joan seem to be okay. At that moment, Lieutenant Huy shouts, "Everyone out. Get into the other plane, and take your flak jacket with you. We're going to leave this chopper here since there are VC in the area. The engine is out of commission. Our left wheel brace is broken."

Sister Joan jumps out and helps the two girls next to her. I put on one of the flak jackets, and grab three more.

I direct one of the boys to the other helicopter, help the boy with crutches to get out and then pick up the helpless child. Moving toward the chopper, I feel like a pack mule trudging up a mountain.

As the co-pilot of the other helicopter runs toward us and signals for us to get into his plane, Lieutenant Huy helps me with the boys. He grabs the boy with the crutches and lifts him into the aircraft. I walk as fast as I can, holding the flak jackets and the boy. Sister Joan and the girls are all running toward the plane as if they are late for a birthday party.

"Everyone get into the plane and sit on a flak jacket," Lieutenant Huy commands.

Upon boarding the plane, the crew chief throws us some additional flak jackets and pats his rear end to signal us to sit on them. Sister Joan tells the children in Vietnamese, "Everyone grab a post on the bulkhead and hold on tight."

Understanding, and being able to speak some broken Vietnamese, I reiterate Sister Joan's command to the children.

We're packed like cattle in the chopper with nine children, two adults, Lieutenant Huy, his co-pilot and crew chief.

Once the plane's crew chief is satisfied that we're all settled and secure, he signals the pilot with a "thumbs-up". The sound of the engine is deafening as it revs up. The chopper struggles to lift off the ground due to the full load. *Come on. Get off the ground.* The plane slowly lifts and is hovering about ten feet off the ground for what seems like five minutes. All of a sudden, it tips slightly forward, looking like a waiter making a bow, and begins to move upward. It's like a slow motion movie. Finally, we are airborne and slowly gaining altitude.

The crew chief is at the "ready" position with his machine gun. He continues scrutinizing the area below as the helicopter moves upward. I flash back to those helicopter flights when we were flying to unknown landing zones (LZ's) during the war.

> As we flew to a "hot" area of Viet Cong concentration, about ten miles from the village of Le My in 1970, the familiar butterflies were floating on air through my stomach. It felt like the start of a mile race during my high school running days when I anticipated how much pain my body would be going through in the last lap of the race. I tried to imagine how we would get through this "race" with the VC.

> As our chopper, with twelve combat loaded troops, flew at tree top level to the landing zone, I didn't know what to expect in the next half hour. We descended to the LZ, and I yelled to my men, "Weapons loaded." The plan of action after landing was rehearsed repeatedly in my head as I gawked at the machine gunner who was intensely watching the area below.

> As the H-34 chopper began its descent to the landing zone, the sound of small arms fire began to fill the air. The "rat-tat-tat" of our crew chief's 50-caliber machine gun returned fire into the trees below. The butterflies in my stomach were quickly removed as my mind sprang into gear with our battle plan just before hitting the ground. The mile race began! Seconds before the chopper landed, I screamed, "Get off. Move to the right and form a perimeter."

The whole scene was chaotic as we jumped off and ran for cover through the red smoke grenade, which marked our LZ. The area was covered with elephant grass, which was good cover for us, but tended to cut any exposed parts of arms and hands due to its razor sharp ends. My men quickly formed our perimeter defense. It was an exercise we had continuously practiced. My troops returned the enemy's fire, much of it blindly, into thick tree areas.

Finally, the enemy fire ceased and the Viet Cong snipers fled. We were flat on our stomachs in the heavy elephant grass. Sweat poured off my face. It felt like a small creek was flowing from my eyebrows to my neck. I passed the word to see if everyone was okay. After a positive response from the squad leaders, we moved out for another six days of grueling guerilla warfare—patrolling and searching for the enemy.

The boy with the crutches next to me begins to cry. I put my arm around him and he leans closer to me. *Where did you come from? What horrors of war have you been through?* A lump forms in my throat. Being adopted myself, I'm thankful that these children soon will be safely placed in a home with loving parents. I know what it means to be taken in by a family who affectionately cares for a child.

During the remaining helicopter ride back to Binh Trieu, I reflect more on the children of war in Vietnam. I remembered the times that some of my fellow marines wandered off with women when we had a day of "liberty" from the war. They didn't always contemplate the consequences that maybe these women would be bearing their child when they were long gone. The pressure and horrors of war blocks out the future events for combat soldiers. Other servicemen actually married Vietnamese women and had children during the Vietnam War. Some of those men were killed in action, and the women couldn't care for their own children. Also, South Vietnamese soldiers, who lost their lives in the war, left children behind. Although the mothers loved these children, many were put in orphanages. The mothers knew that the children would have a better life there. It is estimated that over 58,000 American servicemen were killed and over 2,000,000 Vietnamese civilians lost their lives in the war. The result of these deaths is many orphans.

Although creating orphans is a phenomenon of all wars, this is my war. I want to help take care of as many of these children as possible. I know I can't help all of the orphans, but I especially would like to get as many Amerasians to the United States as possible. If left in this country after the war, these children will most likely have a very dubious life, or be killed. .

Finally, the chopper makes its descent on the original open field from which we took off early this morning. The landing is smooth as the plane touches down and creates the swirl of dust to which we are now accustomed.

"Everyone out," the crew chief shouts.

"Let's get all the children over to the orphanage," Sister calmly tells me.

We unload all of the children, and I pick up the boy who can't walk. All of us hike the two blocks to the orphanage. Sister Nyguen and Sister Elizabeth greet us.

"We were worried about you. What took you so long?"

Sister Elizabeth asks.

"It's a long story. Please help us get the children into the orphanage. They are hungry and tired," I answer.

"John, will you take the boy into the kitchen and get him some food?" Sister Joan asks.

"Of course," I answer as I walk past Sister Elizabeth into the building.

The kitchen is full of children who are already eating. There appears to be many more than when we left this morning. Our one-hour flight to pick up the new children turned into a full day adventure. I set the boy down next to me at the table and realize that I'm famished. In the middle of the table is a large bowl of sticky rice, some pho, and a bowl of fresh vegetables.

The little boy ravenously works his chopsticks into the food. I realize I don't even know his name. Looking at his wrist I see that his name is An. He's such a handsome child, with large round eyes, black hair and smooth light brown skin. Watching him maneuver his chopsticks, I wonder who his parents will be in the United States. Some wonderful adoptive parents will make a good life for this child. How great is it that some remarkable couple is willing to take a child who can't walk.

Sister Joan walks in and sits down next to me.

"Looks like we have more children here than when we left, Sister," I casually state. "Sister Elizabeth says that another twelve children from orphanages north of Saigon were brought here this morning. Have all of these children been processed for adoption to parents in the United States?"

"Yes they have. We've got to review everything, get it approved with Christian Adoption Services, the United

States government and the South Vietnamese government. Then, hopefully, the children are ready to be flown out of here," Sister Joan says.

"I can see we're going to be busy for the next few weeks," I respond.

After the meal, we get the younger children settled as the older children clean up the kitchen.

"We have a meeting in the front room in an hour," Sister Joan announces to us.

"See you then," I respond as I head back to my room for a power nap.

Thirty minutes later, I reach to turn off the alarm on my bedside clock. I think about all the paperwork that we still have to complete in order to prepare the children for their flights to the U.S.

Sister Joan, Sister Elizabeth, Sister Nguyen, Sister Anne Marie and I sit around one of the large wooden tables, waiting for Sister Joan to begin our meeting.

"Are things going okay at the orphanage?" Sister Joan asks Sister Anne Marie when she sits down at the table. "I know you've had your hands full keeping things in order since I've been in and out of here so often."

"We're doing well, Sister. I will say that the number of children continues to increase since the North Vietnamese troops are getting closer to Saigon. The orphanages north of us are getting the children out, especially the handicapped ones and the Amerasians. As you know, the North Vietnamese government doesn't have much use for these kids," Sister Anne Marie replies.

Sister Joan continues, "We have to make sure that our work is all completed on each child before we get them on the airplanes out of here. John, can you work closely with Sister Anne Marie in reviewing the necessary documentation for our United States Embassy and the South Vietnamese government? Sister Elizabeth and Sister Nguyen will assist you."

During the meeting, I notice the urgency in Sister Joan's voice. She continues to emphasize how important it is to get the paperwork finalized as soon as possible due to reports of enemy troops moving quickly south toward Saigon.

"Boom-Boom!"

A whistling sound follows, and then another explosion rocks the building. All of us look at each other, and instinctively we get up and run to the bedrooms to check on the children. Sister Elizabeth and I arrive in one room to find most of the older children gathered in a circle, holding each other's hands. They look up at us as if to say, "Please help us." Some of the babies are crying, but most just lay quietly in their cribs. One of the Vietnamese volunteers adjusts their covering, and makes sure they're all okay.

I walk over to see little Xuan Yen. She looks content as Sister Elizabeth gives her a bottle. *If she only knew what was going on in this country. When she gets to the United States, none of this will be a memory. She's too young.*

An is lying on his bed crying. I go over to him, sit at his side, and put my arm around him. He moves closer to me. His crying turns into a whimper, and he falls off to sleep in the next few minutes.

We spend the rest of the day caring for one child after another. Replacing bandages, soothing wounds, changing diapers, comforting the little children and playing games is becoming a typical routine. I'm worn out when I sit down to our dinner of fried shrimp over a bed of white rice and fresh vegetables. I feel as if I have just crossed that finish line after another mile run.

Following dinner, we perform the usual chores of getting the children ready for bed. However, tonight we have additional children to handle. Some are doubled up on the mats and added to cribs. After we have all the children ready for the evening, I look around the room in amazement. I hear a few whimpers, but no real crying, and there are nearly fifteen children in this tiny bedroom.

When I retire to my room, there are more explosions in the distance. I know we're working hard to get the children in this orphanage processed, but the babies take up to six months before we can fly them out. The sounds of those explosions lead me to believe that we don't have six months. In addition, we can only get a few on the airplanes each day. We're competing with other American agencies, which are sending children to America.

I lie in bed wondering what we'll do if the NVA gets to Saigon and we still have a house full of adoptive children who are mostly Amerasians and handicapped.

CHAPTER

6

The sound of the alarm startles me at five o'clock in the morning. I'm so tired that I sit up and wonder what day it is. Looking over at the pocket calendar on the table, I see it is March 30. The breeze coming in through the window feels like air from a blast furnace. The temperature must be at least eighty degrees. My tee shirt sticks to my clammy body. The humidity is stifling.

After a quick shower and shave, I'm on my way to the childrens' rooms to assist Sister Elizabeth with the babies—feeding, changing diapers, cleaning wounds, etc. She looks like she's been up for hours, but bears her usual smile.

"Good morning, John. The children are okay in here. Sister Joan wants to talk to you in the kitchen."

Hastily I walk into the kitchen and Sister Joan greets me with obvious urgency in her voice. "Enjoy your breakfast, John. We've got to get some kids at a half-way house just north of here, outside of Saigon."

"How far from here?" I ask.

"Only about an hour drive normally. It's about forty miles. I hear the refugee movement out of the northern cities has increased. It may take a little longer," she replies.

Casually, I mention, "I heard on the radio last night that Danang is being attacked by the North Vietnamese and is expected to be overrun by today or tomorrow. People are leaving that city in droves."

"Yes they are," she despondently replies. "They're trying to get out of there by any means possible. South Vietnamese troops are deserting and refugees are getting on boats to flee. Many people crowd the highways, and children roam the streets to fend for themselves. I hear it's pure chaos."

"Where do you get your updates on the movement of the North Vietnamese forces?" I ask.

"I'm in phone contact with my superiors in Saigon who have constant communication with the United States Embassy. They really keep me well informed. They know how critical the situation is becoming."

"By the way, that was quite a trip yesterday, Sister. How do you know Lieutenant Huy?" I inquire.

"Oh...a...I met him a few months ago when we transferred some children here from the Mekong Delta area. He and his family are from Hue, and he's been a helicopter pilot for about four years with the ARVN (South Vietnamese Army). He got his training in the United States. He's been awarded many medals by his country for bravery in evacuating South Vietnamese

Army Rangers from dangerous situations near Da Nang and Hue," she replies.

"Why is he transferring orphans rather than working with the infantry troops now? It would seem to me that he would be needed north of Saigon," I respond.

"He, along with a hand full of other helicopter pilots, was ordered by the South Vietnamese government to help get orphans, especially Amerasian children, out of the country. Maybe his government is trying to look good in the eyes of the American government."

"What about his family in Hue? Who's taking care of them?" I ask.

"He told me that his wife and young son are being watched by some elite South Vietnamese Ranger unit, and he was told they would be taken to Saigon if things get too hot in Hue. I imagine they've left Hue by now since that part of the country has, in all probability, been overrun by the NVA. I just hope he's able to find his family, and can survive all that is going on around us. He's one of the most positive thinking Vietnamese military men I've run into. I pray for him every day, since he puts himself in many perilous situations to help other people," she states with a worried look on her face.

As Sister Joan turns to help one of the children at the table, I look at my food and think of those days I spent around the gracious people of South Vietnam during combat in 1970.

After asking Sister Joan to pass me the pot of coffee, I reminisce about the South Vietnamese people. "You know, the South Vietnamese loved seeing us when I was here in 1970, Sister. They saw us as their saviors from the atrocities of the VC and the North Vietnamese soldiers. Now they've lost our support, and are in a vulnerable situation, desperately trying to get to some safe haven. I feel helpless as I think of their peril."

"I remember talking to one of my fellow officers when he returned to the States after the Tet offensive in Hue in 1968. He reminded me how the Viet Cong rank among the most brutal, callous mass murderers in history. He saw firsthand how they massacred thousands of civilians during that terrible battle," I continue.

"I understand, John. You can see why these people are trying to save their families from possible retribution from the North," she replies.

I feel that in the days to come, I won't be able to comprehend the degree of panic that will confront us.

"Eat up. We're leaving in a few minutes," Sister Joan says as she nudges my shoulder.

"Right, Sister. I'm ready."

After chomping down the breakfast of Quaker Oatmeal covered with raisins and nuts, Sister Joan and I are on our way to the van for the trip to the half-way house.

Our drive into Saigon is relatively uneventful. I watch Sister Joan dodge bicycles, motor bikes and pedestrians in her normal zigzag fashion. Approaching the city limits of Saigon, the number of people in the streets appears to be increasing significantly. They're walking, carrying bundles on their backs, hauling wooden carts full of household goods, and pulling pigs, water buffalo and other animals behind them. Children are strapped to the backs of many of the women. Crowded busses, overloaded with not only passengers but also suitcases, bundles, boxes and a myriad of miscellaneous items stacked on the roof, plug alongside the human movement.

Our van halts. Refugees dart in and out of the traffic. They look like ants haphazardly trying to find their home. Sister Joan weaves the van slowly through a sea of conical hats. Horns honk, people yell, and the sound of children crying reverberates above the commotion. The only men we see, except for South Vietnamese soldiers, are old and decrepit.

"Where do you think these refugees will end up, Sister?"

"It's hard to tell, John. Many of them have been on the roads for days, looking for shelter and safety in Saigon. Either their towns north of here have been overtaken, or the North Vietnamese are approaching their villages. They're carrying everything they own with them. Many wonder aimlessly."

Total despair wraps around the faces of most of these refugees. The women display pronounced worry lines due to the extreme humid climate and coats of dust from the roads. Perplexed, they continue to move and look around as if to say, "Where am I going and what should I do?"

Our van creeps along the road. Children, dressed in filthy shirts and shorts, walk along the street with their hands out, begging for food. Their faces are beset with sorrow, and some look as if they haven't had a meal in days. Desperation surrounds us. Some of them have the round eyes, characteristic of Amerasians.

"How did these children get here, Sister? Where are their mothers?"

"John, they've been left on the streets, mainly because the families have no way to feed them. Fathers, some who may have been American soldiers, are dead or are back in the U.S. The children are abandoned, and have to fend for themselves. God help them."

One little boy, standing on the side of the street, manages a slight smile for us. He holds himself up by one crutch and has a brace on each leg. His soiled shirt hangs over his shorts. He tries to wave to us, but has trouble balancing on his crutch, and pulls his arm down in mid-wave.

"Can we help them, Sister?" I optimistically ask.

"We can't help all of them, but we may have to take some of these street children in before they die of starvation. The Vietnamese government has all but forgotten them. Control of the country is superseding any focus on human suffering. The South Vietnamese government is just trying to exist. It's well aware of the movement of the NVA toward Saigon."

"We've got to help some of them, Sister. Many are on crutches, missing limbs, or look like they have multiple diseases."

At that moment, a young girl walks up to the van and pounds on my side of the door.

With a sad, helpless look on her scarred face, she holds out her hand and says, "Lam on" ("Please").

Sister Joan, in her typical well-prepared fashion, reaches under the seat, pulls out a paper bag, and hands it to me.

"Will you please give her one of the bananas from the bag," she says.

I quickly take out one of the yellow treasures, and hand it to the little girl. She grabs it out of my hand, says "Cam on" ("Thank you"), and quickly runs away. Other children, who are watching us, begin to swarm around the van.

Sister Joan gracefully maneuvers the van at a slow pace through the masses of refugees. More children follow, as I hand out the dozen or so bananas from the bag. Finally, we get a slight break in the traffic, and the van moves faster than the children can run to keep up with us. I watch the complete frustration in their faces as we drive away. I feel helpless as I let out a heavy breathe with total dejection. *What a mess. How are all of these children going to survive? They aren't!*

We finally arrive at the half-way house after a two-hour drive. To call this a house is a stretch. I'm viewing a makeshift structure with a metal roof and cutouts for windows, with no glass. The siding appears to be old plywood from a billboard. The entire building has never seen paint. The foundation consists of rocks, overlaid with planks of wood. The building leans slightly, making it look like it could topple over at any time.

Two young Vietnamese girls greet us and usher us into a cordoned off area which has about fifteen children of varying ages. They're a mixture of Amerasians and Vietnamese. In the corner, there is a cardboard box holding three tiny babies wrapped in light blankets. The infants can't be more than six or seven weeks old. They're skin and bones. They need to be at Binh Trieu Orphanage where we can get them more nourishment and attention. *Oh my God! Does it ever end?*

The smell of urine permeates the room. There are no toys, and just a little furniture—beds, cribs, boxes and floor mats haphazardly scattered between the walls. Flies swarm, and the smell of feces is unbearable.

I'm shocked when I look at the children, many who have rotting teeth, open sores and bloated stomachs.

"We're going to be taking the babies and six other children back to the orphanage today. I'm hoping we can make another trip out here tomorrow to pick up the rest. Kids are being dropped off daily by mothers, and families who can't care for them," Sister Joan states, matter-of-factly.

I know that her heart is breaking, but she's so professional that she won't show any negative emotion to me.

"Boom!" "Boom!"

The entire house shakes. Both of the Vietnamese girls let out a muffled scream, and run to the children, as if to guard them from any danger. Sister Joan and I look at each other, and immediately duck our heads and move to the corner of the room, away from the windows. The concussions from the artillery rounds feel like an earthquake.

As we wait out the barrage, I realize that the incoming armament is probably a few miles away. *Most likely, some Viet Cong or North Vietnamese Army and South Vietnamese Army contact. This is another reminder of how close the North Vietnam forces are getting to Saigon.*

The thunderous sounds from the sky stop. "I'm ready to get out of here," I nervously state to Sister.

"No better time than right now," she quickly responds. "Let's go ahead and take the box with the babies and load the six children which the two volunteers are bringing over to us."

The carton with the three infants feels like it's almost empty because it's so light. Looking at the babies, I notice two are cooing and one is not moving. For a split second, I think about saying something to Sister Joan, but quickly move to put the container into the van. The other six children, ages somewhere from four to eight, follow me and climb into the back seats.

The box with the infants is so small that it fits at my feet in the front seat. Just as I'm about to pick up the motionless baby, Sister Joan jumps into the driver's seat and hastily states, "We're getting out of here quickly. Word is that some North Vietnamese soldiers are moving into this area, and we've got to get these kids out of here, especially the Amerasians. According to the NVA and the VC, these Amerasians have blood of the enemy."

With that said, she fires up the engine, puts the van into gear, waves to the two volunteers, and we're moving back onto the street heading to the orphanage.

"Sister, one of the babies in this box isn't moving," I state.

I pick up the baby and cuddle him in my arm. He's so tiny, he feels like a newborn. I check for a pulse, and realize that there is none.

"This baby isn't breathing. We need to stop and get help," I say.

Sister Joan quickly stops the van along the side of the road, and gently takes the infant from me. She also feels for a pulse. Then, she puts her mouth to the baby's lips and begins to breathe into the baby to try to resuscitate it. After a few breaths into the mouth, Sister Joan, with sad eyes and drooping shoulders, says to me, "He's gone. I'm so sorry."

The older children stare at Sister Joan and the infant. There's fear in their eyes. Sister Joan takes out a small jar of water from the side pocket in the door and pours a few drops on the baby's forehead. She makes the sign of the cross and says, "I baptize you in the name of the Father and of the Son and of the Holy Spirit. Amen."

The older children follow Sister Joan's movement by making the sign of the cross.

I'm stunned. My body is limp. Tears trickle down my cheeks. I straighten up and ask Sister Joan to hand me the baby. She does so, and tells me that we'll take the little one back to the orphanage and bury him in the cemetery there. I wrap the infant in the blanket and gently set the body next to the other babies in the box.

"What do you think caused the death of that baby?" I queried.

"Infant deaths out here are not uncommon, John. He most likely died of malnutrition. The half-way houses have so little food and so many children that they can't keep up with it."

Little did I know that this would not be the last child that would die around me before I left this country.

As we proceed back to the orphanage, I watch the refugees making their way toward Saigon. I wonder how many will make it to safety. How many will die on the way? How many will be killed by the North Vietnamese

or the Viet Cong by artillery explosions? How many will just give up?

I try to avoid the thought of the dead infant lying at my feet. The memory of war begins to flow back into my mind.

> I felt nauseous as I looked at the pile of bodies of those dead Viet Cong soldiers killed in an ambush back in 1970. Many were just teenagers. Arms were hanging by the tendons on some of them. The look in their dead eyes was just a blank stare. A few had no heads at all. It was like a pile of rag dolls, but they were once human beings. Vomit filled my mouth. I turned away and felt as weak as a runner feels after a ten thousand meter run. Death engulfed me. I just stared at the pile, mesmerized by what were once live persons. I wondered about their moms and dads, girlfriends and wives. With that, I turned and spilled my guts on the side of the trail.

A bump in the road jars our van and shakes me out of this dream stupor. I once again look at the box at my feet, and feel nauseous. *That baby too was once a live human being. It seems so unfair.*

As our van limps along among the hundreds of refugees pulling carts, and carrying meager goods on their backs, I observe more young children by themselves, just hanging around along the road. Off to the side of a building, a group of children ravages through a garbage pile looking for a scrap of food. It reminds me of a bunch of rats digging through household trash. Poverty and misery are everywhere.

"These children sure have the instinct to survive, Sister."

"They can be pretty hardy, John. They've learned to fend for themselves for the past few years. My fear is for the Amerasians who won't get out of here. If the Viet Cong or the North Vietnamese don't kill them, their life will be miserable. Now that most of the American soldiers are gone, they represent American imperialism to the North Vietnamese."

"I remember how great those Vietnamese kids were when I was here in 1970. We were their saviors. They loved us, and made us feel like it was so worthwhile being here," I say.

"I understand. They do love us, and they feel we can save all of them. But, it's a day-by-day agony knowing we can only get a limited number of them to adoptive parents in the United States. The war is closing in and time is of the essence," she states regretfully.

I somberly reply, "I know."

With a moment of silence in the van as we slowly trudge along the road, my mind again roams back to the children in 1970.

My Marines felt that all of the children were victims of the war. Protecting children is bred into American servicemen. We had to keep up our guard since the Viet Cong used children as decoys and spies. I remember the little Vietnamese boy who came up to my squad leader with his hand out. Sergeant Jackson handed him a package of hot chocolate mix from his C- ration packet. After Jackson gave him the gift, the boy ran quickly away into a heavily wooded area. As quickly as the boy ran into the bushes, small arms fire was pummeling us, wounding Sergeant Jackson in the leg. The little boy had set us up in an ambush. All hell broke loose at that

moment as our group of Marines set up a quick field of fire, blasting the bushes. Fortunately, the ambush was poorly planned, and we were able to force the Viet Cong to retreat before we had any more injuries. Incidents like that were infrequent, and, although we still treated the children with love, we did it with greater caution.

I jump back to the present as the van comes to a quick stop.

"What's up Sister? I excitedly ask.

"It's a checkpoint by some South Vietnamese soldiers."

"What do they want?"

"They're stopping random vehicles, checking for possible VC," she answers.

"We sure don't look like VC," I quickly remark.

"You're right. But they're also looking for some bribe money."

We pull up to the checkpoint. Sister Joan reaches in the pocket of her slacks and pulls out a handful of Piasters. She casually hands it to the South Vietnamese soldier. He waves us through, and we continue our trip back to the orphanage.

"Hopelessness is setting in. Runaway inflation has hit South Vietnam. Food costs have risen as much as 200% and shortages at the orphanages and half-way houses are becoming critical," Sister Joan states with a sigh.

"The South Vietnamese soldiers are aware of the North Vietnamese movement south. Many are deserting. Bribes are also becoming commonplace. These soldiers know they may have to leave the country if Ho Chi Minh's boys take over," she continues.

We arrive back at the orphanage a little before noon. Sister Elizabeth and Sister Nguyen are waiting for us. Sister Joan tells them about the dead baby. Sister Elizabeth quickly comes over to my side of the van and reaches down for the still baby. She picks him up, making sure the blanket covers the baby. She doesn't want the older children to see the baby, although she understands they know what has happened.

Sister Elizabeth states sorrowfully, "I'll take care of the burial this afternoon. You both need to get a bite to eat and get some rest."

"Thank you Sister," we both say in unison as she walks toward the rear of the orphanage.

I realize I'm damn tired when I sit down at the kitchen table for lunch. There's very little conversation. I'm sure Sister Joan, Sister Elizabeth, Sister Nguyen and Sister Anne Marie are all praying silently for the dead baby.

Sister Joan looks up and states, "John, we'll be leaving to go back to the half-way house in about half an hour."

"I thought we were going tomorrow," I hastily reply.

"Things are getting too unstable. I'm worried about that half-way house being in the path of oncoming NVA and VC troops. Those kids are in danger."

I plod off to my room for my "power nap", continuing to think of that poor little baby who never had a chance to see the world.

The fifteen-minute "rest" is all I need to feel eager to move again.

Sister Joan is waiting in the kitchen. She motions for me to come on over and have a seat at the table. We're the only ones in the kitchen.

She quietly says, "John, things are getting a bit tense out there. We're going to need more Piasters and a little protection. Let's take a walk over here."

With that, I follow her to a closet in the rear of the kitchen. She opens it and I see a large safe. She rotates the combination lock on the safe and slowly pulls open the heavy metal door. Inside there are two Colt 45's and a large manila envelope on the shelf. Sister Joan picks up the envelope, pulls out a handful of Piasters, and hands them to me.

"Put these in your pocket. We may need them this afternoon. For your information, the guns are for our self-defense. You and I are going to each carry one of the 45's with us on these trips, since things are getting more precarious out there," she states.

She hands me one of the pistols and two fully loaded magazines. "Keep this loaded and on you from here on in. Please keep it hidden from the children."

I slip the magazine into the pistol and put it in the large right side cargo pocket of my trousers. The additional magazine slides into my left hand pocket with the help of my sweaty hand.

After picking up the other Colt 45, Sister Joan looks over to me and says, "Let's go get some more supplies for our trip."

At the other end of the kitchen, she opens a large pantry door, and pulls out two large boxes of C-rations.

"Where'd you get these?" I quickly ask.

"The black market in Saigon is as well supplied today as it was when you were in country in 1970. C-rations, military equipment and guns are easy to obtain. The volunteers at the half-way house could use this extra food," she answers.

I pick up the boxes and Sister Joan closes the pantry door.

"Let's go. We need to get back here before dark," she fearfully states, as we move toward the van.

Holy crap. What are we in for this afternoon?

CHAPTER

7

Upon leaving the orphanage in the van, a torrential downpour pummels the roof. It's like being under a cascading waterfall. Sister Joan drives very slowly through the huge puddles of water on the road. We rock back and forth, as she passes over the small lakes. My shirt is glued to me from the humidity. The windows of the van cloud up from the rising heat in the air. My head bobs as I try to fight off sleep.

> I had the same clammy feeling that night in 1970 when I rested in a cemetery. I placed my head against a tombstone of some unknown Vietnamese citizen. Our patrol had stopped for a break, since buckets of rain were dumping from the sky. I covered myself with my poncho, but a trickle of water created a tiny river running down my sticky skin. I began shivering and curled to a fetal position. Lying in a pool of dirty water, I strained to keep my eyes from closing. A nudge from my radioman felt like an electric shock and alerted me that it was time to move again. Two hours had passed. I felt miserable.

The van hits a pothole, which yanks me out of my daze.

"Where are we Sister?"

"We have about a half an hour to go. Looks like you got a little rest."

The rain has nearly stopped, but the humidity is worse. I'm soaking wet, as though I just stepped out of the shower. Beads of sweat trickle down my face and the seat of the van feels like a wet towel.

Large crowds of people gather on the road. More refugees move along. They congregate around the van as Sister Joan moves in and out of the mass of humanity. We are like a whale moving among suckerfish. A teenage girl, dressed in rags, sits on the side of the road. She squats next to a cardboard box cradling a half-naked baby. Sitting to the side of the girl, a young boy touches the infant's hand. The boy is barefoot, and his clothes are grimy and frayed. He tries to comfort the child. The young mother holds out her hands, begging for food.

"John, would you please take a couple of bananas to that woman?" Sister Joan says as she stops the van.

I jump out and meander through the crowd. Feeling her tearful eyes staring at me, I hand her the fruit.

Grabbing the nourishment with dirty weathered hands, she replies in broken English, "Tank Ou."

I let out a sigh of disappointment as I get back into the van. *These are three people who probably won't get out of this mess in one piece, or maybe even alive.* I frown as I look at Sister Joan and sense her frustration as she breaks eye contact with me and lowers her head.

"We can't help them all Sister. Can We?"

"It breaks my heart every time I see these people who have lost everything. I try to keep a positive attitude, but inside I'm a mess. Having you on these trips helps me from completely losing it," she says.

"Thanks, Sister."

"John, we do the best we can. We have to keep moving since the volunteers at the half-way house are expecting us. We need to get those children to the orphanage. I'm sorry."

"It's very hard, but I do understand," I sadly respond as I keep thinking of that poor baby in the cardboard box and the mother and boy just sitting there with no hope.

"Did Sister Anne Marie mention to you that Da Nang fell to the North Vietnamese today? That's about three hundred and seventy miles north of us," Sister Joan states.

"No she didn't," I respond inquisitively. "What happened?"

"We got reports over the radio that artillery and rockets began to hit Da Nang airbase a few days ago. After the capture of Ban Me Thuot in the Central Highlands late this month, mass confusion and lowered morale reined among the South Vietnam soldiers. The NVA captured many aircraft and many South Vietnam soldiers who were assisting their fleeing families. Unfortunately, the ARVN were overrun. Chaos ruled," she states.

"I assume this will cause more refugees to flee further south," I reply.

"Yes it will. Also, I'm told that the fall of Da Nang

is causing wide spread panic and desertion within the South Vietnamese army. The North Vietnamese Army, sensing that victory is theirs, is deploying their reserves and immediately pushing south along the coast in what is known as the 'Ho Chi Minh Campaign', the final thrust toward Saigon."

I'm drained of energy at this point and say nothing in return to Sister Joan. I just stare out the window of the van and watch the refugees along side of us. This reminds me of the helpless feeling that night on Monkey Mountain, watching the explosions on the airstrip at Da Nang.

> We were the highest outpost perimeter for protection of the airbase. The Viet Cong sappers (commandos) were able to covertly get in and blow up F-105 jets and destroy many buildings. I remember witnessing the explosions and gunfire. The Air Force and Marines on the airfield were fighting for their lives. It was like watching a Fourth of July fireworks display. The many detonations created an array of red, green and white sparks followed by white smoke spiraling into the sky. Unfortunately, it was not a celebration---it was war. When it was all over, our Americans were able to save the base, and destroy the attackers. Unfortunately, lives were lost on both sides, and many aircraft were totally destroyed.

"John, are you okay?" Sister Joan asks.

"Yes, I'm okay. Just daydreaming about the war."

Children are everywhere. Refugees pack the streets. They move with heads bowed and total exhaustion flaunting their faces. They're dirty, homeless, miserable... just trying to endure. Women carry children strapped to their backs. Adults and children pull carts full of household goods. Young boys and girls ride water buffaloes. All outside help appears to have disappeared. According to the radio reports, poverty is gripping the country of Vietnam. Stealing and pilfering are rampant. People have nowhere to go.

"This is unbelievable, Sister. Where are these people going to end up? There are so many children and women, but no young men."

"Many of the children will just die, John. The mothers have no way of supporting them. Many of the fathers are either dead or fighting as soldiers. Parents believe the children are better off in orphanages than with them. That's why so many children are dropped off at Binh Trieu and other half-way houses in Vietnam. What the mothers don't realize is the children need love and personal attention as well as food and shelter. An orphanage is not always a good substitute for the family."

"What do you mean?" I ask.

"We've found that many of the children die before the age of six, most of them within the first couple of years. It's just due to lack of this love, personal attention and emotional stimulation. A few of the orphanages and half-way houses in Vietnam lose up to eighty percent of the children. Many died due to this lack of affection."

Emptiness again becomes my companion as I think about Sister Joan's comments. Our hopes to help these children are deteriorating.

The van stops. The congestion caused by refugees, motor bikes, cars, small animals and water buffaloes creates gridlock. Suddenly a woman sets a child on the ground in front of the van and runs away. When I yell at her to come back, she disappears into the crowd. I quickly jump out and pick up the baby. Wrapped in a light soiled blanket, the child is sound asleep. It can't be any older than a year. The infant is silent when I carry it back to the van. I look at Sister Joan. I'm bewildered.

"I guess we have another child for the orphanage, Sister. This is unbelievable!"

"Just hold the baby. We should be to the half-way house in a few minutes. Is the child breathing?" she asks.

The infant starts to open it's tiny eyes. I lightly touch the chest and feel a slight heart beat. A whistling sigh of relief flows from my mouth as I exhale.

"The heart is beating, Sister. I don't even know if it's a boy or a girl."

Finally, the van starts to travel at a crawl. Sister Joan maneuvers in and out of the crowd like a snake moving at the pace of a tarantula crossing the road. At least we're making progress. I look straight ahead, holding a tiny baby on my lap and wonder what else can happen on this trip.

The infant is sleeping in the cradle of my arms when we arrive at the half-way house. One of the young Vietnamese volunteers comes out to the van as I am exiting from the right side. She looks at me with wide-open eyes as if to say, "Why do you have a baby in your arms?"

I hand her the child, and Sister Joan tells her in Vietnamese to get some milk for the infant. The girl quickly walks back into the half-way house with the baby.

"John, we won't be staying here very long. We're going

to be taking the remaining seven children and one infant back to Binh Trieu. Also, we'll be taking the new baby with us. Please take the boxes of C-rations into the house. I'm sure they'll be getting more kids here soon."

Sister Joan gathers up the children and brings them out toward the van. Four girls follow Sister Joan's orders by walking briskly to the van and climb in the back. One boy, who is missing a leg, slowly hobbles to the van on crutches. He smiles at me as two of the boys in the van help him climb up into the vehicle.

Sister Joan walks toward me carrying a cardboard box. I look in and see two tiny babies. She hands the container to me.

"Please put this at your feet in the van. The one on the right is a girl. She's the one given to us on the road. The one on the left is a boy from the half-way house. Both have been given a quick bottle of milk and should be ready for the trip back to the orphanage," she says.

"Are they okay? I ask.

"They appear to be fine. We just need to get out of here. The volunteer girls from the half-way house tell me that neighbors have seen "Charlie" in the area, and they're afraid for the children. They expect more kids to arrive here later. Hopefully, we can get back to pick them up."

"So they still call the VC "Charlie", eh Sister?"

"Sure do," she replies, jumping into the driver's seat. She looks back at the children, takes a quick view of the babies at my feet, and starts the engine.

"Let's go," she says as she waves to the two young volunteers and pulls out onto the road.

The first twenty minutes of the drive back is slow but

steady. I spot a group of uniformed military personnel stopping traffic up ahead. Sister Joan slows the van, and we move in line toward the soldiers.

"What's going on?" I nervously ask.

"Looks like some type of checkpoint."

"It wasn't here on the way to the half-way house, Sister."

"I know. But, they set up these checkpoints at random," she replies.

Sister Joan pulls out some Piasters from her pocket and moves the van closer to the soldiers.

Just then, explosions erupt out in the distance. Blankets of black smoke rise up to the soft white pillows of clouds in the horizon. More explosions. I'm edgy. *Settle down, John. This isn't the first time you've been around artillery.*

The crowds on the road continue to move along, as if nothing new has happened. They appear to be immune to any more fear. The bombing is part of their life. They just ignore it.

"Stop right here," one of the soldiers commands in good English.

Sister Joan immediately halts the van and says, "What's wrong, sir? We're on our way to our orphanage in Binh Trieu."

The soldier is wearing soiled brown khaki pants and a dirty wrinkled grayish shirt. His face has at least two days growth and brown sweat marks are visible along both sides of his face. His black hair protrudes from a disheveled military cap, which is cocked to the side of his head. No rank is visible on his uniform. The scowl on his face gives him the confidence of being in charge. A holster carrying a pistol hangs loosely on his belt.

He moves toward the driver's side of the van, puts his hand on the pistol and says, "Who are these children? Why are you driving them toward Saigon?"

At that moment, I put my hand into my pocket and surround the Colt 45 with my fingers. I fumble around and get my trigger finger in place on the weapon.

Sister Joan responds to the soldier, "I told you I was taking these children to Binh Trieu Orphanage."

"Do you have paperwork for all of them?" he asks.

"Yes I do. But it's at the orphanage."

At this point, I sense that Sister Joan realizes she can't reveal that she has no paperwork for one of the infants.

"That could be a problem," he says as a slight grin crosses his face.

Sister Joan carefully moves her left hand, holding the Piasters, and lifts her arm up so the soldier can see the money. His slight grin turns into a broad smile, which crosses his face like a half moon.

She hands him the money and he says, "Go. Get out of here."

Without hesitation, Sister Joan steps on the gas, and we quickly move away from the soldier. I release my finger from the trigger of my pistol and lift my hand carefully out of the pocket of my trousers.

"I'm sick of these people wanting bribes everywhere we go," Sister Joan states. "These government soldiers are fearful, and everyone wants more money. They think that's their salvation. My concern is that we're going to need additional funds if more panic sets in."

As we move slowly along, the word "panic" triggers thoughts of a situation in 1970 in a little hamlet outside of Da Nang.

> The Viet Cong had visited the village during the night and killed two teachers and the village chief. As we walked into the village the following morning, the look on the faces of the women was one of sheer terror. Tears flowed down the cheeks of the three women who obviously lost some loved ones. I tried to ask them who had killed the teachers and the village chief. Panic filled their eyes as they quickly looked all around, avoiding eye contact with me. Finally, they walked away from me, afraid to say anything for fear of being hurt that night. I knew in my heart that they were concerned for their lives and would not tell me anything. The Viet Cong ruled their lives, and telling us anything could mean death to them in the future.

I'm drawn back to the present when the horn starts tooting. Sister Joan is trying to get some of the throng to move away from us. She moves the van from left to right and then back again to avoid hitting them.

At that moment, a man, who looks like he may be a South Vietnamese soldier, dressed in mucky and ripped brown khaki trousers and shirt, runs along the side of the van and yells to Sister Joan to stop the van.

She continues to drive, trying to ignore the man trotting next to her. He's carrying a young boy in his arms as he continues to run parallel to us.

"Stop, please," he yells. He points a pistol at the window of the van just opposite Sister Joan's face. Immediately she immobilizes the van by jamming her foot on the brake. I quickly put my hand back into my cargo pocket and cling to the Colt 45.

The man pulls his pistol back and says to Sister Joan, "Please take boy. Can't feed. Please."

"We can't take any more children. Our truck is full and we need papers that show the children are orphans," she calmly states.

I draw my pistol out of my pocket and thrust my arm across the chest of Sister Joan, pointing the pistol at the face of the man. His eyes propel open and, for a split second, he appears to consider pointing his pistol at me. But, he turns, holds on tight to the boy, and starts running away from the van.

"Nice job, John", Sister Joan casually states, as if I had given the man a scolding rather than pointing a weapon at him.

" Weren't you nervous, Sister?"

"I was terrified. But I could sense he was desperate, and wouldn't have used his weapon."

"I pulled out the pistol because I felt we couldn't take any chances," I answered.

"Thanks. I'm glad you did," she said, exhaling with a sigh of relief.

After I put the Colt 45 back into my pocket, and Sister Joan continues to drive, I think of the narrow escapes we had during the war.

> As we set up our perimeters at night, we always dug foxholes. Although we were dead tired from patrolling all day, digging the foxholes was impor-

tant as a protection against Viet Cong sneaking up on us during the dark hours. Foxholes were also relatively safe havens against mortar and artillery attacks. It was always better to be safe than sorry. The extra two hours of sleep lost because of digging a foxhole could easily save our lives. I remember the one night looking into the darkness from my foxhole trying to keep awake when all of a sudden mortar rounds began dropping around us. I immediately ducked down, yelling to those near me that we had incoming. Of course they all knew we had incoming! I was so low in the hole that I felt like a gopher hiding from a vicious cat on the prowl. The foxholes saved us, as mortar rounds continued to drop for the next two minutes. Two minutes felt like two hours, but again we had survived the "close call" of death or injury.

I look out of the window of the van and see more military vehicles on the road. They're moving in the same direction as the refugees. All are on their way to Saigon. Many children wander alone. They have no belongings, and many of the older children carry babies. With only a tee shirt, shorts and Ho Chi Minh sandals (open-toed sandals made out of rubber tires), or no shoes at all, the young kids move with the flow of the crowd. *What will happen to them if the country is overrun? Some of them will be survivors, but many of them will die of starvation and neglect.*

"How will they endure, Sister?" I innocently ask.

"They'll find garbage dumps, beg, or do whatever it takes to stay alive. They're pretty durable. I only wish we could take more of them to the orphanage. The problem is that kids are being dropped off hourly at Binh Trieu, and we have to figure out how to process them for adoption. I just hope we can get all the children out safely."

During the last half hour of our drive, I stare into the crowd, and remember Private Tony Martinez and Lance Corporal Billy Clancey discussing their futile situation in 1970.

> "Hey Billy, what are you going to do when you get out of this shithole?"
>
> "I'm going to take a hot shower, have a cold Bud, and sleep forever without an alarm clock," Billy replied.
>
> "How about you, Tony?"
>
> "Me, I'm going to see my girl friend and just lay on the beach all day soaking up the sun. You know, I'm sick of this patrolling all day. I'm going to take a long nap now. Can you cover for me?" asked Tony.
>
> "If I was you, I wouldn't take a nap. You're supposed to be cleaning your rifle for our next patrol. Lieutenant Ellis will be on your ass, and you could get in deep shit," Billy said.
>
> "Listen, Billy, so what if the EL TEE gets on my ass. What are they going to do, send me to Vietnam?"
>
> With that said they both laughed, realizing it couldn't get much worse, and Private Martinez rested his head on his backpack and closed his eyes.
>
> Neither of these Marines knew I overheard their conversation, but I quietly walked away and understood their frustrations with the war.

"We're just about to the orphanage. How are the babies doing'" Sister Joan asks.

The infants appear to be sound asleep among the chaos surrounding us. "They seem very content, Sister."

Sister Joan pulls the van into the front of the orphanage, turns off the engine, and tells the children in the backseat to get out. When I open the front door, the babies both begin crying at the same time.

Sister Nguyen walks over to the van and says, "What have we here?"

"Some new additions, Sister. Can you take them for me?"

"Of course," she says. She picks up the box of infants, and walks toward the front door of the orphanage. *Wow, Sister Nguyen sure is casual about that. I guess she's use to all of this confusion and surprises.*

The rest of the children file into the orphanage. Sister Joan tells them to go to the kitchen for their meal. They're all smiles, even the boy with the missing leg. The mention of food seems to be the catalyst to keeping these young ones happy.

Sitting next to Sister Joan at dinner, I ask, "How did Sister Nguyen get to this orphanage?"

"Sister Nguyen is an interesting lady, John. She was raised in a half-way house in Xuan Loc, which is about 38 miles from Saigon. Her mother delivered her at the house's clinic, and left her there.

"I just can't imagine abandoning a child. At least my mom put me up for adoption when she was pregnant. My adoptive parents were there shortly after my birth. We're so blessed to have been born in America," I reply.

"We sure are, John. The kids over here aren't so lucky. They've been living in a war-torn country for centuries."

"Tell me more about Sister Nguyen," I say.

"Well, the nuns at the clinic named her Chi. She lived at the half-way house until she was around fourteen. She's a very determined person. When she finished her high school education, she went into the local convent, and was able to become a nurse by training in a hospital in Saigon. Her religious name is Sister Yvonne Nguyen. We were able to hire her at Binh Trieu right after she got her nursing credential."

"But she looks so young," I state.

"Actually she's thirty-one years old. She's been working at Binh Trieu Orphanage for seven years. Being an orphan herself, she's dedicated to helping these children make it in life.

"Thanks for sharing that with me. I think I'll head off to bed. Good night."

"Good night, John."

I walk toward my room. There's another explosion far off. Looking out to the horizon, I see more smoke make its way in a rope-like fashion toward the silky sky. More explosions, and the "rat-tat-tat" of a fifty-caliber machine gun, continue to break the silence of the evening.

The orange horizon is turning to grey as the sun sets into the distant fields. The sky is completing its routine of darkening.

How close are the NVA getting to Saigon?, I wonder. *Closer than I think, maybe.*

CHAPTER

8

Unmerciful monsoons batter the orphanage for the next four days. There are a few sun breaks, which create rising heat from the adjoining rice paddies. Humidity envelopes us. Energy evaporates from my body.

Paperwork consumes me. I care for babies and entertain young kids during our sixteen-hour workdays. I'm beginning to wear down. Only a few children are dropped off at our doorstep. The constant downpour deters mothers from visiting and asking us to take their babies.

Arriving at the kitchen at five-thirty in the morning on April 3, I take off my San Francisco Giants baseball cap and sit down at the table. Sister Joan, Sister Elizabeth, Sister Nguyen and Sister Anne Marie all have apprehensive looks on their faces.

"Good morning, John," the chorus of four nuns greets me.

"Morning. Kind of an early meeting today, huh?"

Sister Joan replies, "Yep. Today is going to be another busy one for us. News from the U.S. embassy is that USAID is negotiating with the Minister of Social Welfare of Vietnam, Dr. Phan Quang Dan. He's supposed to expedite getting the orphans out who have the necessary paperwork and are approved for adoption in the U.S. Since things are becoming critical, it's somewhat of a public relations item for both the United States and the Vietnamese government to get these children to the U.S."

"How critical is it?" I gingerly ask.

"Adoptive parents in the U.S. are watching the news, and are well aware that the North Vietnamese continue moving closer to Saigon. They fear for the children that are supposed to be sent safely to them. They're putting pressure on their Congressmen and Senators. Our Ambassador here is also stressing to the South Vietnamese government that getting these orphans out of here will help turn public opinion in the United States in a more favorable direction toward South Vietnam."

"How soon can we get the rest of children on flights to the U.S.?" I ask.

"I'm not sure. The South Vietnamese government also indicates that the escorts, who are mostly American dependents helping the agencies with the children on the flights, can leave without exit visas on flights to the U.S. Vietnamese, Chinese and French are not allowed out of the country now," she states with a worried look.

"Why is that?" I respond.

"Because the South Vietnamese government wants to

limit exportation of the Vietnamese, Chinese and French since most of them are Vietnamese citizens.

"What about Sister Elizabeth and Sister Nguyen? Will they be able to leave?"

"I'm confident I can figure that one out when the time comes. Right now, we have to get the children and volunteers organized and their papers finalized. Our embassy tells me that flights will begin in about two to three days. Ed Daly's unauthorized flights of the World Airways planes to get children out of Danang and Saigon have caused a public outcry in America. He took it upon himself to get the World Airways flights to and from Vietnam, without any approval from the U.S. government. After landing in Danang, masses of refugees ran toward his plane, trying to get on, anyway they could. One man was hanging onto the wheel well when the plane took off. Obviously, he was killed. It was an ugly scene," Sister Joan replies.

"It's been all over the news about his flying babies out of that area," Sister Anne Marie states.

After a rather quick breakfast of oatmeal and fruit, I, along with the sisters, retire to the office in the back of the orphanage and attack the mounds of paperwork. I start to daydream as I continue typing and editing various government forms. The boredom of those daily patrols in 1970 leaks into my mind.

> My twelve-man patrol had been walking since six o'clock in the morning, searching for Viet Cong troops, which our intelligence officer indicated, were in the area. After six hours of slow movement and total concentration, we had seen nothing but

a couple of water buffaloes and a few Vietnamese civilians. Boredom started to set in. Knowing how dangerous tedium can be in a combat environment, I ordered my patrol to set up a perimeter for the next two hours and take a rest. Six could sleep and six would stay awake at all times.

After a short rest, I reviewed my topo map, and decided to send my two American Indian scouts to find a position in which we could move at dark to set up for the evening. The Indian scouts were skilled at finding protective areas for the stealthily movement required in the pitch black of the night. Moving at night to another position assured us of a fair amount of protection against an attack from the Viet Cong who may have spotted us during the day. Although the VC may have heard us move after dark, they could not pinpoint the exact perimeter we set up. Thus, attacking us at night could be risky. This "cat and mouse" guerilla warfare was somewhat of a game, but a very deadly one if you couldn't outsmart the enemy.

At around three o'clock that afternoon, we again began patrolling the countryside, regaining our alertness after the short rest. The "ping-ping" sound of bullets hitting the dirt near the front of the patrol shattered the monotony of our movement. My Marines moved in the direction of the sniper shots, and they opened fire with the fifty-caliber machine gun into a tree line on our right. The semi-automatic sounds of M-16 rifles could also be heard as a background noise to the machine gun. After about thirty seconds, I gave the cease-fire command, and there was dead silence. As I listened and looked with my binoculars, I gave a hand signal to move in the direction of the sniper fire. A half hour of searching proved futile, as the sniper had evaded us. No more boredom. Adrenaline was pumping through all of my veins. Our movement after dark that night was done with precision.

Sister Joan nudges me out of my muse and asks, "How are we doing on the Xuan Yen file? I plan on shipping all of the babies are out of here soon with the older kids."

With Sister Joan looking over my shoulder, I quickly rifle through my stack of papers and pull out the Xuan Yen file. Paging through the paper-clipped information, I state, "I'm not sure, but I'll review it and have it ready to go shortly. I thought the government won't let infants out of here right now."

"That's true. But, with the urgency of the NVA moving closer, the main office is telling me to have all the children ready, no matter what the age. Let's just keep moving through these documents so we're ready when necessary," she replies, sensing that I had been taking a break with my daydreaming.

At that moment, Sister Anne Marie comes running into the room and says excitedly, "President Ford just announced on TV that 'Operation Babylift' would be implemented and the United States government will assist in the evacuation of orphans from Vietnam. It sounds like the White House is being bombarded with appeals to help get the orphans out of Vietnam after hearing about Ed Daly airlifting kids to America. All of a sudden, there's sympathetic public opinion and enthusiasm by Americans to help us get our children out of Vietnam. The report is that President Ford declared he would cut the red tape and other bureaucratic obstacles preventing orphans from coming to America. This is great news!"

I'll always remember April 3, 1975, when our President finally comes to our aid. I'm relieved. I almost start to cry, but hold back the tears of joy. Sweat gathers under the rim of my black Giants cap. I've been back in Vietnam for just over a month, but it feels like a year considering what we've accomplished. I realize that we now have a huge job of getting these children out of here in a very short time period.

"Let's get back to work," Sister Joan states matter-of-factly. "We've got a lot to do. Plan on some more late nights for the next few days. We also need birth certificates, wristband ID's, passports, visas, and emergency travel documents for each child."

"What about the children without birth certificates—the ones from the street or the ones dropped off by their mothers or soldiers?" I quickly ask.

"I'm not sure, John. Prepare as much as you can on each child. I hope President Ford meant it when he said he was going to streamline the paperwork for these adoptions. He said he plans to airlift over 2000 children to Travis Air Force Base near San Francisco and to other West Coast air bases."

The monsoon rains take a break, but not the heat. While I'm working at my desk, perspiration drips down my temple. The Vietnam summer is approaching. The seat of my pants is sticking to the chair and sweat is forming under my arms and soaking into my cotton shirt. *Wow, I forgot how hot this place could be.* I turn on the portable fan on the desk to refresh my face with the slight breeze it creates. I look out the window. The sky has turned from grey to black, and a slight drizzle begins pinging on the tin roof of the orphanage. The temperature feels like it's dropping slightly, but I'm still sweating. Staring at the water-beaded window, I think about the tortuous climate back in 1970.

> Our patrol got ready to move that morning near Monkey Mountain, The steam rose off the ground like a sheet being lifted off a bed. It had rained most of the night as we kept our typical one man alert in each foxhole. I moved around to check on the men and my jungle utility uniform stuck to me like a latex glove. The cotton material of the jacket and trousers of the green utilities absorbed sweat like a sponge. We'd been in the field, patrolling for five days. The daytime temperatures had stayed around one hundred degrees, with intermittent rain occurring almost every day. My clothes were literally rotting away. We couldn't wear underwear because it would chafe our skin as we continuously were on the move. The clothes hung loosely and were always wet. I could smell my own body stink, which meant that it must have been a rancid odor to anyone around me. When we jumped on the evacuation helicopter, I knew the crew chief had to hold his breath due to the putrid stench. However, we were all in the same boat, and I knew, when we got back to the battalion area, that we could throw away our clothing, shower, and get brand new garb.

Returning to reality, I ask, "Sister Joan, how many of our children will be getting out of here on the military planes authorized by President Ford?"

"I'm not sure. I figure we have at least three hundred children to process between our orphanage and the children from the half-way houses. Also, more children could be dropped off on our doorstep by the panic of the refugees. We just have to keep working to get as much documentation as possible completed for each child. The

Amerasians and the handicapped will have priority as far as I'm concerned. But, I plan to get all of the children out of here. You know, when the French occupied Vietnam in the 1950's, children sired by French military personnel were entitled to French citizenship after the war. I hope the U.S. can follow that path when we get these kids to America."

"I have the file on Xuan Yen. Her paperwork looks good. We have a birth certificate, which shows where she was born. There's no mother's name since her mother left the clinic after the birth. The rest of her file is complete, so she's ready. She's pretty young for a long flight to the United States," I say.

"I'm sure she'll be okay, John. She's a healthy baby, and looks to be quite strong. I'm more concerned about Binh, the boy who we call a 'failure to thrive baby'. He has me worried. I want him on the first flight out of here. His adoptive parents are very excited about his arrival. Please check to see if all of his documents are complete as well."

"I've checked his papers, and he's ready to go. Also, I've gone through Trun's paperwork, and he looks good. He's such a bright light in this orphanage. He can't walk, but he acts as if he's Superman with those crutches, moving through the beds offering to help the others. These kids amaze me," I respond.

"Will you also check on Ah, the other young man who can't walk? He too should get out on an early flight, if possible," she says.

"Sure. I'll get right to it, Sister."

I know Sister Joan wants to get the handicapped children and the babies out of here with the first group.

Although word has come from the "higher ups" that healthy children will be airlifted out first to show how well the children have been cared for, Sister Joan continues to stress to us that we're getting the most "needy" out as soon as possible.

These little children are becoming family to me. They've been through hell, yet they act like they're getting ready for a vacation. I think about how lucky I am to be able to be part of helping them get a better life in America. *I guess it **is** like going on vacation to them.*

I continue to work into the evening following a dinner of pho, fruit and vegetables. This evening is hot and humid, and my body is as sticky as syrup. I keep wiping my hands on my trousers in order to keep the moisture off the papers on the desk. Mosquitoes are circling above like helicopters forming to attack. A lizard is climbing the blank wall off to my right. *This climate brings out all of the creepy creatures.* It reminds me of living in the bush during the war.

> I can't forget that very hot and humid afternoon while taking a break with my small patrol. I leaned against a tree, and seconds later jumped up screaming. I felt like my right leg was being poked with a hundred needles. I began slapping my leg and pulling up my utility trouser at the same time. Dozens of red ants were feasting on my bare skin. The ants were having a banquet on me. I quickly rubbed them off and got away from the anthill on which I had been sitting. I continued to soothe the surface of my skin, by rubbing my hand up and down over the little welts caused by the buggers.
>
> The weather was heaven for critters. Many times on patrol, we would walk right up to a huge web, with

a spider the size of my hand staring me in the face. My heart would stop for what seemed like a full minute, until I remembered I was bigger than the spider, and whipped it down with a stick. Between the spiders, snakes (of which many were very poisonous), leeches, ants, lizards and other unnamed insects, I realized the Viet Cong and the North Vietnamese Army weren't our only enemy.

"Bang-bang-bang!"

"Boom!" "Boom!"

The sound of small arms fire and small artillery explosions jolt me. I run to the window to see where the blasts occurred. All I see is a lazy drift of smoke climbing into view a few miles away. *Man, the North Vietnamese are getting closer. I hope Sister Joan realizes how hot things are out there.*

There's no significant crying in the orphanage. Glancing at my watch, I see it's 9:36 PM. It appears most of the children are used to the sounds of war, and they manage to sleep through the chaos.

Our orphanage is around ten miles from Tan Son Nhat Airport, which is near the center of Saigon. The North Vietnamese are not far outside the city. We're told that the South Vietnamese are putting up a good fight, but that it's inevitable Saigon will be taken within the month if the NVA continue their aggressive movement through the country. If Saigon falls, there's little hope that the Amerasian children, or any orphans, will continue to be allowed to evacuate the country.

By eleven o'clock PM, I'm exhausted. Walking into the kitchen for a cup of coffee, I see some of the nuns are also there. They show signs of total fatigue, since they also have been working all day and much of the evening. I pull up a chair next to Sister Nguyen and ask, "How long has Sister Elizabeth been at Binh Trieu Orphanage?"

"About a year and a half. She's very dedicated to helping these children."

"I can see that, Sister. Where's she from?"

"Actually, she's not far from home. She was brought up in Cholon, Saigon's Chinese District. It's a big market center. Also, it's a 'black market' area, trading in US military items. Both of her parents were killed in a fire when their market was burned to the ground. Sister Elizabeth was rescued from the fire and was brought to an orphanage when she was around ten years old."

"When did she join the order?" I ask.

"My understanding is that she was influenced by the nuns in the Catholic orphanage to go into the convent after she finished high school. She told me she always wanted to work with children, especially orphans. So, after her training, she ended up working at various orphanages in Vietnam. Lucky for us, she was sent here not too long ago."

Sister Joan walks into the kitchen and says, "Let's check the children and get a good night's sleep. We'll have another demanding day tomorrow. The tempo of the evacuation is picking up. Adoptive parents in the United States are continuing to put pressure on their Representatives and Social Service providers to get their adoptive children to America. It appears that President Ford is quite emphatic about making this happen."

"How soon before we can get children on a plane?" Sister Nguyen asks.

"The government announced today that a C-5A

Galaxy Air Force cargo plane was ordered to fly to Saigon for the first official 'Babylift' to America. That plane will be here tomorrow. I expect we can get our children on it. We also have about twenty Amerasians and handicapped children coming from a half-way house a few miles from here," says Sister Joan.

"How many can we get on that plane, Sister?" I query.

"Hopefully over fifty. That means the children in our orphanage plus around twenty from the half-way house, who have been processed and will be arriving here early in the morning. Other agencies like Holt, Friends of Children of Viet Nam, and Friends for All Children are among the agencies that will also have children for the evacuation. We have to share with these and other organizations. I'm told that this cargo plane holds over 300 persons. President Ford stated that all of the planes for the 'Babylift' will be specially equipped with oxygen, seat belts, food, and emergency medical equipment. The total trip to the United States is about twenty-four hours. I think the plane has one stop at Clark Air Force Base in the Philippines. This long flight could be a strain on many of the children."

Eruptions of pounding in my chest catch my breathe. *Let's hope they all make it alive?* The reality of that wish puts me in a trance. I continue to think of those innocent little children whose lives we are now trying to save. I don't want to go to bed now. I need to get more of their papers reviewed so they'll get out of here. My mind goes a mile a minute, but my body is exhausted. I realize I had better get a couple hours of sleep.

I walk to my room and roll onto the bed. I'm asleep within minutes.

I pop up from my pillow with a jerk, still thinking about getting the children on that first plane out. Looking at the clock, I see it is four o'clock in the morning. I'm wide-awake. I crawl out of bed, take a quick shower, pass on shaving, and wander into the kitchen. Sister Joan is sipping a cup of coffee and studying some documents.

"Morning, Sister. Looks like you're also anxious to get things moving today."

"Yes, John. We need to have the children who are going on the flight out of Tan Son Nhat Airport to the tarmac by noon today. I've been on the phone a good portion of the night, talking with some of the other adoption agencies. The politics are overwhelming. I finally convinced the coordinator of the flight that we have fifty-eight children ready to go. I've reviewed all the paperwork and we should be okay to get those children on the plane.

"I'm ready to go," I reply.

"On our way to the airport, we've got to stop at the Vietnamese Ministry of Social Welfare to show them we have documentation for all of the children. I know we'll be getting more children the next few days from half-way houses in the area, from refugees and from soldiers dropping children at our doorstep; but, we're going to get the ones who are now ready on this first flight," she states earnestly.

"What else can I do to help you get them ready for transportation to the airport?"

"At this point, let's wake up the other Sisters and volunteers, get the children fed, and prepare them for the trip. The children from the halfway house should be here soon. We should get on the road by eight-thirty at the latest."

My adrenaline continues to pump vigorously. My arms twitch and my legs tingle. I walk down the hall and knock on the doors of the other nuns and volunteers. I then go into the children's rooms to wake them and begin getting the older children ready for breakfast.

Shortly thereafter, the orphanage bustles with activity. The children are sitting at the kitchen table eating their bowls of rice, and the nuns and volunteers feed the babies. Excitement permeates the air. Children chat in Vietnamese and they sense that something good is happening to them. Some of the babies cry amongst the lively talk in the room. Sister Nguyen, Sister Elizabeth and Sister Anne Marie scurry around, preparing the infants for transport to the airport. The nuns pack diapers, milk, blankets and all the items necessary for the trip. Sister Joan tells the older children to get themselves ready as soon as they finish their breakfast.

As Sister Elizabeth walks toward us, holding a tiny child, Sister Joan says, "Sister, you and John will be accompanying the children on the first flight to America. Both of you have authorization to return to Vietnam on one of the Air Force flights after you get at least a day of rest in the States. Make sure you have your passports and papers in order."

Sister Elizabeth replies, "But Sister, I would rather let some of the others go on that flight. I know you need help with the later evacuees."

"I'm sorry Sister, but I really need to have both of you

on the plane to care for our children so they are processed correctly when you get to America. I have all the paperwork. I'll be able to get an exit visa for you since the South Vietnamese government knows you will be coming back."

I listen to Sister Joan's comments to Sister Elizabeth, and continue to get the children ready. I'm excited to be going on the first official flight out. I'll get a chance to see my parents and my sister, and be able to tell them what is really going on with this 'Babylift', and how critical the war situation is in South Vietnam.

At around seven o'clock, three vans from the half-way house pull up in front of the orphanage. A Vietnamese woman jumps out of the driver's side of the lead vehicle, walks over to me and introduces herself as Sister Celeste. She's about five feet tall, and barely looks older than a teenager. She has the deep black circles under her eyes of a person who has seen little sleep and has been working extremely hard. She exhibits a warm smile.

I greet her and introduce myself. "Sister Celeste, I'm John Ellis. Very happy to meet you. Have the children had any food this morning?"

"Nice to meet you, John. Yes. The children have been fed. I'd like to give all the papers for adoption to Sister Joan before we leave for the airport."

"Come this way, Sister. Sister Joan is expecting you. Did you encounter any resistance or delays in your trip here?"

"We were stopped once by some South Vietnamese Army guards, but they were satisfied to let us proceed after accepting the envelope with Piasters."

Once inside, Sister Celeste and Sister Joan greet each other and proceed to the kitchen. The entire staff of Sisters and volunteers is sitting at the kitchen table.

"Okay, everyone," Sister Joan raises her voice to the group. "We have fifty-eight children to get to Tan Son Nhat Airport by noon. I'm not sure how much confusion there will be at the airport, but I want us to be as organized as possible. We've got to stop at the Ministry of Social Welfare in Saigon prior to entry to the airport. Each of us is responsible for the children in our specific van. We don't want the Vietnamese government holding us up any longer than necessary. This first flight out is critical. We have seven vans—three from the half-way house and four of our own. It's going to be a bit cramped."

In her typical command presence voice, she continues, "Let's move out at eight-fifteen sharp. Sister Elizabeth and John will be accompanying the children to America. They'll be back in a few days. The paperwork is in the office. Make sure that you pick up a packet for each child who will be in your van. Any questions?"

The room is silent. I hear the faint voices of children in the other rooms and a few babies crying. *Wow. Fifty-eight kids to the airport with the correct paper work. This is overwhelming!*

After a few moments, Sister Joan continues, "Okay, let's start getting things ready to go."

I head to my room to pack up the few belongings for the trip. This is an historic day. I'm thrilled being able to help these children, like the ones I admired so much when I was here in 1970. With a broad smile on my face, I recognize I'm making a difference in this country. I can only imagine the anticipation and emotion of the adoptive parents in the United States waiting to hear if their children are going to be on this first flight of the "Babylift".

My nerves are unraveling. I ponder about what this day is going be like.

CHAPTER

9

"John, will you join me," Sister Joan waves with her arm up and hand moving toward her. *Looks like it's time to go to the airport.*

She slips me a Colt 45 and says, "I got this from the storage room. Keep this concealed. There's no telling if we'll need it. I'm sure there'll be many checkpoints to deal with on the way. I have both American dollars and Piasters, if needed." *Wow, I feel like I'm getting ready to move out on patrol again.*

With bags under her eyes and accentuated tired wrinkles enveloping her face, she sighs with a deep breath, "Sister Elizabeth and Sister Nguyen have been working since early this morning getting the children ready for this flight to the United States. The kids need to be dressed in clean clothes. We want them to look their best for their adoptive parents."

I stare at the exhausted face of Sister Joan. She's

running on adrenaline. In a hurried manner she snaps, "Sisters, would you please start loading the children?"

The two nuns immediately begin putting the brood on the vehicles in an orderly mode. The older boys and girls help with the younger ones. Cardboard boxes provide a riding place for the babies. They are positioned in rows next to each other on the floors of the vans. Trun moves to my van on his crutch and is smiling like a child on the way to Disneyland. He's a boy on a mission and senses that he's on his way to a better life. Binh is walking with Sister Elizabeth and has a sad look on his face. He's not sure of his future. Despite the pain from her burned arm, Chi helps the sisters. She's only able to use her right arm since the left one is still wrapped with gauze. She grimaces as she assists the younger children. This doesn't stop her from producing a half smile.

I pick up An, crutches and all, and carry him to the lead van. "Sister, these kids are so patient. They amaze me every day."

"Most of them have been through some type of hell, and they feel they're on their way to heaven," Sister Elizabeth replies softly, with love in her voice and warmth in her eyes.

The vehicles, with me driving the lead van, are lined up in the front gravel area. It looks like a caravan ready to haul a group of kids on a field trip. Sister Joan sits in the "shotgun" seat. Stress lines furrow across her face. Below her feet are two cardboard boxes holding four tiny babies. In the back seats, young voices ring with the everyday chatter of children.

We begin our drive onto the main highway to the airport. Crowds of refugees congest the road. The vans move like snails finding their way through heavy brush.

"How long will it take us to get to the Ministry of Social Welfare office, Sister?"

"We should be there in about an hour. I have all of the documents in my briefcase. I do hope they don't delay us too long. As you know, we need to be at the airport by noon. It's vitally important that we get these children on this first plane to America. This morning all the TV commentators were talking about how adoptive parents are anxiously waiting for these children coming on "Operation Babylift."

As the vans creep along, a Vietnamese woman, wearing a bamboo conical hat and dressed in nothing but rags, pounds on our van and holds up her child to us. She yells in Vietnamese to Sister Joan. Sister Joan shakes her head and signals with her hand for the women to go away.

"What does she want?" I ask.

"She wants us to take her child. I wish we could. But we just can't take all of them", she states with a sad tone to her voice and a wounded look on her face.

The pounding on the sides of the van by other women continues as we gradually weave through the refugees. My stomach aches for these ladies. I wonder what will become of them and their children as the NVA continue to approach Saigon.

"John, we've got one more stop to make before we get our papers checked by the Vietnamese government. Remember me telling you about my friend, Jane Ronquist, who is a kindergarten teacher in Saigon? She's going to be an escort on this first "Operation Babylift" flight out. Then Jane plans to visit her mom in San Francisco for a few days before her return to Vietnam. She's been a great help to me in the past on my trips to the states. We'll pick her up at the school. I know she'll be ready when we get there, so there won't be any delay," Sister Joan says.

"Okay. How far to the school?"

"We're almost there. It's up the road about another mile." Sister Joan shakes her head back and forth while looking at the crowd streaming on the road. "Hopefully we'll be there within the next half hour," she sarcastically replies.

"Whoosh!"

"Thump!"

"Ka-Boom!"

Loud explosions burst from the direction of the airport. A huge black cloud of smoke ascends into the horizon. The thump of a mortar round shakes the ground. My legs tremble like a racehorse. *This is getting a little too close for comfort.*

The van continues to move at what feels like walking speed. I think about that last day in Vietnam in 1970 as I was on my way to the airport to leave the war.

> I was riding in the lead jeep along Highway One to the Da Nang airport for my trip out of the war. Highway One was normally checked for mines every morning. However, the minesweepers didn't get to the highway that morning. Our caravan, which consisted of ten vehicles, was travelling around five miles on a road that I knew could be filled with explosive devices. We were carrying supplies to

the airport. I tried to keep my shaking arms and chattering teeth as quiet as possible. All I could think about was our jeep exploding on my last day in Vietnam.

As we limped along, I was half standing so I could jump out if we hit a mine. I really knew that it would be too late to jump if there was an explosion, but I was ready. I tried to act casual in front of my driver, but I'm sure he sensed my nervousness. Hell, he had to be edgy too! How could they not have checked for mines today, I thought. This is crazy. I survived being shot at for months, but here I am getting blown up on Highway One. I couldn't stop worrying. I silently prayed.

Finally, the airport was in view. Only a quarter of a mile to go. I held my breath for what seemed like an eternity. As we pulled off Highway One onto the tarmac at the Da Nang airport, I jumped out of the jeep and felt like kissing the ground.

"John, here's the elementary school. You can pull into that parking lot on your left," Sister Joan loudly says to me.

"Got it, Sister. I was kind of daydreaming."

"Yes, I noticed," she states matter-of-factly.

The other vans follow us into the parking lot, and Sister Joan jumps out. She heads across the meager playground to the one story yellow stucco school building. With urgency in her voice, she shouts over her shoulder, "Keep everyone in the vans. This shouldn't take too long. I'll be back in a few minutes."

I check the babies on the floor in the front seat and tell the Vietnamese volunteer in my van to watch them and the rest of the children while I walk back to the other vehicles. It amazes me how calm the nuns, volunteers and the children appear. More explosions erupt in the distance. I tell the drivers that Sister Joan will be back shortly, and that everyone should stay in the vans.

Within a few minutes, Sister Joan and a young woman run toward me. They climb into the van, and Sister Joan says, "John, this is Jane Ronquist. Jane, this is John Ellis."

"Nice meeting you, Jane", I politely reply.

"My pleasure, John", she says with a bright smile.

We quickly shake hands. Sister Joan moves to the back of the van and immediately starts talking to one of the older children. Jane moves to the seat next to me. She's about five feet four, has deep blue eyes, and auburn hair tied in a ponytail. She's dressed in brown cargo pants and a light green blouse, and appears to be about my age. In another time and place, I might be asking her out on a date.

We back out of the parking area and resume our trek to the airport. Looking out of the corner of my eye, I say, "Jane, who are you teaching at the school?"

"I teach mostly Americans, and a few Vietnamese. The program is funded by the Catholic Church."

"How long have you been doing this in Vietnam and how do you like it?"

"I've been here for about three years. I came over with my father, who's a doctor working here for USAID. I love it here. The people are so gracious and thankful for our help."

"What'll you do when you get to the States?" I ask.

"My plan is to see if I can pick up some funds and beg for supplies for my school. I've done this in the past and have had a lot of success due to the generosity of Americans. I'm a bit concerned now, since the North Vietnamese are moving so quickly into the south. I don't know how long we're going to be able to keep the school open," she responds.

"What do you mean?"

"Well, the American children are already starting to leave with their parents and the Vietnamese children will be at risk, because most of their parents work with the South Vietnamese or the American government."

"What about your father? How long will he stay here?" I ask.

"This week the United States government ordered him to return to the States. They feel it's getting too dangerous for him to continue administering medical help to the South Vietnamese. He's supposed to be on the first plane leaving. I'm also going to be an escort for orphans leaving on that flight," she says.

"We sure appreciate your help," I state with optimism. "I'll be on the flight too."

"Great," she answers with a soothing smile. "You're sure fortunate to be working with Sister Joan. She's amazing. She keeps this operation moving in the right direction. I've known her for a couple of years and I'm astonished how much she accomplishes with the orphans."

"She's a dynamo!" I grin.

We continue our sluggish journey to the Ministry of Social Welfare Office, and I think about the many wonderful people who are helping to get these orphans out of Vietnam to a better life. Their life work is helping others to succeed, not worrying about their own welfare. They're a special breed.

I bring the van to a complete halt. We inch up to four South Vietnamese soldiers blocking the road. Sister Joan comes up toward the front of the van, opens the door, and jumps out. She quickly walks up to the one who appears to be in command. I put my hand in my pocket and place it on the handle of my Colt 45. Sister Joan is very animated, with her hands helping her talk to the soldier. She reaches into her pocket and cautiously slips some bills into the soldier's palm. With the pointing of his finger, he signals her to return to the van.

"Nice job, Sister. You're pretty good at bribing."

"It's become part of the job. I'm just glad that they accepted the money. We need to move on quickly. These crowds are stifling." She then climbs into the seat directly behind me. I start up the van and we continue our slow progress to the Ministry of Social Welfare.

"I'm really excited about getting this first group of children out of here on the plane today," Sister Joan spurts out. "The civilian in charge of coordinating this first flight told me that he wants to send only the healthy and older children, so we can show how well we take care of these orphans. Being the rebel that I am, I don't agree with that. As you know, I've chosen to bring the most severely handicapped and tiny ones out first. They're the most needy in my opinion."

Jane jumps into the conversation. "What'll they do

to you when you arrive at the airport with these handicapped children?"

"Who cares? It'll be too late for anyone to turn the children away. What are they going to do—send me to Vietnam?" she blurts out with a laugh.

"Good point, Sister," I say with a smile. "That reminds me of the response we often heard during the war. *This woman is something else!*

She points, "There it is, John. You can pull into that parking lot over there. You and I will go in with the paperwork. Please tell Sister Elizabeth to watch the vans and keep the children inside. Jane, you can wait for us here."

Jumping out of the driver's seat, I run back to the vehicle behind me and relay the plan to Sister Elizabeth. I jog to catch up with Sister Joan who is already on her way into the two story grey and white stucco building flying the yellow and red South Vietnamese flag. After finding the entrance to the Ministry of Social Welfare, we proceed to a well-furnished office. It's quiet, and the smell of freshly cut flowers flows from the vases neatly placed on tables throughout the waiting room. A portrait of South Vietnamese General Van Thieu decorates a beautifully wood paneled wall.

A young Vietnamese secretary, sitting behind a polished oak desk, greets us. "Goot morn. Can help you?" she says in broken English.

"Hello. My name is Sister Joan McKenny. I'm here to get clearance for children from the Binh Trieu Orphanage for the flight to America."

"Yes. Colonel Phan be with you moment. Please seat."

Within a few minutes, a Vietnamese man, dressed in a well-pressed army uniform, walks into the room. He stands about five feet-two, is well shaven, and has a broad smile on his face. He presents his hand to Sister Joan. "Good morning. I am Colonel Phan. I am the head of this district for the Ministry," he states in very proper English.

Sister Joan also extends her hand and acknowedges, "So nice to meet you Colonel." She nods to me, "This is John Ellis."

I also shake hands with Colonel Phan, and Sister Joan hands him the documents for the children.

With wrinkled brow, and looking at Sister Joan, he declares, "I have bad news, Sister. The Minister of Social Welfare has removed you and the children from the first flight. Another agency was given priority. It has to do with politics."

"What? No! This must be a mistake! We were promised that our children would be on this flight. I'll to talk to the Minister myself!" Sister Joan angrily replies.

I'm afraid that isn't possible, Sister. The commitment is made to the other agency."

Her voice thick with disgust, and tears running down her face, Sister uncomfortably says, "When will we be able to get them on a plane?"

"We'll try to get you on the next flight. The demands to our Minister are coming in on a daily basis. We're doing the best we can, Sister. I'm so sorry I cannot get your children on this flight."

Stunned, Sister Joan backs up slightly. She bows her head and begins to sob. With her hands on each side of her face, and her voice full of embarrassment, she slowly blurts out, "I...am...so...sorry, Colonel. My disappointment is overwhelming. I so much wanted those children on that first flight. I just don't want to let them down."

With that, Colonel Phan replies sympathetically, "Sister, I will talk to the Minister about your situation, and ask him to schedule your children as soon as possible."

Sister Joan pulls herself farther away from Colonel Phan, and regains her composure. "Colonel, you know that John, Sister Elizabeth Chen and Jane Ronquist are scheduled to be on that flight as escorts today."

"Yes, I know, Sister. They have been cleared to go on the flight. Additional escorts are needed since there will be so many children on the plane. You can take the adults to the airport right now."

She reluctantly responds, "Thank you. We'll use one of the vans to take them to Tan Son Nhat. The others will be sent back to the orphanage."

After getting Sister Elizabeth into our van and explaining the situation to her and Jane, I look at Sister Joan, commenting, "Things will work out Sister. Hopefully the next flight will be leaving tomorrow."

"I hope so. But, I've been around these government officials long enough to know that we're not home free yet."

"I really feel bad about going on this flight without our kids. I know Sister Elizabeth feels the same way," I say.

"It's okay, John. You'll be back in a couple of days. Hopefully, we'll be getting our children on to planes by then."

The other vans head off in the opposite direction as we begin the remainder of our journey. After a short ride, I spot the airport on our left. A column of vehicles is waiting to get through the completely fenced and guarded entry. I pull the van in line and count the number of vehicles and motorbikes in front of us. It looks like we are number eight in the row. The heat becomes stifling, even with the windows wide open to help get a cross breeze. Air conditioning is not an option in these vans. *I sure could use that South San Francisco damp breeze I remember from the time I drove to the interview in the City. Wow. That seems like years ago.*

Jane checks the babies in the box at her feet, and lifts one of the infants to her lap. She reaches for a bottle in the sack next to the door, and begins giving the child some fluid—part water and part milk, I think. She props up a bottle in the cartons at her feet for each of the other babies. The tiny ones seem content and the van inches forward every few minutes. The rest of the children in the van are relatively quiet considering Sister Joan told them that they would not be going on this flight.

Finally, we approach the guarded airport entry and a South Vietnamese uniformed guard walks up to us. His uniform is sweat stained under his arms, and beads of perspiration are dripping from his dark side burns. A cigarette hangs loosely in the corner of his mouth, reaching toward his nicotine-stained goatee. His thin, lanky posture reminds me of a picture of Ho Chi Minh which I saw in the newspaper yesterday.

I hand him the folder, which Sister Joan had just given me, for Sister Elizabeth, Joan and me for our trip. The guard takes the file. He walks back to the wooded guard shack and confers with another soldier.

After about two minutes, he returns, gives the papers back to me, and says, "No good. You not get on airplane."

At that moment, Sister Joan grabs the folder from me, and gets out of the van. She walks over to the guard and, with her arms waiving in various directions, talks in rapid Vietnamese. During this time she points to Jane, and me and then to Sister Elizabeth. The talk continues, until Sister Joan comes back to the van with a look of frustration on her face.

"He said that the only plane going out today is a United States cargo plane, and that it has all of the escorts on board. I told him the three of you are supposed to be on that aircraft. He said he was sorry, but he can't help us. Finally, I was able to convince him, with bribe money of course, that you are scheduled to be on that plane."

"Here are the papers for you, Jane and Sister Elizabeth for boarding, John. When you get to San Francisco let our agency know the situation here and tell them that we, hopefully, will be getting children on one of the next flights. I do hope your father is on this flight, Jane. The three of you can go over to that jeep. They'll take you to the airplane. I'll take the van and children back to the orphanage."

Jane, Sister Elizabeth and I jump out, and pick up our carry-ons.

Sister Joan climbs into the driver's seat. "Have a safe trip. God be with you!" she yells at us, as she backs up and begins turning the vehicle around.

We trot over to the designated jeep. A young, yellow-toothed South Vietnam soldier greets us with a smile. He slowly drives the jeep toward a huge United States Air Force plane. I recognize the aircraft as a C-5A Galaxy. I'm fond of airplanes and know many of the military ones. This is one of the largest cargo planes in the world. It carries tanks, large equipment and helicopters. The cargo hold of this airplane is the size of a large gymnasium. Although the C-5A has had some problems in the past with the rear doors, it's been used successfully for transport for the Air Force due to its capacity to carry many troops and large equipment. Ironically, its crews know the plane as FRED (fucking, ridiculous, economic/environmental disaster) due to its maintenance/reliability issues and large consumption of fuel.

As we approach the plane, the jeep stops in front of four United States Marines who are dressed in camouflage utilities, and wearing flak jackets, combat boots, and steel helmets. Each carries an M-16 rifle. One of the marines walks over to us and asks for our passports, which we proudly display to him. In normal Marine tradition, he refers to us as "Sir and "Ma'am".

"Semper Fi, Marine," I proudly state.

"Semper Fi Sir," the Marine quickly responds.

A loud boom sounds in the background. At that moment, the Marines surround us and motion us to get to the airplane. I hear the "crack" of some rifle fire and the "pop-pop-pop" of automatic weapons, which sound like a string of igniting firecrackers. Other people, who are preparing to board the aircraft, are running, and confusion surrounds us as we sprint to the rear door of the C-5A.

An Air Force sergeant helps the three of us onto the plane. As we enter the "gymnasium", the number of children placed throughout the cargo area stuns me. The inside of the plane has netting on the floor and cargo harnesses are securing the children. Many look sad and some smile. All of them look bewildered. The adults appear to be Americans—probably wives and dependents of United States government employees.

I look around and realize that this is an historic moment. People in the United States must be glued to their television sets, as we are the first official airplane out of Vietnam on President Ford's "Operation Babylift." This is a unique event—a time when many threads of the Vietnam War are joined together in a humanitarian effort. It's one of the extraordinary events of the twentieth century. It suddenly strikes me that I'm a small part of it.

Yes, this is an important flight, but none on board realizes *how* important.

CHAPTER

10

Children line the steel floor of the two-story C-5A airplane. They sit and lie on blankets. Adults hold and comfort the young ones. Oxygen masks and life rafts are not visible. Toys and supplies are scattered around the lower deck. Crates of diapers and medical supplies border the walls of the plane. Boxes with infants rest in rows side by side, with harnesses stretching across the cartons. *This is a mass of humanity crowded onto the floor of a gym ready to take a twenty-four hour flight. It looks damned unsafe.*

The Loadmaster, an Air Force Tech Sergeant, dressed in camouflage utilities, signals me to move to the front of the plane. Then, with the movement of his hand upward, he gestures for me to proceed to the second level.

Advancing toward the metal stairwell, he says to Jane and Sister Elizabeth, who are walking next to me, "Ma'am, you two can stay on this deck and help with the older children. We need to secure these kids as best we can." Pointing toward the front, he says, "That group over there needs some help."

Moving past Jane and Sister Elizabeth toward the flight of steps, I gaze back at the throng of scattered children along the floor of the plane. *It looks like a huge nursery in the middle of a concert hall.*

Upon arriving on the upper deck, I stare at the filled spaces along the bulkhead. Children are tightly strapped two or three to a seat. Most look to be from two to eight years old. Some cry, and others look confused.

"Sir, would you make sure the older children along the sides are fastened in? Please fill all the empty seats with two or three kids each. The other volunteers will take care of the babies," an Air Force Sergeant commands.

Each seat, which normally holds one person, secures at least three younger or two older children in place. The infants rest in cardboard boxes with seat belts across the top. Some of the volunteers bottle-feed the babies. Many of the infants are skinny and malnourished. The cabin vibrates with a cacophony of voices. Grownups calm the children, and many of the helpers have their arms around the young ones. Escorts, agency workers and Air Force personnel all show signs of fatigue as they work non-stop. The lack of air conditioning combined with the humidity enhances the smell of dirty diapers and urine. *This is beyond the call of duty for volunteers!*

"Sir, will you help me quickly secure the rest of these children?" a young Air Force Sergeant shouts over to me. "We have over three hundred personnel on board, and the pilot wants to get this bird out of here before some VC hits us with a mortar or small arms fire!"

"Of course. How many orphans are aboard?" I ask.

"I believe we have around two hundred and thirty. The rest of the passengers are adults—government employees, crew and volunteers."

"You guys are doing a great job. It looks like you got everyone aboard in an orderly manner, and the volunteers are working feverishly with the younger children," I state as a compliment, although it appears that the plane is overloaded with passengers. *I know this C-5A was not designed to carry this many personnel, since it's basically a cargo plane.*

"Thank you, sir. We're used to moving quickly and loading this aircraft under stressful conditions. Actually, getting personnel into this cargo plane is a bit more confusing than loading combat vehicles. The twenty-four hour flight to the U.S. isn't going to be too comfortable for you passengers. Excuse me, sir. I have to notify my superior that this deck is secure for takeoff," he replies, walking away.

There are a few oxygen masks on this deck. I know there aren't enough toilets to handle over 300 people. *I hope we can manage to take care of all these kids on this long trip.*

After getting back to my seat next to the children, I think about Sister Joan and her commitment to this wonderful cause. She's a remarkable person. Her life is helping others. I've never heard her complain, unless it was to improve the orphans' situation.

The front and rear doors of the C-5A slam shut. The whirring of the four turbo-fan engines makes the entire airplane shudder. I feel the power of those jet engines as the pilot revs them up prior to moving onto the taxiway. I can't see out of the plane so I'm imagining where we are as the aircraft jolts forward. The giant shakes as it creeps along the concrete.

My armpits are soaking wet. I can only imagine how the children near me must feel. The high temperature inside the plane is sweltering.

Waiting for the plane to take off, the intense heat in here takes me back to 1970. I keep thinking about the whole war effort.

> The S-3 intelligence officer, Major Kaper, was debriefing me in the battalion headquarters outside of DaNang. I was exhausted from a week of patrolling. He kept asking questions about the NVA locations we had discovered, and how many enemy were in the area. I responded with the number and locations. We also talked about the total war effort. We both agreed that the United States had never lost a major battle during the war, but the pressure from Washington and the American public made it look like the North Vietnamese were winning the war. I was soaking wet from the constant humidity in the air. The debriefing took at least an hour. I could smell my own body odor since I hadn't had a shower for days. I just wanted to finish our meeting, get a shower, and take a rest in one of the tents at the battalion command post.

The airplane stops prior to final take off, and I'm back to the present. I'm concerned about the South Vietnamese who we are going to be leaving behind when this war is over. We didn't lose this conflict. We just pulled out, and left the South Vietnamese army and people to fend for themselves. My stomach growls. I have a sick and queasy feeling. Is it the heat? Is it my frustration with this war?

Is it the many orphans? I'm confused.

The engines again power up. The aircraft is ready for takeoff. I look at my watch and see it's about four in the afternoon. Sitting in this large metal tube with no windows is like being on the spinning ride at a carnival in which you can't see out. You know you're going to be moving around in circles and the gravity will hold you against the wall.

The engines become louder as they suck fuel from the wing tanks. The C-5A rolls forward, and our speed increases. The big airplane is travelling down the runway at full speed now, and I feel the lift off as we gradually leave the concrete surface. I'm exhilarated. The air in the cabin becomes a little cooler, and the beads of sweat on my face are chilly.

Wow! We're airborne, on our way to the United States. I can't wait to see the faces of the children and their new adoptive parents when we land. Also, maybe I can get to know Jane a little better once we get to the States.

I look at the small boys and girls sitting adjacent to me. Some are smiling. Although most of the children are clean and wearing clothes without holes, they look like a group of poor children from the ghetto. Their malnourished bodies, messed up hair, and dark marks under their eyes are evidence of a rough past. The children are silent, seeming to be mesmerized by the liftoff of the airplane.

Explosions erupt outside, but they seem to become more distant as we gain altitude. I begin to relax. My body falls into a stupor. The excitement of getting to the airport, loading onto the airplane, and watching all the activity of the children and adults, catches up with me.

I lean back and start to nod my head, half-sleeping and half-paying attention to what's going on around me.

"Boom!"

A thunderous sound echoes from the back of the lumbering airplane. My eyes pop open. Adrenalin flows rapidly through my body. I'm trying to figure out what's happening. The plane moves back and forth, right and left, like a fish in slow motion. It makes a turn, but it's acting like there's very little control. *It's probably a minor problem, I rationalize.*

"The rear doors have blown out! The captain has lost control of his steering mechanism! Put on the oxygen masks! Then help the children with theirs. They'll have to share masks. Secure yourself and hold on tight!" shouts the Air Force Sergeant, who is getting instructions through his earphones.

"How high are we, Sergeant?" I scream.

"We're at about twenty-three thousand feet and some forty miles from Saigon. He's trying to get back to Tan Son Nhat to land. When we're on the ground, get to the lower deck, and help the children out the doors as quickly as possible. The captain thinks he can make the runway!" he shouts.

A fog immediately forms in our cabin from the decompression. The air in the plane cools and condenses. I'm light headed. I put on an oxygen mask, and move to put them on the children next to me. There aren't enough. I move the oxygen from child to child. Some of the children are groggy.

"Hold on!" I yell in both English and Vietnamese to the children.

Screaming and loud banging reverberates from below. I'm terrified. I grab the seat belt harness with both hands, close my eyes and begin to pray. I think about those combat days.

> Waiting in the ambush sight that black night made me tense. Our patrol crouched low in the thick grass near the road. The drizzling rain patted the top of my helmet as I tried to focus on any movement to our front. After two hours of silence and fear, chaos erupted. A mine explosion on the road signaled the presence of an enemy patrol. Machine guns, small arms fire and hand grenade explosions caused tremendous confusion through the misty evening. Yelling and screaming saturated the once soundless night. Orders were yelled. Sounds of 'Corpsman' filled the air. My mind sharpened as my Marines performed their trade well.

My eyes open quickly. The plane loses altitude as it sways back and forth like a glider trying to deal with heavy winds. Terror and fear engulfs the eyes of a young girl. She has gauze covering both of her arms. She reminds me of Chi. My breath comes in short, sharp gasps.

The plane continues to descend. The noises below sound like things are flying around inside of the airplane. The aircraft bounces through the air.

Please, God. Let us get through this okay. I want to see my family. I want to live.

The C-5A vibrates. The front of the plane slants downward. I'm helpless. *We may not make it.*

Then, everything starts to slow down. What must have been only a couple of minutes feels like an hour. I continue to pray and my hands are numb from holding tightly onto the harness. Time stops.

At that moment, the plane skids along the ground. The straps on my harness pull my body in all directions. The loud banging and smashing sounds are horrific, as if the plane is breaking up. My hands dig into the arm rests next to my seat. Scraping and screeching sounds, like those from a horror movie, engulf the plane. The grating sounds suddenly stop. It feels like we are airborne again. I wait for another impact. Battering sounds fill the air as if something is pounding on the side of the plane. Children scream. There's more scraping and crashing below me. Time then stands still. Everything seems to be in slow motion again, as I watch things around me flying and turning in various directions. All of a sudden, the entire plane is turning sideways. Crashing and smashing sounds, like explosions, surround us. Everything turns black. The thought of war flashes back to me.

> Have I been hit by a 50 caliber round, or was it shrapnel from the incoming mortar explosion? Lying on the ground, I'm half-awake. I hear myself yelling, "Get the children out! Help them!" My shirt is soaking wet. My head is floating in space. I'm weightless. Is this the final minute of my life? Scenes reel out before me like a movie stream.

Suddenly, I realize it's not 1970 when that 50 caliber machine-gun round grazed my shoulder. I've been knocked unconscious, and am returning to the present in an open field, lying in a pool of dirty water. I shake my head and slowly sit up in the middle of a rice paddy. Mud sticks to my clothes and face. My shirt and pants are torn. I must have been out for a long time. I'm totally dazed. My eyes try to focus. Everything is blurry. I look around and squint. Crying babies recline on the ground. People run by me. Airplane parts lie scattered around me. Black smoke billows toward the sky. I slowly stand up and walk unsteadily over to a woman who is picking up a scream-ing baby. Miraculously, the baby looks okay. My eyes become clear.

" Shit! Where...am...I? What...happened?" I slowly ask in a completely bewildered state.

"The plane crashed. We're helping the wounded!" the woman shouts to me.

I suddenly realize where I am. My mind becomes more alert. Checking myself over for any wounds, I don't find any. I'm stunned by what I see. I can't believe I'm alive and looking at complete destruction around me.

The scene is mind-boggling. The C-5A is broken into many pieces. Parts of the plane burn. The smell of smoldering fire fills the air. As I try to run and help, I fall down into the sludge. Bodies of little babies are spread over the rice paddies. Huey and H-34 helicopters are in the distance. Ambulances, with red lights blinking, are parked, far from the airplane. I see the airport runway off to my right. *Why don't they get over here and help us?*

As I continue to come to my senses, I realize at that moment vehicles can't get through the mud of the rice paddies. Everyone around me seems to be trying to help. People run to and from the airplane. Confusion reigns.

"What can I do?" I ask an Air Force woman who has a torn sleeve on her tarnished uniform and a stream of blood creasing the side of her face.

"Just search for anyone alive around the plane. Many

have survived, but we need to move quickly," she states. She limps away carrying a young child.

Through the body parts scattered on the ground around the wreckage, I keep searching, looking for any sign of life. A little boy sits in the mire holding a baby. I quickly dash over to him, pick up the baby, and grab the boy by the arm. Looking for a helicopter, I notice blood is oozing from the side of the boy's head. His ear is missing. I quickly take off my shirt and tear a piece of the cloth to tie around his head to stop the bleeding.

I ask him in Vietnamese if he is okay. "Yaa (yes)," he replies.

I walk in the direction of the choppers, and hand over the two children to a Vietnamese woman. She takes the boy by the hand. I place the infant in her other arm. The baby appears to be alert. The woman continues toward the helicopters with the two children.

Walking back to the airplane, someone signals for me to help him get some victims. Smoke surrounds the plane, which makes any rescue attempt more difficult due to the lack of oxygen in the air. As I near the aircraft, I see some of the passengers in the airplane still strapped in their seats, which were ripped off the floor and turned on their side. Some are unconscious. Blood is everywhere. Screams and crying reverberate throughout the plane. The inside of the C-5A looks like the aftermath of a bomb explosion.

"Help me," cries a little girl strapped to her seat. She has a severe gash in her arm. Her face is covered with blood. I quickly release the seat belt, and gingerly pick her up. I hand her off to a South Vietnamese soldier next to me.

Two young children lie on the floor, their broken bodies lifeless. Stepping over them, I trip over two tiny infants. Amazingly, they're alive. I carefully pick them up, and crawl through the jagged side of the plane. I walk to a Vietnamese volunteer who takes the children to a waiting H-34.

An American volunteer sits on the ground with her head in her hands and, crying, she says, "This is awful. So many dead and injured. We need to get them all out. My God, please help me."

I couch down next to her and look at the dirt-covered face, and soiled utilities. She's about thirty years old and her shoulders are shaking from her short sobs. "Are you hurt? " I ask.

"I'm okay, I think," she answers in a soft voice.

"Dammit. Get up! I need to get back to the airplane and see if we can help," I respond coarsely to see how she will react.

She slowly gets to her feet, and seems to have a second wind. "Yes. Let's get over there and help them. I'll follow you," she says.

We arrive back at the ripped and torn fuselage of the aircraft and begin to wade through the tangled metal heap. I move into the mess and tell my companion, "There's some children over there that are trapped. I need your help to get them free. Follow me."

Inside, we find two kids ensnared beneath a metal brace, which has crushed the legs of one of them. The other child appears to be unconscious. I pull on the metal brace, and it starts to bend. The lady, whose name I don't even know, removes the two children from under the piece of steel.

"Let's get them out of here," I command.

She picks up one of the children and I gather up the comatose one. As we exit the broken fuselage from the opposite side of the aircraft, the child starts to wake up. *Oh my God! Maybe he's okay. I hope.*

I see helicopters in the distance, and realize they can't land next to the crashed airplane because of the miscellaneous wreckage and huge amounts of water. Treading through the swamp carrying the child, I see other kids lying in the mud. Two young boys sit up, staring blankly with their mouths open. Motionless infants loll in the muck. Many are naked. Some are headless. I keep moving, trying to get this child to one of those helicopters. I'm torn with emotion since I can't stop to help anyone else now.

"Keep moving in the direction of the choppers," I yell to my partner.

After trudging through the mire, we find a South Vietnamese soldier wearing a flight suit. He tells us he's a crew chief from one of the helicopters. We hand him the children and I turn and say," Let's go back and get the children lying on the ground."

"What about the kids in the plane," she yells back.

"Let's just keep working until we save them all," I quickly answer.

Americans and Vietnamese volunteers, Air Force personnel, South Vietnamese soldiers, and emergency workers all around us search for survivors. Bodies are everywhere. Babies stretch out, half-buried in the mud. Mangled bodies lay on top of each other—some children and some adults. Pools of blood mingle with the muck. Baby bottles, diapers, clothing, and comic books are disbursed throughout the rice paddies. My stomach rumbles. I'm nauseous. I walk away from the woman and vomit.

"Here's a child who's alive!" she shouts.

Running over to her, I see the child half-buried in the mud and crying softly. He appears to be unhurt. I'm ecstatic. We carefully help him stand up, and he begins to walk with us. He looks to be about four or five years old, and his face and most of his body are covered with crud. His slanted eyes open wide with joy.

"*Cam on* (thank you)," he says in Vietnamese.

"*Yaa* (yes)," I reply as I pick him up and hold him, listening to the beautiful sound of his heartbeat against my chest.

Walking in the direction of the helicopters with the young boy in my arms, I'm viewing a scene, which is out of a horror movie. Dead bodies, blood, body parts, pieces of wreckage, toys, clothes—it's all unreal!

After spending a couple of hours helping with the rescue effort, my volunteer associate departs on a helicopter with some injured children. The smoldering fires of the wrecked airplane lift their white clouds toward the pink skyline of Saigon in the distance. Volunteers and South Vietnamese soldiers have been working with us all afternoon. I don't know how many passengers died and how many are missing from this crash.

"John, are you okay? We thought you were dead," cries a female voice from behind me.

When I turn to look, Sister Joan is standing next me. Off to the side, I see a Huey, which she has just exited. She has a look of both relief and despair on her face.

"I'm okay Sister. This has been a horrible day. So many lives lost," I answer with much dismay.

"I'm so happy you made it, John. I thought you were dead. Sister Elizabeth and Jane are still missing. One of the helicopter pilots who dropped me off said the plane first hit the ground and skidded. Then it bounced up in the air for about a half a mile. It flew across the Saigon River before ramming into a dike and breaking into several pieces upon final impact in this rice paddy. When the plane hit the second time, the fuel tanks on the wings ruptured, touching off the fire. The bottom cargo area of the plane took the greatest impact."

"Oh my God," I reply, falling to my knees. "Sister Elizabeth and Joan were in the cargo area."

"No…No…No!" cries Sister Joan. "That can't be!"

Putting my arms around her, she rests her sobbing face on my shoulder.

"They may have made it, Sister. Let's not give up yet," I reply with empathy.

Moving slowly away from me, with tears continuing to flow down her face, she says, "I know you're right, John. We'll keep praying."

I sit down on one of the dikes in the rice paddy with my hands over my face. Tears creep down my soiled face.

I look up at Sister Joan and slowly ask, "Do you know

what happened, Sister? Does anybody know what caused the plane to crash?"

"No one seems to know too much at this time," she replies. "I tried to get some answers out of the helicopter pilots, but all they could tell me is that it could've been a mechanical problem, or possibly VC sabotage."

"Shit!" I respond. "Sorry...Sister. There are many injured passengers still out here. We've got to get back to the plane, and get them out."

"Are you up to it, John?"

"I'm pretty beat, but I'm not leaving here now. Let's get going."

Sister Joan hands me a flashlight. "You may need this since we only have about an hour of daylight left."

We slog our way back to the plane. For that next hour, we continue to view mangled bodies of children, some dead and some injured. We both carry and assist the wounded through the rice paddies to the waiting Hueys. I hope and pray that we'll find Sister Elizabeth and Jane. Dusk gradually takes over, and the sun and the evening darkness close in on us.

"Sister, I think we've done all we can for now. I can hardly see anything in the murky water of these rice paddies. I think we'd better get ourselves to one of the choppers now."

"I agree. I hate to leave this scene, but we can't really do much more right now. The emergency people and the South Vietnamese soldiers will most likely be here all night protecting the area from the VC and looking for survivors," she answers dejectedly.

Walking back toward the waiting helicopters, I'm

trying to figure out what really happened to the Galaxy C5-A. I wonder how many children were killed and if, by some miracle, Sister Elizabeth and Jane made it. Hearing that the bottom cargo area took the brunt of the crash, I'm not too optimistic about either of them surviving.

I wonder if it was a mechanical failure on the C-5A, or was it sabotage by the North Vietnamese or Viet Cong?

CHAPTER

11

Approaching a waiting helicopter, I see scattered items from the wreckage. Pages of a Mickey Mouse comic book, boxes of diapers, cushions from the plane, baby bottles and a myriad of cardboard boxes and torn items litter the scarred rice paddies and dikes.

Adults—both Vietnamese and Americans—search around the remains of the plane. They look for bodies and help the injured and stunned children. Some carry dead and mangled bodies toward the choppers. The horror blurs my mind. I'm surrounded by death. I think of that day in 1970 when the VC ambushed us.

> After the chaotic ambush, I stared at the VC prisoner's face. It was covered with blood. We were in the smelly cavity of what was once a church, waiting for the helicopter to take him away. I was quivering as I looked into his hateful eyes. My finger was tense on the trigger of my Colt 45, afraid he might try to kill me if I turned my head, even though he could no longer walk. His legs, blown apart by a shotgun

157

blast, hung by tendons. His trousers and shoes were a deep blood red. I wanted to say, "I'm sorry," but he and his comrades had just killed one of my men and injured four others. I felt confused and sick to my stomach.

I'm drawn back to the present and turn to see the cockpit of the C5-A. It's separated from the rest of the airplane, but it's in one piece. *I wonder if the pilot survived the crash.*

Our camouflaged helicopter sits with the rotors idling. The crew chief, an American, hands me a brown T- shirt. I quickly take the garment and pull it over my head, gratefully stating, "Thanks so much."

"You okay sir?" he yells.

Realizing that I'm alive and not injured, exhaustion sets in. I lean against the metal bulkhead inside the chopper, exhale and respond, "Yes sir. Thanks for your help. Who are you guys? Are you Marines?"

"Not exactly, sir. I'm a former Marine and the pilots are Army. We now work for Air America. We're just trying to help get people out of here before the NVA take over Saigon."

"What the hell made our plane go down?" I ask.

"It's too early to say but it wouldn't surprise me if the damn VC sabotaged it," he answers loudly above the clatter of the idling engine.

"Oh crap. What a way to start an evacuation of children!" I angrily shout.

After Sister Joan and seven other passengers from the crash sit down in the helicopter, the crew chief puts on his head set. He yells, "Hold on tight!" as he gives the pilot a "thumbs-up".

The chopper commences lift off, and the rotors hum like tuning forks. The plane rises and makes a left turn into the wind. Looking out of the open door, I witness the mangled wreckage of the C-5A. Parts smatter the banks of the Saigon River. White smoke ascends into the cloudless sky. People walk around the wreckage. The whole picture is that of complete destruction. Finally, we're airborne. I begin to think again about the destruction of this whole war.

> In 1970, as our jeep was moving down Highway One to the regimental headquarters, I watched the young children scavenging through the Army's dumpsite, digging for scraps of food. It was like watching ants moving in and out of their quarters on an anthill. Homes along the way were just piles of rubble. Roads were nothing but potholes and mud. I continued to reflect on the desperation war causes for civilians-both adults and children. Both sides are fighting for a cause, but one of the greatest consequences is the destruction of homes and the devastation of the lives of people.

Flying toward Saigon, the sky becomes slightly rosy from the lights of the city. Explosions thunder in the distance as our helicopter descends for a landing at Tan Son Nhat Airport. When the chopper touches down, the crew chief shouts, "Get off!" Jumping from the aircraft and giving him a "thumbs-up" at the same time, I jog toward one of the Quonset huts about fifty yards away. Adrenaline keeps me going. Sister Joan and the rest of the passengers follow closely.

The building bustles with doctors and nurses tending to patients. Children are crying. Persons on stretchers move by us. The smell of medicine and decaying flesh is overpowering.

"John, you need to have a doctor or nurse check you over," Sister Joan states.

"I'm okay. My bumps and bruises aren't bad. Others need to be taken care of before me."

"What's wrong with him?" an Army nurse interrupts.

"I was on the plane, but I'm okay," I snap.

"Sit down, sir. I can check you over to make sure you really are okay."

The nurse proceeds to ask me simple questions. She takes my blood pressure, checks my heart rate, and goes through the normal procedures of giving a swift physical checkup.

"I think you'll survive. A doctor isn't available to check you now. You can see they're dealing with some critical patients in this room. I do think you should get a thorough physical when you can. "Making eye contact with me, she says, "You're one lucky man, sir."

"Thank you ma'am," I reply as we walk out of the hut.

Sister Joan points to a van parked off to the side. One of the volunteers from the orphanage sits in the driver's seat. Sister Joan jumps into the passenger side and I get into the seat directly behind her. The young Vietnamese volunteer quickly fires up the engine and we are on our way to Binh Trieu Orphanage.

My head begins to bob, due to drowsiness, as we zig-zag through the streets of Saigon. In my stupor, I can't stop thinking about the chaos at the crash site. I reflect on the bedlam of war itself.

> That misty day, we started to enter the village to help the children and women with their routine medical needs. The village was peaceful. All of a sudden, small arms weapons were being fired at us. Although trained in situations like this, we were caught by surprise. It was similar to an ambush. I quickly yelled to my squad leaders to position their men to handle the fire, and return it with the tracer rounds loaded in our weapons. Confusion reigned for a few minutes, until we moved on the offensive. VC had infiltrated the village, and were using the women and children as shields. We quickly surrounded the village and were able to drive the handful of Viet Cong away. When we finally sorted things out, we found two dead women and four injured children who needed medical help. The village residents were terrified, and some women were screaming as they tended to the injuries caused to their children. Our medic ran to help the children. Two had knife wounds in their legs and one had a head wound. One child was seriously wounded in the stomach and blood oozed through her brown soiled shirt. Women in the village were running around, signaling with their arms for us to help them. One woman grabbed my arm and pulled me over to an injured girl. My medic was with me, and he quickly attended to the child. Again, blood, death and confusion encircled us.

The van hits a bump in the road and jolts me from my half dream. Sister Joan says, "Sorry. She's trying to avoid all the rough spots, but these roads are lousy. We hit one of the holes squarely."

"That's okay. I think I got a bit of a nap, although I can't get the sight of those dead bodies and all the mayhem out of my mind."

"I totally understand, John. That was a horrendous mess. It's a miracle that not everyone on the plane was killed. You're blessed to be alive. I'm devastated that Sister Elizabeth and Jane were not found. I pray that they are possibly still alive, and by tomorrow we'll have some good news."

"Me too," I respond, knowing in my heart that their survival is not likely.

The ride back to the orphanage is slow due to the continued crowd of refugees on the roads. Darkness doesn't seem to matter to the moving refugees. The area around Saigon is very congested.

Sister Anne Marie and Sister Nguyen are anxiously waiting for us at the orphanage. Looking cautiously at both of us, Sister Anne Marie asks, "It's so good to see you. John are you okay? We heard about the crash. Where's Sister Elizabeth and Jane Ronquist?"

Sister Joan quietly responds, "We don't know if they made it, Sisters. When we left the crash scene, they hadn't been found yet. Please pray that they may still be alive."

"Oh my God!" escapes from the mouths of both of the nuns in unison.

"Soldiers will continue the search through the night. We should know more in the morning. I think John could use a bit of food right now," Sister Joan says.

"Come into the kitchen. The girls are preparing a meal for you, hoping that you would be arriving here soon," Sister Anne Marie answers.

Sister Joan, with her voice cracking and tears streaming down her weary face, leads us in a prayer, ands asks God to take care of Sister Elizabeth and Jane.

My belly growls. I'm starving. The steaming bowl of rice, a plate of chicken and another platter of colorful vegetables make my mouth water. Reaching to serve myself, I notice my arms are very inflexible. My entire body aches, but my stomach is controlling the entire system. I fill my plate and begin to nourish myself with the wonderful meal.

"Does anyone know what caused the crash yet?" I again query Sister Joan.

"Information is sparse as far as I can tell at this time. Rumors are flying about a possible sabotage by the Viet Cong, but no one knows for sure. We should have more information by morning."

"I sure hope it wasn't caused by the VC. This could put a damper on continuing the entire Babylift," I respond.

Sister Joan replies, "I'm hoping to get more information tonight from my contact at the embassy. I think you need to get some sleep. I anticipate that by the morning we'll have some better information.

"Thanks. I'm going to take you up on getting that sleep."

Walking back to my room after a most satisfying meal, I can't help thinking about Sister Elizabeth and Jane. *I hope to God they didn't suffer. This damn war is so unfair!*

I'm shaking when I wake up and look around my room. The clock on the table shows it's eight o'clock in the morning. I jump out of bed and look out the window at cauliflower cumulus clouds against a bright blue sky. My body is stiff. I lose my balance. My right arm pushes against the wall, saving me from tumbling to the floor. *Slow down John.*

I move cautiously to the shower. Then, giving myself a needed shave, and getting into some clean clothes, I walk into the kitchen.

Sister Joan is sitting at the table looking over a pile of loose papers as I approach and ask, "Have you heard anything regarding Sister Elizabeth and Jane?"

The sad look on Sister Joan's face gives her answer before she responds. "They didn't make it. The embassy called earlier to tell me they've accounted for all the survivors and they're not among them."

"I'm so sorry, Sister. I was hoping for better news."

"God bless them. They were doing the work they loved."

"I know," I helplessly respond. "How about Jane's father? Do we know if he survived the crash?"

"Jane's father is fine. He actually walked away from the crash. The girl at the embassy knows him personally, and she said he's fully alert and not injured. She also told me that of the three hundred and forty-two people aboard, seventy-eight orphans haven't been found. A hundred and fifty of them did make it. Twenty adults were pulled out of the wreckage alive. Many were lost. These were dependents, escorts and Air Force personnel. Some of the unaccounted were either dead in the fields, or trapped in the smoldering wreckage of the plane. Most of those in the lower cargo area were killed. Some were sucked out of the C-5A when the rear doors blew off."

"Was it a VC sabotage?" I ask.

"Although the area near the crash is partially controlled by the Viet Cong right now, there's no indication that it was sabotage. We should know more for sure in a couple of days. I understand from the newscast that a team of investigators from Thailand has been ordered to the site today. You know, that plane was supposed to end up at Travis Air Force Base in California. President Ford was going to meet the plane and take the first baby off as a gesture of support for "Operation Babylift." Who knows what'll happen now. I just hope the whole thing isn't cancelled. I'm devastated by the losses on that plane. I can only thank God that our orphans got bumped from that flight."

I'm glued to the television much of the day, although the reception is poor. The scenes from the crash site are grueling. The rows of body bags near the crash sicken me. Those little children don't deserve this. Many had already been through hell and then this. I'm frustrated as I watch the clean up along the Saigon River. I again think of those rows of body bags back in 1970.

> Three helicopters were lined up at the landing zone to pick up the dead bodies. I counted twenty body bags. These were all young American Marines who were fighting for our country. I sat on the side of the hill watching this sight with a heavy heart. Why them and not me, I kept asking myself. Their lives were so short. I knew what the phrase, "War is Hell," meant. Tears trickled down my cruddy face as the crews of the helicopters loaded the body bags onto the choppers to take these brave men to their final resting place.

The announcer on the television states that President Ford proclaimed that the Babylift would continue. He says the President is determined to get the Vietnamese orphans to America. I'm relieved.

The following day we continue to prepare the children for evacuation. We get word from the American Embassy that all C-5A's are temporarily grounded until the cause of the accident can be determined.

During lunch, I state, "It appears that the crash was not sabotage. Military experts on television are saying that the probable cause of the accident is due to a defective latch on the door at the rear-loading platform. As the pressure from within the aircraft grew, the improperly latched door blew out, followed by the ramp and other pieces of the plane. Some of the hydraulic systems were destroyed as the control and trim cables to the rudder and elevators were severed. It's incredible that the pilot was able to get the plane turned around and make any type of landing."

"He did an amazing job of even getting that plane headed back toward the airport," Sister Joan replies with a sigh of relief.

"I know the C-5A has had problems in the past. In aviation circles, it's known that the locking system frequently malfunctions on its giant cargo doors. They are so wide that three jeeps can drive through them abreast. Supposedly this plane has been embroiled in controversy for years," I mention with some authority.

"How do you know that?" Sister Anne Marie quickly asks.

"I'm kind of an airplane buff. In the States, I subscribed to a couple of military magazines, and like to keep up on the latest info on weapons and airplanes."

"As much as the accident is a tragedy, I hope your

theory, and the military experts on TV are correct, John," Sister Joan replies as her voice cracks.

"Me too. It depresses me that these malfunctions can't be corrected. So many deaths due to mechanical problems. What a waste."

I add more information from the television. "The report on the news says that C-141's will be replacing the C-5A's. These planes are a bit smaller, but they will be used for the continued Babylift. Also a Pan American 747 is scheduled to pick up a load of children to be taken to Travis Air Force Base in California."

"That's great news. I'm supposed to hear from our agency today. I'm hoping our children will be going on one the flights out of here tomorrow," Sister Joan excitedly says.

One of the volunteers signals Sister Joan that she has a phone call. Upon her return a few minutes later, Sister Joan informs us that our children will be leaving on a plane in the morning.

"Will our children be going on the 747?" I query.

"No. Another agency is assigned that plane. Our main office in Saigon told me that our first group will be going out on a C-141. We'll need to get everyone ready to leave early tomorrow. We have to be at the airport by ten o'clock in the morning. Also, there are more children coming by vans and by helicopters to the half-way houses. Volunteers will be getting those kids to our orphanage daily," Sister Joan announces.

"I'll have all seven vans ready for loading in the morning, Sister. What time will we be leaving?" I ask.

"We need to get out of here by six o'clock AM. Let's plan for delays. The checkpoints are increasing and we may get stopped for other insane reasons by the South Vietnamese soldiers," she says with irritation.

After another day of routine paperwork, I arrive at dinner to find the tables filled with children, chattering away. Sister Joan is at another table with some young Vietnamese volunteers.

Sitting between Sister Nguyen and Sister Anne Marie, I decide to find out a bit more about Sister Joan.

Nodding in her direction, I ask, "What brought Sister Joan to Vietnam. Can you tell me about her?"

"What do you want to know?" replies Sister Anne Marie.

"I understand she's from Iowa and has been in Vietnam for three years. She seems very experienced. What led up to her being here? She must have had many responsibilities over the years."

"Yes, she has. She's extremely dedicated to this job. She was a farm girl in her youth in the States, and went into the convent in Ohio, after getting her college degree at the University of Iowa. She comes from a large family—seven children, I believe. Sister Joan's a loving person and told me she always wanted to work with children. After completing her studies at the convent, her first assignment was in Africa. I think she was there for four years, working with impoverished families."

"How'd she get to Vietnam?" I ask.

"After her tour in Africa, they sent her back to the convent in Ohio. I believe she was then sent to get a

Masters Degree at Ohio State University. Upon completion of that, the order decided to send her to Vietnam to run this orphanage and set up a group of half-way houses to care for orphans created by this war. She's been here since 1972, and has created wonderful lives for many distressed children. She's a dynamo. Sister Joan's a true leader and has gotten many adoptive children to the United States in the past three years. I think her goal is to get every orphan out of here. She's one courageous woman and has done much."

"I can see that. She's a tireless individual, committed to her work. Love courses through her veins. Thanks for filling me in on her past," I say.

"You're welcome. You know she wouldn't tell you any of this herself. I found out most of this information from people who have worked with her."

"I know. That's why I asked you."

Sister Joan walks over to our table and says to the three of us, "We need to do some paperwork after dinner to make sure we have everything in order for tomorrow. Our documents have to coordinate with the adoptive parents' papers, which our agency in the states sends us. Sister Anne Marie, will you help get the children ready for bed? Sister Nguyen, John and I will work in the office."

Sister Anne Marie replies, "Will do Sister," as both Sister Nguyen and I nod our heads in agreement.

"Do you have any idea how many airplanes will be departing tomorrow?" I ask Sister Joan.

"I don't know. My boss, Father Raymond, will meet

us at our main office in Saigon. He told me on the phone today that we can take all fifty-eight of our children out on one of the flights. Volunteers and escorts from the Saigon office will be there to meet us as well."

"According to television reports, there are both military and commercial flights coming in to take out embassy personnel, dependents and orphans," I state.

Sister Joan responds, grimacing, "My gut feeling is that it's going to be chaotic at the airport. I'm concerned with delays on the way. The refugee problem is overwhelming. Also, the embassy representative tells me that some of the South Vietnamese Army and their dependents are starting to panic. They, as well as those who worked for the U.S., fear for their lives. They're all trying to get out of the country."

"I do hope there's some order at the Airport."

"Don't bet on it. We're talking life and death situations if the NVA overrun Saigon. Let's just hope we can get all of our kids out of here before that happens."

After a couple of hours reviewing the permits, ID's, nametags, visas, etc. for the children, I head to my room. The orphanage is abnormally quiet, as if the children sense they are going to a better place. I hear a few whimpers from infants, but the lack of the typical chattering and playing is deafening.

My alarm clock is set for four-thirty in the morning. Looking out the window, I see some red and white small-arms tracers arcing through the dark sky. Loud explosions reverberate as well. I tense up. The fighting between the NVA, VC and South Vietnamese Army is getting way too close for comfort.

I turn off the light, lay my head softly on the pillow, and think about tomorrow when this wild journey will continue.

CHAPTER

12

The bed shakes me awake. I jump out and, instinctively, hit the deck. Explosions erupt outside. I crawl to the window, look out and see white smoke flowing up into the black sky. Fully awake, I get to my feet and walk, bent over, to the bed and stare at the clock. It's four in the morning. The calendar next to the timepiece shows it's April 7.

The angry blasts outside subside. I cautiously lie down for one last rest before my daily schedule and begin thinking about what Thich Nhat Hanh, the Vietnamese Zen Buddhist Monk wrote: "Every morning, when we wake up we have twenty-four brand new hours to live. What a precious life: we have the capacity to live in a way that these twenty-four hours will bring peace, joy and happiness to ourselves and others".

I hope the next twenty-four hours will bring those precious things to us.

The sound of, "Time to get up," followed by a couple of knocks on my door, bumps me out of my laziness.

I depart for the kitchen by five-thirty, and eat a delicious bowl of pho. The warm noodles and tender chicken swimming in fresh vegetables, followed by a hot cup of Vietnamese Weasel coffee, bring a new life to my weary body.

"Sister Joan, are we definitely going to get kids on one of the flights? This war is getting too close!"

"I've been promised that we'll get our fifty-eight children on a plane today. I'm ready and confident that we've crossed all the "t"s and dotted all the "i"s. No one is going to stop this determined lady," she replies to me, and loud enough so all those at the table hear.

"What time are we planning on moving out?" I ask.

"Let's start loading the vans in about half an hour. We're required to be at Tan Son Nhat by ten o'clock. Remember, we also have to stop at our main office before we get to the airport. It was pretty crowded in this orphanage last night, and more children are expected to arrive today," she responds.

At that moment, Sister Joan leans over and softly says to me, "Make sure you have your pistol with you for the trip."

Walking through the halls after breakfast, I look in and see the rooms crowded with young ones. Babies are in boxes side by side on the floor and some of the older children are sitting two to a mat.

At six-fifteen, we're loading the seven vans. Some of the babies cry as we carry the boxes to the vehicles. The older children help us pack the little cardboard containers, containing the infants, onto the floors in front of the passenger seats.

"Let's keep moving. We need to get everyone in as soon as possible," I tell the older children.

By seven o'clock, we have all of the children squeezed into the vehicles. Looking into the horizon, I see a clear blue sky with animal cracker clouds floating aimlessly. The temperature rises fast as a necklace of sweat forms around my throat.

"Sister Joan will be in the lead van. After our stop at the Christian Adoption Services office to pick up the final documents for boarding the plane, we'll head straight to the airport," I inform each driver as I walk down the line of vehicles.

With the vans carrying eight or nine children each, we are ready to begin another journey to freedom for these kids. Sister Anne Marie gets into the passenger seat. We are directly behind Sister Joan's vehicle. Our trip toward the airport is very slow again due to the continued stream of refugees on the road. We're in high spirits, knowing these kids are getting out of here.

"John, what made you come back to Vietnam?" Sister Anne Marie blurts out.

"What...I...ah...I guess I had a desire to help the children of this country," I sheepishly responded.

"Really? That's a pretty gallant cause."

"Actually, after being back in the states and getting my Masters Degree, I thought about all of the children I had seen while here in 1970. My life didn't have a lot of direction in the States at the time. I had a job with San Mateo County in the social welfare department. It was rather boring. I saw an ad in the San Francisco Chronicle for a social worker needed in Vietnam at the Christian Adoption Services. After discussing the job with Bob Darcy at the San Francisco office, I made the decision that I could help the children I had so admired when I was in this country before. So, here I am. What about you, Sister? How'd you get here?"

"Oh...I was one of those spoiled kids growing up. My family lived in California—LA area. I'm an only child, and my dad was the CEO of a big company. We had the good life—big house in Brentwood, church every Sunday, and all the things I needed. I went to exclusive private schools. After college at UCLA, I bummed around, trying to find myself. I was involved with the wrong crowd and got into drugs. After hitting bottom, so to speak, I woke up one day and realized that this wasn't a good life. At that point, I decided to make something out of myself. When I told my parents I was going into the convent, they were a bit shocked, and figured I wouldn't last. Well...I did. After my training, I worked in Cleveland, Ohio with foster children who had mental and physical problems. After about twelve years in the Midwest, I was transferred here by my order. That was about a year ago. I love working with Sister Joan. It's so inspiring. Wow...I'm sure I told you way more than you wanted to know."

"Not at all, Sister. That's a great story. Thanks for sharing it with me."

The heat permeates my clothes as we slow to almost a walk. I'm sweating, and the perspiraton streams down my back, staining my shirt. My whole body is slippery.

We continue to plug along and I remember that slimy feeling from my combat days.

> We moved at night on patrol. The darkness was moist and warm. My clothes were always wet from the heat. The sweaty utilities added an extra couple of pounds to my weight. I recall that night we moved across a deep stream. We were all chest high in the river. Great! More water to carry on our backs when we get to the other side! I felt something sticking to my legs, like suction cups. I focused on the opposite river bank, which I could hardly see. I tried to avoid thinking about the snakes, lizards and other dangerous creatures swirling around my legs in the water. When we reached the other side, I quickly pulled off my trousers to find leeches clinging to my skin. I breathed a sigh of relief and pulled them off one by one. They were butt-ugly creatures.

"John. Look out," shouts Sister Anne Marie. A small bundle rolls in front of the van, followed immediately by a woman with her child.

"What's going on?" I respond.

I quickly hit the brakes and the van bumps to a stop. The woman picks up her package and steps out of the way. I reply with a slight cough, "Sorry, Sister. I was daydreaming a bit."

Putting my foot lightly on the gas pedal, we move at the pace of a tired turtle. Up ahead is a roadblock with some South Vietnamese soldiers holding up their hands. As we approach, I glide my hand into my pocket, feeling the steel of the Colt 45.

"Sister, get those Piasters and the cash out of the glove box. Keep them in your pocket. We may need them soon," I hastily state.

We approach the checkpoint. Two soldiers signal Sister Joan to stop her vehicle. I halt immediately behind her. One of the soldiers, who appears to be in charge, walks toward her. He's slightly overweight, wearing a neatly pressed khaki uniform. A black leather holster, carrying a pistol, hangs loosely from his belt. Sister Joan exits her van. I jump out and walk forward when the South Vietnamese soldier approaches.

Sister Joan asks the soldier, "What's the problem?"

In very good English, he responds, "Where are you going? My name is Captain Long Nguyen."

"We're on our way to the airport. These children are flying out of here today," she states as she points to all of the vans.

"I will escort you to the airport," states Captain Nguyen.

"We have no more room for passengers," Sister replies.

"I am going with you," he repeats as he puts his right hand on his holster.

Sister Joan, seeing the movement of the Captain's hand, says, "You can get in my van. It's quite crowded, but I think we can squeeze you in."

"John, we should be okay. They'll let us pass now," Sister Joan tells me as she slowly walks to her van.

When I get back to my vehicle, Sister Anne Marie asks with confusion in her eyes, "What was that all about?"

"That South Vietnamese soldier is an officer and he pretty much ordered Sister Joan to take him to the airport. Television reports have been noting that the South

Vietnamese army is getting nervous about the movement of the North Vietnamese toward Saigon. The commentators talked about the panic starting to set in with the ARVN troops. They said that some of the soldiers are trying to get out on some of the Babylift airplanes. I guess 'rank has its privileges'. Who knows what'll happen when we get to the airport."

We arrive at the Christian Adoption Services Office at around nine o'clock. Driving into the small gravel parking lot in front of two run-down, never-seen-paint Quonset huts, I spot a canted wooden sign above the door of the one on the left indicating we are at the main office. The other vans follow, and park alongside each other. Sister Joan gets out of her van, and walks over to me.

"John, you and I will go in. Please tell the others to wait here. We should be out in a few minutes."

Walking to the other vehicles, I tell the drivers to sit tight, and we'll be back shortly. I notice Captain Nguyen is not moving. He has slumped down in his seat and avoids eye contact with me when I walk past him.

Sister Joan and I step into the Quonset hut. The air inside is cool due to the swamp coolers which hum like bees giving a concert. The interior walls of the office are sheet-rocked, and gleam with bright white paint. It gives the building a feel of being larger than it really is. The reception area has brownish carpeting and a brown leather couch. The receptionist, a young Vietnamese girl, is dressed in a traditional red and yellow ao dai. She is sitting behind a grey metal desk. She greets us with a warm smile.

"Can I help you?" she says in perfect English.

Sister Joan replies, "Yes, we've come to see Father Raymond to pick up our papers. I believe he's expecting us. My name is Sister Joan McKenny and this is John Ellis."

"Of course. Father Raymond is waiting for you. Please follow me."

Sister Joan and I move with her to the rear of the building and stop at a walled off office. The receptionist knocks and a voice responds, "Come in."

Upon opening the door, we're looking at a handsome man about fifty years old, dressed in black trousers and a grey short sleeve cotton shirt with a Roman collar. His hair is salt and pepper grey and he stands about six feet tall. He moves from behind a metal desk piled with papers and a half-filled coffee cup.

"Sister Joan. So nice to see you."

"Nice to see you, too, Father. This is John Ellis, who has joined us this year."

Extending my hand to the priest, I respond, "It's a pleasure meeting you Father."

"Nice meeting you, John. Please, both of you have a seat," he replies after shaking my hand. He pulls up a chair next to us and sits down.

Sister Joan quickly states, "We have fifty-eight children in the vans outside ready to go, Father. I've got paperwork on all of them. Who are we suppose to meet at the airport prior to getting on the assigned plane?"

With hesitation, and a slight frown, he replies, "Sister, I have some bad news for you. The US Embassy called me this morning saying that our children won't be going out today. There was some confusion regarding other agencies having priority over us. I'm hoping we can get our kids on a flight tomorrow or the next day."

At that moment, Sister Joan rises from her chair and, with a look of total bewilderment on her face, loudly states, "What…what do mean? We're not going out today?"

Father Raymond also stands up and faces Sister Joan and says, "My hands are tied, Sister. I tried to tell them we're prepared, but it was to no avail. We'll get the children out soon."

With her eyes wide open and staring at Father Raymond, Sister Joan's voice raises to a high pitch, "I don't buy this, Father. We've been working too hard to be sent back to the orphanage again. You've got to convince them that we need to put our children on a plane today."

"Sister, please calm down. I'm doing my best. I know the urgency to get the children to the US."

Sister Joan cuts off his comment and moves closer to the priest. Tears swell in her eyes. She loses her composure and starts swinging her arms at Father Raymond's chest. "I need to get these children out today! I can't stand these delays! What does it take to convince the officials that it's our turn? We've worked hard to get the paperwork completed. We deserve to go now!" she shouts as wet streams flow down her face. She pounds on his chest with her fists.

I quickly walk over, put my arms on Sister Joan's shoulders and pull her slightly backward, trying to calm her. Father Raymond attempts to put his arm around her.

She shrugs both of us away. Finally, Sister Joan slowly moves, and melts into her chair. She glares at Father Raymond. Silence bounces off the walls.

After a few moments of total quiet, I say reassuringly, "Sister, we'll get the children out. I know we can do it."

Father Raymond adds, "We will, Sister. This is only a temporary delay."

"No! That's not good enough. I want these children out today! Their lives are in danger. We can't keep waiting! I'm sick of these delays," she shouts back.

I put one hand on her shoulder. She bows her head. With a delayed sigh, she looks up, accepting my condolence with complete dejection in her tired hollow eyes. Wiping the tears away with a handkerchief, which she pulls from her pocket, she slowly says, "I know...I...ah...I lost my cool. I'm sorry. This is so disappointing. These kids are my life. What do we do now?"

Father Raymond moves toward her and says, "I'm confident that we'll get the children on a flight in the next couple of days. Many agencies are in the same boat as us. We just have to wait our turn. I'm working hard to make it happen. You'll have to take the vans back to the orphanage, and I'll call you when the first flight is available."

"Okay, Father. We'll head on back," I reply as I stand up and grab Sister Joan's arm.

"Thanks, Father. Again, I...ah...I'm sorry I let my emotions get the best of me. Please let us know as soon as possible regarding the next flight," Sister Joan states.

Upon our exiting the office, Father Raymond calmly

replies, "I totally understand, Sister. I'll be talking to you soon. Be careful on your trip back to Binh Trieu."

Walking toward the vehicles, I say, "Sister, are you okay to drive? I'm sure I can get one of the volunteers to drive your van back to the orphanage."

"I'm fine John. Would you tell the rest of the drivers that we're heading back? I'll talk to Captain Nguyen about our situation. He'll probably want to be dropped off at some other checkpoint."

After telling the other drivers the situation, we're on the road again to Binh Trieu. Upon approaching yet another checkpoint, I see Captain Nguyen jump out of Sister Joan's van and casually walk over to the South Vietnamese soldiers. *I assume he will give them some story about escorting us somewhere.* Sister Joan's van pulls up to two soldiers. Her hand comes out of the driver's window as she gives one of them some money. He then signals for her to move forward. Captain Nguyen stays at the checkpoint. We follow in line, passing the two soldiers who are eagerly counting the bills handed to them. One waves his arm, signaling us to continue.

We arrive back at the orphanage about an hour and a half later. After helping unload all of the children and getting them to their rooms, I head into the kitchen and turn on the TV. The volunteers feverishly begin to prepare lunch, since they didn't expect the children back.

I listen to the TV above the clatter of dishes. CBS's Dan Rather is reporting on the Babylift situation. He's describing President Ford's support of the Babylift. He mentions that Air Force C-141's, C-130's, foreign carriers,

and some US commercial airliners will be flying to Tan
Son Nhat Airport in Saigon for the next few weeks to take
orphans, embassy personnel and foreign workers out of
Vietnam. He reports that South Vietnam is crumbling.

When Sister Joan walks into the kitchen and sits
down next to me, I say, "I notice a few more children are
here since we left. I sure hope we can get most of them
out of here soon."

"We will John. I know Father Raymond will do his
best to help us. He's under a lot of pressure from the
main office in San Francisco. Also he has to deal with
the politics of the South Vietnamese government, our
Embassy and the other adoption agencies."

"Did you get a chance to check any of the new arriv-
als?" I ask.

"Yes I did. About ten more children have arrived
here. Most of them are sick. They have diarrhea, upper
respiratory afflictions and assorted viruses. Some are so
sick they may not make it. They won't be able to go with
us on the first flight. Hopefully, we can get them out in
a few days, after we give them some needed care," she
states with sorrow in her voice. Then, she gets up and
leaves the kitchen. I begin to think back to 1970 when we
all wondered if we would make it out alive.

> Corporal Watson didn't make it. Those young bod-
> ies of Viet Cong didn't make it. Although sickness
> wasn't our greatest fear during those combat days,
> death was. We joked about making it through the
> war and then being killed after we got back to the
> states, from falling off a deck, or from a crash on the
> freeway driving home. The humor kept us going.
> We always joked about "short timers" (ones who

had only a few weeks left before heading home). It was always a scary joke. I remembered Lieutenant Fargo, whose tour was up and was preparing to go home. With only two weeks to go, he was killed in an ambush. He didn't make it either. The fear of death was ever present.

I'm startled by a dish crashing on the floor in the kitchen. The children begin to arrive for lunch. Sister Anne Marie sits next to me and says, "Those new children are really sick."

"Yea, Sister Joan already told me. I hope we can save them and get them safely to America."

"Me too. But a couple of them probably won't make it through the night," she sadly relates.

"Excuse me Sister. I need a little fresh air," I state while getting up from the table.

Ambling through the orphanage to the front door, I think about all of the lives we are affecting in this orphanage. I wonder how many of these children will make it to their adoptive homes. I ponder about the mothers who gave birth at the clinics, and left the infants, never to see them again. How about the fathers? Do some of them even know they had children? Will these children ever be able to find their roots when they get older? Probably not.

Just as I get to the front door and walk outside to a blast of warm air, I hear "Boom," "Whoosh," and "Boom" in the distance. These war sounds are becoming more frequent. The NVA continue moving south, and things are getting increasingly stressful around here.

Explosions break up the quiet of the day. After a few minutes, I stride back to the kitchen and listen to Dan

Rather tell the American public that the North Vietnamese are continuing to destroy and take over cities north of Saigon. Pictures of actual combat flash on the TV screen.

Sitting next to Sister Anne Marie at the table in the kitchen, I say, "Things don't look good, do they Sister?"

She replies, "Rather says this country will most likely fall to the Communists within days. Thousands of refugees are clogging up the roads to Saigon. Chaos and hysteria are rampant. I'm concerned about us getting through the masses on the way to the airport."

Reassuringly, I reply, "We'll get there. Even if we have to move in the pre- dawn darkness, we'll get there."

Sister Joan sits next to me and says loudly, "Let's make sure we're ready to depart at any time in the next couple of days. I have a feeling that we won't have a lot of notice when it's time to go to the airport."

We all nod our heads in agreement. After lunch, I head back to the rooms to help care for the children. It's another exhausting day at the orphanage. I bathe a dozen tiny kids, change at least twenty diapers during the afternoon and bring a ragged doll to a lonely girl. Two of us spend an hour changing bandages on children with burned limbs. I toss a rubber ball back and forth with the older boys and help the volunteers distribute our meager supply of medicine to the sick kids. After having a quick dinner, I help get the children to bed, do my normal paperwork, and by ten o'clock, head for my room.

Being sleep deprived, worried and concerned about getting all the children out of here alive, I lie down on my bed and pass out.

CHAPTER

13

The building vibrates like a bass drum. I jump out of bed and peek out the window. Beyond the rice field, white tracers skim through the black sky. Rocket and mortar explosions resound in the distance. The echoes of battle continue for a few minutes before there is complete silence. I surmise that there was an ambush a few miles from us. The clock shows me it's two-thirty in the morning. Although I'm concerned about the proximity of the conflicts between the North Vietnamese Army (NVA) and the South Vietnamese Army (ARVN), fatigue wins out. I crawl back into bed, and plop my head on the pillow.

The alarm ring jerks me out of my stupor at five o'clock. The remaining morning is chaotic at the orphanage due to more children arriving.

At lunch, on April 8, Sister Joan walks into the kitchen and announces excitedly, "We're scheduled to get some of the children out tomorrow. The plane is supposed to depart at seven o'clock in the morning, which means we'll have to leave very early."

"What time?" I ask.

"Probably around four o'clock. It could be dangerous, since the VC are operating at night. But we have no choice."

Concerned, Sister Nguyen asks, "Are we going to send some of the volunteers on the plane? Television reports are saying the South Vietnamese government is restricting the number of Vietnamese getting out on these flights."

"I have paperwork for our volunteers who work here. We'll get some of them on the flight. I'm a bit concerned about those arriving from the half-way houses. But...ah...I'll figure out how to get them out as soon as possible," Sister Joan replies. "Before I forget, Lieutenant Huy is bringing in some children with a volunteer from a remote half-way house near the Mekong Delta. His helicopter is supposed to arrive this afternoon. John, can you accompany me to the landing site?"

"Of course. How many more flights will Lieutenant Huy have to pick up children?"

"Based on my phone conversation with him yesterday, this will be his last flight. His family made it to Saigon safely. He's planning to meet up with them, and then he's going to stay in Saigon. He's been reassigned to ground duty there."

After lunch, I return to my normal routine of working with the children. Sister Joan walks into the room and says, "It's time to go. Lieutenant Huy should be at the landing site in about twenty minutes."

Near the open field where the helicopter is scheduled to set down, a dot approaches in the hazy blue sky. As we move into a trot toward the landing area, the chopper descends. When it gets close to the ground, the dust becomes blinding. I shut my eyes and turn away as the plane settles into the field. As soon as the helicopter blades are set to idle, Sister Joan and I turn and walk to the door.

The crew chief and a young girl, who looks like a teenager, jump out of the helicopter. The girl carries a baby and the crew chief helps unload six other children. The volunteer is very attractive, and has the round eyes of an Amerasian. She approaches Sister Joan and hollers in good English, "My name is Theresa. We're from the half-way house near Tan Ngai Village. You must be Sister Joan whom I've heard so much about. Thank you for taking in our children. I had to leave the area since the VC are getting close to taking over. The nuns at the half-way house feared for my safety."

"Welcome, Theresa. We need to get these children to the orphanage. We're just a few blocks away. Theresa, this is John Ellis."

"Nice to meet you, John."

"Likewise, Theresa. As soon as the helicopter leaves, we can walk the children over to the orphanage."

At that moment, Lieutenant Huy jumps out of the pilot seat, walks to the open door, jumps off the chopper and comes over to us. His flight suit is soiled and it looks like he hasn't shaved or showered in days. With a smile on his exhausted face, he says, "Good afternoon, Sister." He stretches his arm out to shake my hand and says, "Hi, John. Nice to see you again."

"Very nice to see you too, Lieutenant. Thanks for bringing these kids. I hear you're heading back to see your family after this flight."

"Yes. It's been quite an experience these past few weeks. But, my family made it safely to Saigon, and I'm looking forward to seeing them. I miss them dearly. The NVA and VC are making it more difficult to get these orphans from the remote areas. We've taken fire many times. I feel lucky to still be in one piece."

After the children are gathered around Sister Joan, she says, "Lieutenant Huy, have a safe trip back to Saigon. God be with you and your family. Thank you so much for your help."

"You're welcome Sister. Take care of those precious kids," he answers as he climbs onto the chopper, waving as the crew chief shuts the door.

The helicopter blades begin their slow twist, and erupt into a full whirlwind. The chopper engine goes to maximum power. The H-34 shakes in response and dust lifts from the earth like a tornado. The children and adults on the ground turn their backs to the helicopter and their hands cover their faces.

Upon liftoff, the plane makes a slight bend into the wind, and then becomes fully airborne. I turn and watch the rescue plane leave us. In just a couple of minutes, the helicopter again becomes a spot in the horizon.

"Okay. Let's head over to Binh Trieu," I direct. "Theresa, the children can follow Sister Joan and me. Have they had any lunch?"

"Yes. We fed them before the helicopter picked us up."

Back at the orphanage, Sister Anne Marie shows the newly arrived children their bedroom. Theresa, Sister Joan and I head to the kitchen. After pouring myself a cup of coffee, I ask Theresa, "How bad is the war situation near Tan Ngai?"

"Things are a mess out there. The VC have been firing rockets into the region almost every night. Also, we've been seeing less and less of the South Vietnamese soldiers in our towns. I'm afraid the NVA and VC may overrun my village anytime. I don't know how the halfway house will care for additional children coming in every day."

"I only wish we could get more of them here," states Sister Joan. "But, our main office in Saigon tells me that the helicopter flights have all but stopped because of the continuing movement of the North Vietnamese toward Saigon. I fear that many orphans will not make it out of here."

"Do you think we can make another trip to the halfway houses near Saigon to pick up children, Sister?" I ask.

"I just don't know, John. Between trying to get the kids to the airport and the continuing arrival of children here, I'm doubtful that we'll have the time."

Looking over to Theresa, I inquire, "How long have you been in the Tan Ngai Village area?"

"Oh...ah...I was born in Vinh Long Province, and my parents settled there during the French occupation of Vietnam. My mother told me that my father was a French soldier who was killed during the war. I was going to a French school when the Viet Minh forces killed my mother. I was seven years old at the time. That's when I was put in the half-way house. I lived there until I was old enough to work as a full-time adult. I've been there ever since."

"Sounds like the nuns took good care of you."

"They were very kind to me there, John. Prior to getting to the half-way house, I had to put up with physical and mental abuse because I was not considered a native Vietnamese. The people in the area were not very fond of mixed blood children."

"Sorry to interrupt, Theresa," Sister Joan says. "We're very happy to have you here. We're scheduled to get over fifty of the children to Tan Son Nhat Airport early tomorrow morning. We won't be able to get you on the plane then, since I won't have the correct papers for you yet. But, I'm confident I can get you out on a later flight as an escort."

"Thank you, Sister. I'm here to help in any way I can."

With approximately eighty children in the building, the noise level increases. Children chatter. Some sing and some laugh. There isn't enough room at the kitchen tables for everyone. A group of children sits on the floor in the Vietnamese "squat" as they eat their rice with chopsticks. The older children get plates, bowls and glasses for the younger ones. They also help the handicapped. *These kids never cease to amaze me as they selflessly assist each other, with so much love.*

Sitting next to me at dinner, Sister Joan looks over and says, "Since we'll have to leave around four tomorrow morning, it'll be fairly hectic getting the children ready.

I want to make sure that Xuan Yen, Binh, Chi, An, and Trun all get on that flight."

"Sister, I thought that the South Vietnamese government didn't want children under six months old leaving the country. You know, Xuan Yen is only a couple of months old. Have they changed their tune?"

"Yes. Since things are getting hotter in the country and the North Vietnamese are threatening Saigon, the South Vietnamese government has loosened up on the rules. We're not restricted anymore on age."

"Is Xuan Yen healthy enough for the flight? She had a fever and diarrhea a couple of days ago," I say.

"I checked her this afternoon. She seems to be back to normal. By the way, did I tell you I met her adoptive parents on my last trip to the States? The family lives in California, has three boys, and is really looking forward to seeing Xuan Yen. Her adoptive mom and dad helped me babysit some orphans at the San Francisco Airport. The orphans were on their way to some of the Midwestern states. I told the parents that I would be tagging a girl for them. At the time, I didn't have a specific child for them, but now we do. Should be a wonderful family for this little girl."

"That's great, Sister. I'll make sure those kids are all ready in the morning. Do we have the required wrist bands marked?"

"Yes. You, Sister Nguyen, and Sister Anne Marie, can put on the wristbands before they go to bed. We have a busy evening. I would like all of us to meet in my office in about an hour."

About fifty minutes later, I walk into Sister Joan's office and notice that she bears a blank look. The lines on her face look like stress fractures in a pane of glass. Tears streak down her cheeks.

"What's wrong, Sister? Are you okay?" I ask.

With her head lowered, and starring at the floor, she replies, "I have some terrible news. I just received a phone call from the American Embassy. Lieutenant Huy was shot down on his flight to Saigon. The embassy always had close contact with him since he did so much work for the orphanages. I'm sick."

My stomach drops. I'm stunned. This couldn't have happened. I'm paralyzed for a second. Sitting down, I take a deep breath and start to say something, but nothing comes out of my mouth. Head in hands, I recall a horrendous sight from 1970.

> We had called in a medical evacuation helicopter to pick up three wounded marines and six body bags. The landing zone was still under hostile fire, but the chopper, as usual, didn't let that stop them from helping their brothers. We had a perimeter defense around the landing zone to protect the H-34 on its landing. A second helicopter circled above for support. The rescue chopper landed safely. Marines quickly loaded the body bags and helped the wounded marines on to the aircraft.
>
> The chopper bounced into the open sky as small arms fire pelted the air from the surrounding brush. The marines fired both machine guns and rifle fire into the bushes to help protect the departing helicopter.
>
> Looking into the sky, I saw smoke coming out of the H-34's engine. The plane appeared to be limping through the sky but slowly gaining altitude. A

sputtering sound continued from the engine, and at that moment, the chopper turned sideways and began to fall out of the sky. My stomach sunk and I froze as I watched the helicopter crash into the tree line. I heard a loud breaking sound but no explosion.

I shouted to my first squad to follow me in the direction of the crash to see if we could help. The second squad provided fire protection for the departing marines. The small arms fire from the bushes had all but stopped. The crash scene was frenzied. The chopper was lying on its side. The door was crushed. The pilot and co-pilot were out of the plane, trying to get back inside the main body of the aircraft through the windows. My corpsman and I ran to the chopper to help the pilots. The rest of the squad formed a defense perimeter around the helicopter.

Unfortunately, the crew chief, and the three wounded marines never had a chance. They were all crushed by the impact of the plane when it hit the ground on its side. We cleared the area for a landing zone. I radioed the rest of the platoon to meet up with us, and we called in the second chopper to take out seven dead bodies. I sat down away from my troops. I felt nauseous as tears of sorrow and frustration flowed down my face. *Those guys were so close to getting home.*

"John. You okay?" Sister Joan asks.

"Yeh. I'm fine. Sorry for the daydreaming. I'm upset hearing about Lieutenant Huy."

Glassy-eyed and with a heavy sigh, Sister Joan comments, "He was such a good man. Oh, how he will be missed."

Slowly, she continues, "We're going to leave at four o'clock tomorrow morning. Are all the wristbands on the fifty-eight we are taking to the airport?"

Both nuns, who had also come to Sister Joan's office, reply at the same time, "Yes."

"As soon as the children are settled, all of you need to get some sleep. We'll use all seven of the vans in the morning. I have volunteers to drive as well as John, Sister Nguyen and Sister Celeste. Sister Anne Marie, you'll be going on the flight as the supervisor for our group. When you get to Travis Air Force Base in California, you can turn the children over to our staff there. I'm told by our office here that you can get a return Air Force flight within a day of landing there."

Sister Anne Marie asks," Do we know what kind of airplane we're going on, Sister?"

I interrupt with, "The TV has been announcing that C-141's are coming into Tan Son Nhat today and tomorrow. They also mentioned that Xuan Loc, about forty miles east of here, has been under attack by a large NVA unit. I think they hit the area yesterday."

Sister Joan's eyes open wider. "Whoa! That's pretty close. Did they say how the ARVN troops are holding out?"

"All the report said was that the South Vietnamese are putting up a good fight, but that they're outnumbered by at least six to one."

Sister Joan responds, "That doesn't sound good. We have a lot of kids to get out of here. I just hope the ARVN can hold out for a while. I feel like our days are numbered."

"John, you know a lot about airplanes." She pauses

and asks, "How big are those planes and how many passengers do they hold?"

"I know the C-141's can carry large vehicles, missiles and troops. They also carry paratroopers and can drop cargo and troops out the large rear door while in flight. I believe the plane can be outfitted for around a hundred and fifty passengers. It's a huge Air Force jet with swept-back wings.

With a smile, Sister Joan says, "Thanks. I guess it'll be able to take our fifty-eight children."

"You bet, Sister."

"See you all at three o'clock breakfast tomorrow morning," she says.

After tossing and turning for a few hours, the alarm blast surprises me at two-thirty in the morning. I slip out of bed. My tee shirt is soaking wet and sticks to my skin. *No cooling at night like at home in California.*

On my way to the kitchen, I hear the chatter of children filling their rooms. Two of the volunteers, with tears in their eyes, quickly walk by me. I follow them into the bedroom and see Sister Nguyen holding a still baby. One of the volunteers takes the infant and leaves the room.

"What happened, Sister?"

"Another two babies died last night, John. These are the third and fourth ones this week. They were in terrible shape when we got them. It never seems to end," she replies with a heartbreaking look on her face.

"What's causing the deaths?"

"Mostly measles. Also, bacterial infections following the measles are fatal to so many babies in this country."

"Where are they being buried, Sister?"

"In a cemetery about a half mile from here. Cemeteries are a safe haven for many. They're so sacred to the Vietnamese that even the VC hold a reverence for them. Actually, many of the refugees and local citizens go there to avoid rocket and incoming artillery attacks. We have a local gentleman who picks up the babies. Burials have to be quick due to this humid climate," Sister Nguyen replies.

Back in the kitchen I down a cup of black coffee and eat a bowl of pho. I'm now fully awake. The children, who will be going to the airport this morning, gobble up their dishes of pho. The volunteers feed the babies.

"John, this is going to be an interesting trip to the airport," Sister Anne Marie says. "With the VC out at night, I just hope we get there in one piece."

"I think we'll be okay," I say. "Hopefully, the main road to the airport will have some South Vietnamese troops guarding it. The TV reported last night that more ARVN soldiers are moving closer to Saigon due to the continued overtaking of outlying towns by the North Vietnamese Army."

"I hope you're right. I'm worried for the children. You know I'll be praying the whole way there."

Sister Joan walks into the kitchen, sits down next to me and says, "Have you got your weapon?"

"Yes, I do. Are we ready to load up the children?"

"I'd say in about ten minutes we can begin. Would you go tell Sister Nguyen, Sister Celeste, Sister Anne Marie, and the rest of the volunteers that we are almost ready to go?"

"I'm on my way. Will you be riding in the lead van with me? I'll drive."

"Yes, John. I'd like to be in front in case we run into any checkpoints, which I think is very likely. I've got plenty of money in order to try to avoid any delays. It's a little dicey going in the dark, but we really don't have much of a choice."

After rounding up the nuns, the volunteers, and fifty-eight children, we head outside toward the vans. The night is warm and humid and the sky is black. The big dipper and surrounding stars watch over us as we all begin to board the vehicles. Again, the older children help the handicapped ones, and adults carry babies in cardboard boxes and put them on the floors in the front seats. I hear rocket explosions in the distance. Some of the babies cry. The older children seem to ignore both the rockets and the wailing of the babies.

Sister Nguyen is loading her vehicle, and calls out, "Trun. Come over here. You and Chi can come in my van."

Trun hobbles on his crutches, and Chi, with her arm still wrapped in gauze to protect her burns, walks toward Sister Nguyen. Climbing into the van, Trun trips on a large rock as he nears the door. When he starts to fall, Chi quickly turns and grabs him with her bandaged arm. With a muffled cry, she lifts him from his fall. Helping him into the van, tears slowly flow down her soft brown skin.

"Are you okay, Chi?" Sister Nguyen asks.

Chi quickly turns her head away from Sister Nguyen,

and shakes her head to indicate she's okay, and continues to help Trun get in the van. I can see that Chi is in agony from the pain in her arm. I'm again amazed at the determination of these children and the love they have for each other.

"Boom!"

The ground shakes as some type of artillery shell explodes. I look into the sky to the north. White and red tracers from small arms fire are visible. The "rat-tat-tat" of fifty caliber machine guns breaks up the silence of the night. Some of the older children begin to cry. We continue loading the vans.

Looking over at Sister Joan, I ask, "Is Xuan Yen in our van?"

"Yes. I just put her on the floor with another baby in the front seat. I also have Binh in the back of our van with one of the volunteers. I'm worried about him. He has a slight fever, but I don't think we can afford to leave him at the orphanage any longer. 'Failure to Thrive' children are always at risk. He needs professional medical attention. I'm hoping they have a doctor on the flight to look after him."

I walk down the line of vans to check with all the drivers. Passing Sister Nguyen's vehicle, I notice that one of the volunteers is putting An in one of the seats. He has a smile on his face as I amble over and pat him on the head.

More explosions discharge. Walking up to the lead van, I look through the open window at Sister Joan, who is shuffling through some papers. "We're all ready, Sister."

Looking up casually, she says, "Thanks. Let's go. We

should see daylight in a couple of hours. Hopefully, the main roads will have some ARVN protection for us."

"We'll make it, Sister. This is a big day for these children," I reply in a quivering voice, as I turn on the ignition and aim the van toward the main highway into Saigon.

Jesus, I hope we make it.

CHAPTER

14

My concentration level is at its peak, waiting for something to happen as the string of vans moves toward the airport. I'm anxious as we drive down the deserted highway in the dark with our lights off. At fifteen miles per hour, I feel like we are going through a haunted house in which a ghost will pop out and scare us at any moment. Small arms fire and artillery explosions echo in the background. *So far. So good. We should be at the airport in about half an hour. This journey is like being on patrol at night during the war.* My mind begins to wonder.

> The eleven of us were moving across the mountainous area to set up a perimeter defense for the night. We moved with the stealth of a mountain lion, trying to keep as silent as possible.We put one foot at a time gently upon the ground in front of us. Our faces, rubbed with charcoal, blended into the darkness. We traveled about a mile. It took over

an hour. My senses were razor sharp. I heard every sound of the night. We stopped dead in our tracks when a tree branch moved or any noise came out of the bushes. It could be an animal, the enemy, or just the wind.

The journey was exhausting, even though we moved at the pace of a tired turtle. Constant focus on covertness during this movement was draining on the body. Finally, we approached our objective. We set up our defensive position for the night, taking great pains to be as quiet as possible. I looked at my watch. It was one o'clock in the morning. I was weary, knowing that I would only get about two hours sleep before preparing to move out on patrol at daylight.

"Boom!"

"Rat-tat-tat!"

My body jerks. I put my foot on the brakes. The sounds are in the distance, but I'm still jumpy. Tracers, looking like a stream of lightning, dash through the sky.

Older children in the van whimper. Some of the younger ones cry, as they crouch down in their seats with their hands over their faces. Sister Joan checks the babies at her feet.

The dark marks under her eyes and the sharp wrinkles on her face accentuate when she turns her head toward the back of the van, and says, "Quiet please!"

"We're getting close, Sister. I see some lights out there. I think it's the airport."

"I sure hope so, John. It's spooky driving through this cloud of darkness without headlights."

I spot the outline of some planes ahead. The few lights

around the airport create eerie shadows, making the air-planes look like black buildings lined up on a street.

"There's a checkpoint ahead," I say. "I assume those are South Vietnamese soldiers?"

"Yea, they are. Looks like a lot of people are hanging around the airport fence," she replies.

Driving closer to the checkpoint, I see hundreds of refugees camping out, surrounding the entrance. The concertina wire on the fence, which circles the entire tarmac, keeps all unauthorized persons away from the airplanes.

Steam from the humidity rises up from the airfield as the reddish sun creeps up toward the cloudless sky. The black planes turn grey, and the Air Force symbols become visible. Slowly, the van lurches forward to the checkpoint. With the sun lighting up the area, refugees start walking over to the van, staring at us with desperation in their eyes. Some plod along with us as we approach the main gate.

A South Vietnamese soldier pushes people away from the gate as he waves his arm, signaling us to move up to him. Six soldiers, all carrying M-16's and wearing steel helmets, stand around the main gate.

"I'll get out and talk to the guard," Sister Joan states as she opens the door before I come to a complete stop. She jumps out and trots over to the soldier. She begins talking, with hands moving in various directions. The guard looks over the paperwork, which Sister Joan has given to him. He quickly hands the papers back to her and points to an airplane on the tarmac.

Followed by two of the South Vietnamese soldiers, Sister Joan comes over to me. "They want to check our vans, John. Everyone is supposed to stay in the vehicles until they are satisfied that all the passengers are legitimate. I don't know how they're going to do that," she says with a disgusted look.

The two soldiers, glaring at me, board our little bus. The children are now quiet, with terrified looks on their faces. After a minute or so, the uniformed men leave our van and move down the line, going into each vehicle. Sister Joan walks behind them and patiently waits as they check everyone. Finally, the two soldiers say something to Sister Joan, and she returns to the front seat.

"The one in charge said we can proceed to that airplane," which she points out to me.

"It looks like we're finally going to get these children out of here," I say.

"It looks that way, John. But, this is just the beginning. I'm worried. We've got many more children to take care of. I just hope we can survive this mess."

"We will. Let's keep pushing. I'm happy that we made it this far."

"Me too," she replies, breathing out loudly through her lips.

Driving in the direction of the C-141, I'm partially blinded by the rising sun against the now clear blue sky. Heat rises from the runway and the humidity makes my shirt sticky.

The whistling sound of a rocket screams overhead. An explosion erupts near one of the C-141's. The van jolts.

Another blast follows. Jeeps and armored personnel carriers move rapidly in the direction of the rocket launch. Children start shouting, "VC coming. VC number 10!"

I know from my days in the war that when someone yelled, "VC number 10", it meant that the Vietcong are nearby, and they plan to hurt someone.

"I'm just going to keep moving to our plane. Hopefully we can get the children on and get out of here," I say to Sister Joan.

Approaching the airplane, with the caravan following like a twisting snake, I see four U. S. Marines walking toward us. One of them motions us with an arm signal to drive up to the rear of the plane. I feel more secure now, knowing we're dealing with American servicemen. The C-141 looks enormous up close. The massive grey swept-back wings are almost touching the ground. It looks like a large squatting bird.

Stopping at the giant rear door of the aircraft, I stick my head out of the window and address the Marine. "Where do we put the children?"

The marine, dressed in camouflage utilities, wearing the three stripes of a sergeant on his sleeve, and carrying an M-16 over his right shoulder, says, "You can unload them here, sir. They can walk in this rear door, and the attendants inside will help you get them into seats. The babies will be at least two to a seat."

"Thank you. Are we going to get these kids out of here okay?"

"Yes sir. We've had some incoming periodically, but the ARVN have a good defensive perimeter set up around the airport. We just have to load the planes quickly. The pilots will get these big birds off the ground in a hurry."

"We'll get them on right away, Sergeant."

Unloading the children and moving them into the C-141 goes fairly orderly. Other busses and vans also unload children and help them into the plane. Adults hurriedly carry babies. The older children help the younger ones and the handicapped. Air Force personnel instruct volunteers and escorts where to put the children in the plane. The rear door of this plane opens into a huge gymnasium-type cabin. There appears to be over a hundred seats along the bulkheads, and a large open deck area in the middle.

Sister Joan carries the box holding Xuan Yen and Binh. I'm holding An in my arms as we walk into the plane and look at children sitting two and three to a seat, with seat belts across their laps. Boxes, holding two or three infants wrapped in blankets, line the floor of the plane. Many of the babies are sleeping. Some smile as they suck their fingers. Blankets drape over the older children. Some have looks of confusion on their faces. Others chatter in Vietnamese to each other.

"Where should I put this box," Sister Joan asks one of the female Air Force Tech Sergeants.

"Over here, next to these older children. I'm assigned to this area. I'll take care of them. We have bottles, diapers and blankets for them."

"Thank you so much, Sergeant," I answer while carrying An to a seat next to one of the older children.

The plane is nearly full. Volunteers sit with children

strapped in seats. Escorts and Air Force personnel scurry around checking on the babies and getting everyone ready for takeoff. I head back to Xuan Yen and Binh.

"How are they doing, Sergeant?"

"Looks like they're ready for their freedom flight to America, sir."

With tears forming under my eyelids I respond, "Please watch these two carefully. They're special to us. Her name is Xuan Yen, and the boy's name is Binh. Xuan Yen's big black eyes focus on me, and she smiles. Binh just stares, with a blank look. *God, I hope Binh makes it. He doesn't seem to want to live. This "failure to thrive" syndrome is debilitating.*

"I'll take care of them. These children are in good hands here," she replies happily.

I bend over and give both Xuan Yen and Binh a kiss on the forehead and whisper, "May you have a great life in America."

Quickly we depart the plane, and I see Sister Anne Marie boarding with Chi. Trun is following her, limping along with his crutches. His smile is irresistible.

Stopping in front of her, I say, "Sister, have a safe trip. We'll see you in a few days. This is a momentous time for these children. God bless America."

"Thanks. We'll see you soon," she replies as she gives both Sister Joan and me a hug. We both move to Chi and Trun, give them an embrace, and then walk toward our van.

"Boom!"

An explosion shakes the ground near the C-141. I

look in the direction of the blast. It's close to an airplane parked about a hundred yards from ours.

"Is everyone aboard, Sister?" I nervously ask.

"Yes. I've done a head check, and they're all on the plane. Sister Nguyen and Sister Celeste should be back in their vans, and all the other drivers are ready to go back to Binh Trieu."

Other vans and busses turn around and head toward the main gate. The rear door of the C-141 is closing, like a white blanket spreading over a bed. The Marines direct all the vehicles to leave the area around the plane. Driving away from the large grey bird, I hear its jet engines fire up. Our van wobbles from the vibration. Reaching the gate, I stop the vehicle and see that the giant bird is moving. The same soldier, who gave us entry, signals us through the gate. We proceed, and pull off the road after about four hundred yards. The trailing vans follow our lead.

"Let's stop and watch the takeoff, Sister."

"Sounds fine to me," she answers wearily.

The C-141 taxies to its departing runway. The engines rev up to full power. The plane starts moving, picking up speed as it lumbers down the concrete surface. The wings start to lift and the nose of the plane gradually comes off the ground. Looking like it's moving in slow motion, the aircraft is now fully airborne. "Rat-tat-tat!" Tracers fly through the air. My heart drops. Oh no! The freedom plane continues to gain altitude. The machine guns and small arms from off the runway continue shooting at the ascending plane. White tracers are soaring over the wings of the aircraft. It makes a left turn and then a sharp right turn, trying to avoid the small arms fire. Finally, the plane maneuvers another left turn and begins to minimize in size as it changes into a dot. I take a deep breath, look over at Sister Joan, and say, "Wow, am I glad they're on their way."

She replies, with a shaky voice, "Me too. Our prayers have been answered. Let's get back to the orphanage."

I think about the great welcome these children will get when they arrive at Travis Air Force Base and San Francisco. There'll be crowds—happy adoptive parents and relatives awaiting them. I flashback to my arrival in San Francisco after the war.

> The Boeing 707 landed at San Francisco International Airport around seven o'clock in the morning. I was so thankful to be back in America, safe and sound. Walking off the airplane, I felt the cool San Bruno air blow in my face. It was like heaven, after leaving the dripping humidity of Vietnam. My mom, with tear-streaked face, was in the terminal to greet me. My cousin was also there to welcome me home. Other Marines coming off the flight experienced the same type of reception from relatives.
>
> As I walked through the airport, I saw some young people, many of the males with long hair and beards, shaking their fists at me. Others were dressed in multi colored shirts. Men, wearing loose fitting pants and women in ankle length skirts, were carrying signs which read 'Baby Killers'. Another sign said 'Murderers'. I was both mad and depressed. What do those people really know about war? I didn't kill any babies. I didn't murder anyone. I just was trying to do my job in Vietnam and bring my troops home safely. Do these people

know what it's like to have someone trying to kill you? They're crazy. I fought for them. I was furious. I felt like running up to them and punching them in the face.

My cousin said to just ignore those protesters and keep walking. I was very disturbed. I knew there was unrest in the states about the war, but I didn't think it would be so brutal. It was very disheartening. My heartbeat was racing.

What a sad homecoming, I thought. I was glad to finally get away from the airport and arrive at my home in San Bruno.

"Those children are sure going to have a great welcome when they arrive in the states, Sister," I blurt out as I put the van in gear and step on the gas.

"Yea, they sure are," she calmly replies as her head bobs forward in a sleep-deprived manner.

On the slow drive back to the orphanage, I inhale two candy bars. I figure this will be my lunch for today. We arrive back at Binh Trieu about two o'clock. A group of about thirty refugee women are milling around in front of the orphanage. Most are dressed in virtual rags. Many have babies or young children strapped to their backs.

One of the volunteers walks over to our van and speaks to Sister Joan in Vietnamese. With a concerned look on her tired face, Sister Joan says, "These women want to leave their children at the orphanage. They don't want their offspring to be raised by the communists of North Vietnam. Since many of the children are Amerasian, they're afraid the NVA will harm them. Many of the women told me they'll kill themselves. They're frantic."

"I can't see us leaving their children on the street,

Sister. Can we somehow process them in order to get them out of the country?"

"Yea, we can, John. Unfortunately, some of these kids are probably so unhealthy they won't last but a few days. On the other hand, we have no choice but to take them in. You, I, and Sister Nguyen can start bringing them into the orphanage now."

"I'll go ahead and start lining up the mothers so we can get the children inside, Sister."

For the next four hours, the three of us, plus the volunteers, continue to help the anxious mothers leave their children in our hands. Many of the women hopelessly wail as they leave their loved ones with us. The little children who are able to walk come to us with worried looks on their soiled faces. The babies feel almost weightless as we carry them inside and put them in cardboard boxes.

"This place is filling up again," I say to Sister Nguyen as I give her a tiny infant.

"Yes it is. How many does that make, John?"

"This is the last one, Sister. Number thirty-two. Do we have name tags on all of them?"

"Yes. We had to give some of them American names, since not all of them were with their mothers. A boy in the other room says his name is Ba. He's Amerasian. One of the volunteers told me he was left at the front door of the orphanage this morning. No one knows where the mother is. Would you mind going in and tending to him, John? He seems pretty upset."

"I'm on my way. I'll see if he's okay."

The small boy is crouched in the corner of the room.

He looks about four years old. Tears trickle down his dirty face. His T-shirt is full of holes and his mud-covered shorts are in shreds. He has a full head of black hair and is wearing a pair of "Ho Chi Minh" sandals.

Slowly I ask, "Is….your….name…Ba?"

In fairly good English, he replies, "Yes. My name Ba. Will I get to 'Merica? Will Marines come? VC kill me?"

I sit down next to him and put my arms around him. I look at him fondly. "You will be safe here, Ba."

He returns my look with his round black eyes wide open. "Tank you," he says as he puts his head against my shoulder. We remain there for the next few minutes. One of the volunteers comes over to us and takes Ba's hand. She walks him out of the room and into the kitchen for dinner.

After a quick shower, I'm back in the kitchen for dinner. After accompanying my dinner with fresh Weasel coffee, I eat and enjoy the juicy guava, bananas and papaya from the overflowing bowls on the table. I'm constantly amazed at the abundance of food available at the orphanage. Also, a recent shipment of medical supplies arrived here from Saigon. Sister Joan mentioned that funds are constantly available for food and supplies from the office of Christian Adoption Services.

Looking over at Sister Joan and the other nuns, I inform them, "I heard on the radio today that the NVA have rolled through Nha Trang and Cam Rahn Bay on the coast. They're having their way with the South Vietnamese troops."

"Are the ARVN going to be able to hold off the North Vietnamese, John?" asks Sister Nguyen.

"I'm not sure. President Thieu has asked the U.S. for more support, but our Congress doesn't want to give more aid. Too many people in the United States oppose the war. So far, over 57,000 Americans have died in this conflict, and the U.S. just wants out completely. According to the report I heard, the CIA says that the ARVN are strong enough to hold off the North Vietnamese until at least 1976. Word is that the U.S. wants to accelerate getting Americans out of the country, but Ambassador Martin is optimistic that the existing South Vietnamese Army can hold its own. Frankly, I'm a bit skeptical about his optimism."

"Whoosh!"

A mortar explodes in the distance.

"Boom! Boom!"

Artillery shells hit the ground far off.

"Rat-tat-tat!"

Machine gun sounds whistle through the air near the orphanage.

"Wow. That sounds relatively close," I say to the nuns.

"That's for sure. I hope the CIA is correct in their assumptions about the ARVN," Sister Joan replies.

"John, I got a call earlier from a half-way house about ten miles east of here, in the direction of Xuan Loc. They're having more NVA and ARVN clashes near them, and feel they're going to have to abandon their quarters. They don't have a vehicle to get out. I'd like to have you and Sister Nguyen go up there to get the two Vietnamese volunteers and six children. Are you both up for that?"

In unison, Sister Nguyen and I respond, "Of course."

"If it's okay with Sister Nguyen, we can leave first thing in the morning. Do we know the ages of the children at the half-way house?"

"I'm told they have three very sick infants, and three other children, around five or six years old, who are relatively healthy," Sister Joan replies.

"Okay, Sister. I'll load up the van with some diapers, blankets, milk, baby bottles, fruit and C-rations. Also, I've got my trusty Colt 45 and an envelope full of Piasters. We should leave at sunrise tomorrow."

"Let's bring some medical supplies also. I think those kids may need it. I'll see you at breakfast, John," Sister Nguyen says. "I'm going to get the children ready for bed before I retire for the night."

Sister Joan, with coffee cup in hand and a very serious look on her face, says, "Be careful on this trip, John. Things up there are pretty hot."

"You bet, Sister. Don't worry. We'll get those kids back here safely. I just need some directions to the exact location of the half-way house," I reply with confidence.

After loading the van with the necessary supplies and picking up some extra rounds in the safe for my Colt 45, I head off to my room. Looking at the clock, I see it's already eleven o'clock. I set the alarm for five in the morning. Laying my head on the pillow, I think about how critical things are here. I believe the North Vietnamese are stronger than our Ambassador's office wants us to believe. I don't think we have much more time.

CHAPTER

15

The alarm rings at five o'clock. A glance at the calendar shows me that today is April 10, 1975. I jump out of bed, take a shower, shave, and head to the kitchen by five-forty-five.

Walking over to get some hot oatmeal, I greet the nuns who are already sitting at the table. "Morning, Sisters. Sister Nguyen, are you ready for our journey today?"

"Sure am. What time do you want to leave?"

"I think we can get out of here shortly. Let's shoot for six-fifteen. Hopefully, that'll get us back by noon."

After breakfast, Sister Nguyen and I walk to the front door of the orphanage. A group of women with babies and young children welcome us. It looks like they have been here all night. Some balance bamboo poles on their shoulders. Baskets loaded with fruit, vegetables and other household goods hang on the ends of the long shafts. Most of the women wear conical hats and are dressed in rags. Many have infants strapped to their backs and some squat on the ground, breast-feeding their babies.

When I walk out the door, a woman carrying an infant comes up to me, and holds her child out toward me. Many shout in Vietnamese through their betel nut stained teeth. They push their infants and children toward the orphanage entrance. I know some of these children are orphans and some are sons and daughters that the mothers can't feed and shelter. I have an empty feeling in my stomach as I think about the agony these women must be going through.

We move to the van, and the sun alters the black sky to grey. A pink haze in the distance indicates that today will be another hot one. I can already feel the heat penetrate my skin.

"Let's go Sister. We'll have to let Sister Joan handle these refugees. I don't know how many more kids our orphanage can hold."

"I don't know either. I believe Sister Joan is planning to take more kids to the airport in the next few days. She told me that she's going to keep pushing to get as many children on planes as possible. We're going to need complete papers on all of them before letting them leave this place," she says.

"I know," I reply, as we both jump into the van, and begin our drive to the half-way house. "I expect that we'll be there in about an hour or so. I hope that we won't have too many delays due to the people streaming toward Saigon. If I keep the van moving, we should be able to weave our way there at a relatively decent pace."

"Right," Sister Nguyen responds hesitantly.

There are hundreds of refugees on the road; many more than on our last trip. Some water buffaloes, carrying children, are walking alongside women and old men pulling carts full of household goods. The sea of conical hats moves randomly among motor bikes, bicycles, trucks and vans. Most of the refugees wear tattered clothes, and many carry bamboo poles with hanging baskets. This mass of humanity clogs the road. I toot my horn as the van weaves between the throngs of people. We continue to move slowly in the right direction.

A woman walks along with us and shouts, "Nhin. Toi Doi. Cam on." (Look. I'm hungry. Thank you.) She holds her baby up to us. She looks desperate. "We can't stop. You know that," I say.

"I know. It's just gotten out of hand. These refugees are frantic. Some have probably travelled for miles, and they know that the North Vietnamese may hurt or kill them and their children. They know they're on the wrong side in this war," she replies softly, with her voice cracking.

Another woman pounds on the van. More hold up their children signaling for our help. After about half an hour of this constant beating on the side of the van and steady shouting, we approach a checkpoint. Two white wooden sawhorses block the road. Sentries wave four people on bicycles around the barricade. Two South Vietnamese guards, both with cigarettes dangling from the corners of their mouths, are waiting for us. I maneuver the van up next to them. An M-16 dangles over the shoulder of each of their wrinkled and dirty uniforms.

One of the guards leans on my window and says, "Where going?"

I immediately inhale his nicotine breath, and respond, "We're headed to a half-way house to pick up children for our orphanage."

"Passports," he snaps.

Sister Nguyen quickly hands me her passport, and I give both of the packets of documents to the guard. He looks them over, and with hesitation, says, "Very dangerous up there." He points in the direction we are faced. "What else you have for me?"

I reach into my pocket and pull out a handful of Piasters. I hand the wad, equivalent to about twenty dollars, to him.

With a broad smile, he responds with a breath of smoke through his yellow- stained teeth, "Tank you. You may go."

I put the van in gear, slowly move around the sawhorses, and drive back into the tangle of refugees. The road narrows and turns to dirt. We move through an area of heavy brush and coconut trees. There's a smattering of run-down shacks along the road.

"Boom!" "Boom!"

The van shakes. People on the road scream and disperse in all directions. A fountain of black smoke shoots up above the tree line. I stop the van.

"Whoosh!" "Boom!" "Rat-tat-tat!"

Artillery explosions, mortar rounds and small arms fire echo in the distance.

"Get out! Under the van!" I yell.

We both jump out. Sister Nguyen runs around the

front of the vehicle, and we hug the ground next to the driver's side. The clatter of a machine gun continues for about a minute. Eventually, the explosions terminate. Refugees are lying in the road. Some cry. Women stretch out over their children. Some recline under their carts. Finally, the noise of the weapons ceases.

"Let's get back in the van. Sounds like the conflict is over," I state with apprehension.

We climb back into the van and continue moving slowly in the direction of the half-way house. My shirt is dirty from lying in the dust and all of my clothes cling to me from the unbearable humidity.

"I thought the VC and the NVA retreated to tunnels and the jungle areas during the daytime," Sister Nguyen says.

"It used to be that way. But, the size of the North Vietnamese Army in this area is so large now that small battles are going on daily. Since the VC and NVA are very powerful, they no longer have to hide during the day. It's no wonder the half-way house has to be evacuated. I realize how much danger they're in."

"How much further?" she asks.

"Looks like about another couple of miles. I'll be glad when we get there. We need to load everyone up quickly, and head back to Binh Trieu."

I notice more South Vietnamese soldiers up ahead. They're walking towards us and mingling with the refugees, trying to look inconspicuous. Many have no weapons, and amble along with their heads lowered. Their uniforms are dirty and torn. Many are not wearing any helmets.

Sister Nguyen points to a wooden shack, constructed

of distressed wood siding and covered with a metal roof. "There's the half-way house up ahead."

I pull the van to the front of the building. Two Vietnamese women run over and start chattering in Vietnamese to Sister Nguyen. She gets out and walks with them to the house. I follow them. As I get closer, I realize they're just teenagers. When I get inside, my eyes widen in astonishment. Three cardboard boxes with an infant in each are lying on the floor. One of the babies has a bloated stomach and sores covering its body. The other two look like skeletons with a coat of skin. The three older children, who look about five years old, squat on the wooden floor. All of them have deep-seated hollow eyes and look undernourished. They're all barefooted, wearing shorts, but no shirts. They're black Amerasians.

"John, the girls tell me that there have been many explosions around here for the past week. They're frightened."

"Let's get the children and the young ladies into the van. Give them some of the C-rations. The babies will need milk," I say.

The children hold tightly to my hands and arm as we walk to the van. The girls and Sister Nguyen each carry one of the cardboard boxes. Sister puts one at her feet in the front seat. The young women get into the back of the van, holding the other two boxes. I help the older children into the vehicle. Sister passes the milk cartons, some bananas, and C-ration boxes to the rear. She then takes a milk container and pours the liquid into one of the bottles, which she brought from the orphanage.

"Are we ready to move out?"

"Ready, John. Oh my God. This baby's in terrible shape," she says while cradling the infant in her arms and putting the bottle into the tiny mouth.

As I back the van away from the bungalow, explosions erupt off to the east. A black cloud ascends into the hazy grey sky about a mile away. Quickly, I put the vehicle into gear, and we're on our way back to the orphanage.

With pronounced wrinkles on her forehead and eyes squinting, Sister Nguyen says, "Looks like more ARVN soldiers are walking toward Saigon."

"Yea, I heard on the radio that many of the South Vietnamese troops are deserting and trying to get back to their families. Many fear that the North Vietnamese will retaliate against the ARVN's wives and children."

I'm tense as we proceed along same area where we had to jump out of the van. Beads of water trickle down both sides of my face and sweat from the heat of the day blurs my eyes.

"Rat-tat-tat!"

Red tracer bullets fly across the front of the van. I slam on the brakes.

"Everyone down on the floor!" I scream.

Sister Nguyen leans forward and down, covering the box containing the infant. I stretch across the seat toward her.

"Ping-ping!"

Two bullets hit the side of the van. Someone in the van screams. The children are crying. The noise is incessant and fear reigns in our vehicle. Finally, the weapons stop firing after about a minute.

"Don't get up yet. Stay down." I yell to everyone as I move my hands in a downward direction.

People in the street begin chattering. I slowly lift my head and look out the window. Refugees get up off the ground and pick up their goods. Children whine and women lean protectively over their young ones. Gradually the groups continue moving on their pilgrimage to Saigon. No one appears to be hurt.

"Everything looks okay. We can go now," I say as I turn on the ignition, and we start moving.

Looking over her shoulder to the back of the van, Sister Nguyen shouts, "John, one of the girls is hurt!"

I quickly stop the van and shut off the engine. One of the young workers is holding her blood soaked sleeve and sobbing. I immediately get out and run around the front of the van to get to the back door, open it and jump in.

"You okay?" I dumbly ask.

She moves her head back and forth and continues to whimper. I sit next to her and gingerly lift the injured arm. She grimaces with pain and shakes. I slowly pull her sleeve up to her shoulder. Her soft skin is cut open. Blood oozes toward her wrist. One of the side windows of the van is shattered.

"Sister, hand me those gauze pads, some tape, and the medicated cream in the glove compartment. Also, there should be a small bottle of alcohol there. It appears she has a flesh wound. The bullet sliced through the side of her arm. Looks like it came through the window. She's very lucky. I should be able to stop the bleeding."

Passing me the supplies, she says, "Thank God. Is everyone else okay?"

"Looks okay back here."

After I clean the wound and put on the bandage, the girl closes her eyes and breathes out a deep sigh. She manages a slight smile and says, "Tank you." Tears slowly trickle down her auburn face. The three children stare at me. Terror is evident in their wide-open eyes. Tears dribble along the cheeks of the other worker. She wraps her arms around both of the cardboard boxes. I lean over and grab the children's' hands, and gently squeeze. With a smile, I nod my head up and down and say, "Okay."

I slowly back out the van door and walk to the front. Passing Sister Nguyen's door, I utter, "I think she's going to be okay. It'll be painful, but she seems to have calmed down." Sister Nguyen moves her lips in prayer while I'm speaking.

"Wow. We need to get going. Let's hope that we don't have any more shooting," I anxiously say.

In the next few minutes, the van again wades through the horde of people desperately hoping to find some form of safety. I reflect on the shooting incident. Things happen so fast in war-torn areas. I remember approaching an unnamed village with my platoon to give medical aid to the civilians in 1970.

It was mid-day, and this was a goodwill mission. We had been told that some of the villagers were wounded the previous night. The VC had attacked the village, killing a schoolteacher and hurting some women and children. As we walked cautiously to the thatched-roofed community, the sound of small arms fire and machine guns suddenly filled the air.

I yelled to my squad leaders to hit the ground. Tracer rounds flew overhead. Squad leaders screamed orders. I was stuck to the dirt, like a band-aid pressed against my skin. The red tracer rounds kept us down. Confusion reigned for a couple of minutes as I tried to figure out where the firing was coming from.

Finally, I yelled to the first squad leader to prepare to envelope the village from the left. At that moment the gunfire stopped. No one moved for at least thirty seconds. Gradually, I lifted my head up with the rest of the platoon. All the Marines had their weapons at the ready position.

I gave orders to spread out as the squads circled the village. Arriving at the meager huts of the residents, the women were shouting "VC gone! VC number 10!" This outrage by them meant that the VC were dangerous, mean and bad.

Fortunately, we had no injuries and were able to take care of the wounded villagers. We couldn't find any VC.

A woman walks along the van on Sister Nguyen's side. Through the open window, she holds up something wrapped in newspaper. Her hands are black with grime. Her ruddy face looks like cracked leather. Through her black tarnished teeth, she says, "Baby. Take."

"No. No," Sister Nguyen says and waves her hand in a slapping motion to the woman.

The woman moves away from the van, but then quickly comes back and shoves the wrapped newspaper through the opened window. Startled, Sister Nguyen puts her hands out and the bundle falls from her wrists to her lap. "No. No," she yells as she turns toward the window. The mother runs into the crowd.

"Stop, John. We have to find that lady."

I stop the van and run into the crowd. She's gone.

"She got away, Sister. How's that child?"

"The baby appears to be fine. Oh my God. How do we stop all of this?"

"We don't. Let's get moving. We now have another orphan for Binh Trieu."

Sister Nguyen puts the infant into the cardboard box with the other baby.

Arriving back at the orphanage around one o'clock, I see the swarm of women still surrounding the front door. Sister Celeste comes out to meet us.

"Sister, one of the girls in the back is injured," I tell her. "Sister Nguyen needs to clean and re-bandage the young girl's wound. I think it's okay, but I'd feel better if she checked it over carefully. Would you please help us get the children into the orphanage."

"Sure, John. What happened?"

"Things are pretty hot out there. The North Vietnamese are advancing faster than we think."

Sister Celeste and I off-load the young children and babies. Sister Celeste picks up the cardboard box from the front floor of the van. She puts her hand on the tiny chest of one of the infants, and bends her head down next to the baby's mouth.

With a look of shock on her face, she says, "John, this baby is dead."

"Oh no," I shout. "This is crap!"

I run my hand through my hair and close my eyes for a second. The interior of my mouth seizes from instant dryness. After getting all of the young ones into the building, I walk to my room and sit on the edge of my bed. Holding my head in my hands, I feel helpless. *Get yourself together, John. There's a lot to get done.* I slowly get up and head to the kitchen.

The sweet smell of pho welcomes me. After helping myself to a bowl of the chicken and vegetable covered noodles, I walk over and sit next to Sister Joan.

"Hi John. I heard about your trip. Thank God, you're back safely. Our young worker seems to be okay, but she's really shaken."

"It was a pretty harrowing experience. Any more news from the Embassy regarding the NVA movement, and getting more children on planes to the U.S.?" I ask.

"Nothing except South Vietnamese troops are panicking and deserting to be with their families. I'm not sure how much more time we have before this area is overrun. The main office told me that we'll be able to get a group of children on a flight out on the thirteenth. I also expect Sister Anne Marie to be back here on a flight tomorrow."

"I see we have more orphans than when I left."

"We have nearly eighty kids packed in here now. Children are arriving from half-way houses nearby. Unfortunately, five babies died today. The condition of some of these infants is hopeless," she responds, her voice cracking. "Until we leave for the airport in a couple of days, we've got to get as much documentation as possible for these kids. Sister Celeste has got things organized for us. Could you work with her after lunch to get all of the children necklace IDs?"

"Of course. Are we going to be able to satisfy the officials with our paperwork?"

"I think so. Things are getting somewhat more lenient due to the chaos. The main office tells me that if the children are tagged, and we have some form of paperwork that looks official, we can probably get them through."

"God, I hope so, Sister. We can't leave these kids behind."

For the next two days, Sisters Celeste, Sister Nguyen and I work feverishly to get the documents and ID's in order while the other volunteers tend to the children. Sister Anne Marie arrives back at the orphanage on the evening of April 12.

During dinner, Sister Anne Marie continues to answer questions about her trip to the U.S. I sit down next to her, and notice Sister Joan is at the table with three of the Vietnamese volunteers.

"How was the reception at Travis?' I ask Sister Anne Marie.

"It was great. Many volunteers and families were at the base when we arrived. Reporters and TV cameras were all over the place. Buses were lined up to take the children to San Francisco. It was overwhelming. We're definitely making the news in the U.S. I've never answered so many questions to reporters in my life."

"Did you explain how serious the situation is over here?"

"Yes. I must tell you. It's on the news constantly. I wasn't able to stay for too long, since I was resting at Travis before getting another Air Force flight back here. I met with our staff personnel there to inform them of our situation. They did tell me that getting the Amerasian orphans and Vietnamese volunteers out first is critical. I told them that we're working hard to make sure we have documentation on all of the orphans. There are many anxious adoptive parents waiting for those kids. Reports from the higher-ups in the United States are that the military situation is becoming extremely serious. Like I didn't know that," she answers with a slight amount of sarcasm.

With a look of determination, I respond, "We're taking a group of kids to the airport tomorrow morning. Sister Joan has been on the phone much of the day. The main office here reported that some of the South Vietnamese soldiers are resentful that we're taking children out of their country. Some are starting to make things difficult at checkpoints. No telling what we'll run into tomorrow on our trip to Tan Son Nhat."

"How many children are you taking out?" Sister Anne Marie asks.

"We should have about forty. Also, we're sending three Vietnamese volunteers on the flight. They're not returning here, since they're in danger because of working for a U.S. agency. We have to start getting all of our Vietnamese helpers out since the North Vietnamese Army may kill or imprison them if the NVA overrun Saigon. Many of them are terrified right now."

"See you all in the morning, Sisters. I'm going to get some shut-eye. I'll be leading the caravan to the airport. Sister Joan is staying behind to get the next group ready for evacuation. Sister Nguyen and Sister Celeste will be joining me," I say as I get up from the table.

I look out the open window of my room at the eerie darkness. The smell of the refuse dump nearby makes my nose twitch.

"Ka boom!" "Ka boom!"

The flash from the explosions creates a lightning effect against the black horizon. Red and white tracers, like a snake of stars, dart through the ebony sky.

Lying down on the bed, I think about the futility of this war. *What a mess. How many kids will we get out before all of us have to evacuate?* My lethargic mind follows my fatigued body into a deep sleep.

CHAPTER

16

An explosion jerks me out of a deep slumber. I can't tell if it's thunder or mortars. The building vibrates, followed by children crying in the other rooms. Leaping out of bed, I look out the window at the drizzling rain. Immediately, the rain turns into a downpour, typical of the coming monsoon season. Shutting the window, I turn on the light to see its four-forty-five in the morning. I'm in the kitchen sipping a hot cup of coffee by five-fifteen.

"John, what time are we leaving?" Sister Nguyen asks.

"We should get out of here by six-thirty. We'll have enough daylight by then. Four vans should be enough for the trip. Sister Anne Marie, Sister Celeste, and you and I will be driving. Three of the Vietnamese volunteers will be going on the flight, and will be coming with us."

Sister Joan sits next to me and says, "The volunteers

we're sending today are teenagers. Actually, they look younger than that. This'll be to our advantage, since the South Vietnamese soldiers are showing more resentment about letting adults out of the country. We want these girls to blend in with the children as much as possible."

"How are we going to do that?"

"The best we can do is dress them like the children, with T-shirts, shorts and sandals, and put them in the back of the vans. These girls are terrified of the North Vietnamese soldiers. They fear death, and possibly torture, if the South is overrun. Anyone sympathetic to the South Vietnamese could be in serious danger, and they know it. Theresa is also going on the plane. We have full paperwork on her plus a passport, so they shouldn't question her. Since she's part French and part Vietnamese, I feel we need to get her out now. Mixed blood people are not popular with the North Vietnamese."

After breakfast, I help the nuns and volunteers prepare the children for our trip to Tan Son Nhat, as well as make sure that each of the children has their necklace IDs. The rain continues to bombard the tin roof, like pebbles falling on the orphanage.

Daylight peeks through the clouds around six-fifteen, and the deluge subsides to a drizzle. We begin loading the vans, tramping through the mass of puddles caused by the storm. The rain stops, and the thermometer reading immediately rises as the sun climbs above the clouds that resemble moving corsages. Steam rises from the little lakes in the parking area. Beads of sweat develop on my forehead and upper lip. My shirt fuses to my back as I'm loading children into the van.

After I give Sister Nguyen a box containing an infant, Sister Joan shouts to me from the doorstep, "John, have you got a minute?"

I walk back toward the orphanage, and follow her into the office. "We're ready to go. All forty of the children and the volunteers are in the vans," I announce.

"John, I just heard on the news that the North Vietnamese Army has accelerated their movement to overtake Saigon. Rumor has it that this "Ho Chi Minh Campaign" has the objective of celebrating the Vietnamese leader's birthday (September 2) in Saigon. Ambassador Martin has been stating on TV that negotiations can be made with the communist government. He hopes that they'll allow a phased withdrawal for all Americans and helpful locals over a period of months. I think Martin is optimistic. So, be careful. No telling what you'll run into on your trip to the airport."

I reply, "We'll get'em there okay."

"God be with you," she replies, as I walk back to the van.

Theresa is in the right hand seat of my vehicle. She has two boxes at her feet. One contains a sleeping infant and the other is empty. She's bottle-feeding the baby in her arms. "How long will it take to get to the airport?" she asks.

"Don't know. Depends upon how many checkpoints we hit and how many people are on the roads."

Our trek toward Saigon begins well. But, when we hit the central highway to the airport, the refugee situation seems to be more obstructive than on our last trip. The crowds move at a slightly brisker pace. Some water buffaloes, with carts attached, trot along the side of our vans. Children run in order to keep up with the elders. Panic is apparent in their eyes. We meander among the sea of carts, animals, motorized vehicles, bicycles, children and adults.

When Theresa puts the baby back into the empty box on the floor, I ask, "What will you do in the US?"

"I'll be working with our Christian Adoption Services office in Chicago. Have you ever been to Chicago?" she asks.

"Yeah. It's a very nice city. I know you'll like America. The people there will welcome you with open arms," I answer with enthusiasm.

"I'm sad to leave my country. But, I know it'll be so different if the North Vietnamese take over. They wouldn't be good to people like me. I would remind them too much of America," she retorts with sadness in her voice.

Her response reminds me how determined the North Vietnamese and the Viet Cong are to take over South Vietnam.

> There was a bitter look on the captured Viet Cong prisoner's face. His gaze radiated both hate and frustration. He was dressed in rags and looked like he had been in the jungle for months. He weighed about a hundred pounds and carried a pack containing survival supplies and a small ration of cold rice. His AK-47 rifle, which we seized, weighed about ten pounds.
>
> His stare was piercing. Although captured, it was obvious that he was not ready to concede to us. He struggled with us as we tied his hands behind his back. We turned him over to our South Vietnam

advisors. He spit at them and yelled at them in Vietnamese. He was not ready to give up, even though
he was probably going to be tortured or killed by
the South Vietnamese. I knew at that moment that
these enemy soldiers were determined to fight no
matter what the odds.

The babies at the feet of Theresa whimper. She picks up
one at a time to calm them down. The windows of the van
are open to get some cross-breeze through the sticky air.
The noise level outside intensifies. Women with futile
looks and hands in the air continue to beg for food from
us. Some pound on the side of the van and hold babies in
the air, pleading with us to take their child.

Sounds of war continue to echo in the distance.
Explosions and the "woosh-woosh" of mortar rounds
fill the air. Some of the children in our van bawl. The
volunteers comfort the children by putting their arms
around them.

"There's a checkpoint ahead, Theresa."

I reach into the glove compartment and pull out some
Piasters. I then put my hand in my pocket to make sure
the Colt 45 is available.

We move slowly toward the South Vietnamese soldiers. Stopping the van, Theresa and I get out and walk
over to the men. Both have scowls on their faces. They are
rake skinny. A cigarette dangles from the corner of each
of their mouths, and their khaki uniforms are wrinkled
and dirty. M-16's hang from their shoulders.

One of the soldiers starts talking in broken English. I
can almost taste the tobacco as he moves his face close to
me and says, "Where go? You have money?"

I pull out the Piasters and hand him the bills. He smiles and pushes his hand through the air signaling for us to get back in the van. We climb in and I start up the engine. The vehicle moves by the guards and I watch them count their riches.

Our vans continue to bump along toward the airport. Theresa looks over and says, "John, do you know Sister Celeste very well?"

"She's been at Binh Trieu for only a little while. I did get to talk to her a few times about her background. Why do you ask?" I reply.

"I was just curious. She's been so nice to me and makes me feel so welcome here. I'm going to miss her."

"Sister Celeste has been through some rough times. Her family is from Hanoi, and they left the North when Ho Chi Minh decided to fight the South. They are devoutly Catholic, and wanted no part of communism."

"Where did they go in South Vietnam?" she asks.

They settled in Ban Me Thuot. Her father joined the ARVN and never returned home. Sister Celeste joined the convent there and then began working in a half-way house not too far from here. She told me that she fears her mom and sister may not have made it out of Ban Me Thout when it was overrun by the NVA in March," I say.

Spotting the airport in the distance, I say, "I'm going to pull behind that group of buses."

I wave my arm out the window for the other vans to follow me as I move in line. We're now stopped, and surrounded by a barrage of refugees. It's hotter. The sun hides from time to time, obscured by racing white clouds that look like horses flying across the sky. I'm clammy. The noise level in and out of the van is loud and rowdy. Our van slowly progresses toward the gate.

Finally, we're at the entrance. I look around for U.S. servicemen and see none. Three C-141's sit on the tarmac in the distance. Two of the C-141's are surrounded by buses being unloaded with people who are boarding the planes. From the gate, it looks like ants crawling into toy airplanes. Many Hueys and H-34 helicopters are spread across the airfield. A Pam Am 747 rests on the runway ready for takeoff. Jeeps, armored personnel carriers and 6 X 6 military trucks move in all directions. A South Vietnamese soldier, with his M-16 at the ready position, walks over to my side of the van and says in broken English, "How many go on airplane?"

Pointing to the vans to my rear I reply, "Forty children and one adult."

"You have papers?" he asks.

Theresa hands me the master sheet listing all of the children. "This is the boarding list for the airplane," I explain as I show him the paper.

"We check each bus. Need ID tags," he states with authority, and signals to three other soldiers at the gate to move to our vans. I get out, and walk back toward our other vans, following two of the men.

In the meantime, Theresa opens the van door and one of the South Vietnamese soldiers enters our vehicle. Some of the children cry. Others look away from the soldier as he slowly checks the neck ID's of each child. He stops at one of the teenage girls and stares at her. She shyly turns her head. "How old?" he snaps.

"Eleven," replies Theresa.

He hesitates. "She too old," he responds.

"She's on the master sheet here," Theresa says.

"Show me name," he states. She points to the name on the page. The volunteer girl is deadly silent. She holds her breath and displays horror in her eyes. At that moment, a guard at the gate yells something in Vietnamese to our van. The soldier turns quickly and heads to the door. Outside, the sentry shouts loudly toward the other vans. The South Vietnamese soldiers exit and walk to the main gate. The teenager gives a huge sigh of relief.

Following the two soldiers toward our van, I ask, "Did you hear what he said, Theresa?"

"The soldier at the gate told him that we've got to move the buses to the airplanes for loading right now. The plane is getting ready for takeoff. This means we shouldn't have any trouble getting the young teenagers on the plane as well," she answers.

"Great! Let's go!"

We move toward the C-141 pointed out by the South Vietnamese soldier. Crossing the asphalt runway, I see some Marines around the airplane. Letting out a deep breath, I glance at Theresa and say, "Looks like we're okay now. These Marines won't hassle us."

One of the Marines gives an arm signal for us to pull up to the rear of the C-141. Once the four vans move to the rear of the large bird, the Marine walks over to us. His camouflaged utility jacket reads 'Saxton' in black letters on the right front.

"Sir, you can unload the children and start getting

them into the plane now. There are Air Force personnel to help you. Move as quickly as possible. We're loading two planes and they can't stay here too long. The VC like to take pot shots into this place. As soon as the kids are on the plane, you best get the vans out of here," he says with command presence.

"Will do, Marine. Thanks for your help," I reply.

I step out of the van and hustle back to the other vehicles to tell them to start getting the children onto the plane.

We jog with the children to the big rear mouth of the C-141. Other buses and vans unload children and adults into the aircraft. The Air Force loadmaster and a group of volunteers in the airplane assist our children. We're the last group put onto the plane.

I hug Theresa. "Good luck to you. Hopefully, I'll see you when I get to the States. Keep up the good work."

"Thanks, John. God be with you."

A Mercedes Benz pulls up to the rear of the airplane just as I'm about to get into my van. A South Vietnamese soldier, wearing a neatly pressed uniform with two stars on his shoulder, gets out of the back seat. An attractive woman is with him. She holds the hands of a teenage girl and a younger boy who looks to be about four.

In very good English, with desperation in his voice, the ARVN soldier says to the Loadmaster, "My wife and children are supposed to be on this flight. President Thieu gave me the authority to put them on the plane."

The Loadmaster replies, "This plane is full to capacity. We can't take any more passengers."

"I order you to put my wife and children on this plane," the General replies.

"I'd have to take three children off this plane, General. I can't do that."

"You can't take my children off this plane, Sergeant," I interrupt with passion in my voice.

"I don't intend to. This General is adamant that he has priority to board the plane. Right now I have to get the rear door on this baby closed for takeoff."

I watch and listen as the South Vietnamese General and the Air Force Sergeant continue to argue. The General shows the Sergeant some papers and pleads his situation. Finally, the Loadmaster points to the plane, and the woman and two children climb onto the rear ramp to board. The General turns abruptly and walks toward his chauffeured Mercedes.

I exhale with a sigh of relief that none of our children are taken off the plane. I walk to my van, exhausted. *Looks like some of the South Vietnamese are damn nervous about the war situation.*

An explosion at the far end of the runway lights up the sky with a bright yellow and white flash. The van wobbles. Two South Vietnamese armed personnel carriers and a 6 X 6 truck loaded with soldiers head in the direction of the blast.

Running over to me, the Marine shouts, "Get your vehicles out of here now, sir!"

I jump into the driver's seat and start the engine. Sticking my arm out of the window to signal the others to follow me, I step on the gas and turn sharply toward the main gate. The South Vietnamese soldier waves both of his arms indicating we should move through the gate without stopping. Other cars, buses and vans move toward the main gate from different directions. Armed soldiers run onto the tarmac. The sound of the C-141 engines firing up adds to the clamor surrounding the airport. There's another explosion behind us. I hear the "rat-tat-tat" of fifty caliber machine guns. *Shit! We made it this far. Those planes have got to get out of here!*

I pull the van off the road just outside the main entrance. Looking back toward the runway, I see the two C-141's line up for takeoff. A clear jet exhaust flows out of their engines. The lead plane starts to move down the airstrip and slowly lifts into the air. The sounds of machine gun and small arms fire continue. The second plane, with our children aboard, is now at full power and rolls down the runway. It rises into the air like a goose taking off from a pond. Both of the planes make a right turn and disappear into the pillows of clouds.

I puff out a mouthful of breath and yell out to nobody, "Yes! They made it!" I smile.

I stick my arm out the window and wave the vans parked behind me to move out. Our trip back to the orphanage is slow. The stifling heat is unbearable. My shirt is pasted to my back and the seat of my pants is wet. Streams of sweat seep under my arms. Driving through the throng of refugees, the smell of animal dung, body odors and diverse cooked and raw foods saturates the air. My stomach spasms, and a sour liquid floods my tongue. Inhaling and exhaling rapidly, I continue to merge in and out of the sea of humanity in our path.

We arrive back at Binh Trieu around noon. The crowd

of women and children is larger than when we left. Some squat with children in their arms while others just stand around with hopeless expressions covering their wrinkled faces. Children play, and several of them rapidly move chopsticks as they eat rice from wooden bowls.

Walking to the front door, I see Sister Joan and ask, "What are we doing with all of these people?"

With a slight moan she replies, "We're trying to help them. But, the orphanage is loaded right now. As soon as we take some more children to the airport, we can move several of these kids inside. These women will stay here as long as necessary. They have no place to go. They're desperate to get their children out of the country. Many have come from small villages, which have already been overrun by the VC or the NVA. Wow, you look beat. Why don't you go into the kitchen and get some lunch. We're bringing food out to these people."

Sisters Anne Marie, Nguyen, and Celeste, who are standing next to me listening to my conversation with Sister Joan, depart with me for the kitchen. I'm famished. I devour a bowl of pho, and gorge myself with some fresh bananas, dragon fruit, and papaya.

Sister Joan walks in, sits next to me and asks, "How was the trip?"

"Things went okay. The airport's a bit shaky, though. There's VC activity on the runways. Fortunately, the planes made it out okay, but there were mortar explosions and gunfire before and during the takeoff of the C-141's. We had to get out of there pretty quickly after the planes were loaded."

"Thank God. The news today reported that the massive communist force continues to close in on Saigon. Supposedly, there are about a hundred and forty thousand North Vietnamese troops headed this way. They've halted, and are demanding that the U.S. military personnel leave the country immediately. Adoption agencies are being urged to get their staffs out of the country and close down the orphanages."

"What are our plans, Sister?"

"We've got about a hundred children ready to send out of here, and another fifty or so out front that have to be processed somehow. No telling how many more will show up at our doorstep in the next few days. I'm not closing this place down until we get all these kids out of here. We've got to get Sister Nguyen and Sister Celeste and the four Vietnamese volunteers out of here soon. You, Sister Anne Marie and I will have to handle the last group out, whenever that may be."

"How much time do you figure we have?" I ask.

"The news reports that it's a matter of weeks before Saigon is taken over by the North. Thousands of people trying to get out of the country are hounding the United States Embassy. Some have connections in high places with the Vietnam government. Also, the number of U.S. employees and family members to be evacuated has risen to the hundreds of thousands. My office called today and said we can't get anyone on a plane for a few days. It's already April 14th. I just hope we have the necessary time to evacuate everyone. Let's plan to keep working to process and tag as many kids as possible."

We spend the rest of the day working with the children and preparing documents. Around ten o'clock in the evening my head is splitting. I head off to my room to take a couple of aspirin. The sky is clear and dotted with a smattering of brilliant stars. Explosions and small arms fire interrupt the serenity of the evening. Beyond the garbage dump, white and red tracers arc through the air forming a partial rainbow. My head spins. I lie down on the bed, troubled about the intensity of the NVA movement toward Saigon. *I wonder how much time we really have to get out of here.*

CHAPTER

17

It's an active war zone now. The sounds of artillery and bombings increase daily around the orphanage. Red and orange bursts and white tracers interrupt the evening sky, as rockets and small arms fire continue their thunder. The area surrounding us is infiltrated heavily by the Viet Cong. The North Vietnamese Army is overtaking Saigon. I'm nervous.

We spend the next four days at the orphanage trying to keep the critically sick babies alive with food intake and the use of our best medical skills. We tend to the children with various ailments who are waiting at our doorstep. The orphanage overflows with suffocating odors of vomit, open wounds and urine. These kids have a myriad of illnesses and disabilities--bloated stomachs, boils, malnourishment, diarrhea, braces, missing and deformed limbs, and burns. Many are Amerasians. Some won't make it.

Sister Joan gets a call from the headquarters on April 19th telling her that fifty more children can be flown out tomorrow.

Chatting with Sister Anne Marie at dinner, I mention, "We now have all of our children in here ready to go."

"You're right. But, even if we get all of them out of here tomorrow, there's still a crowd waiting with young ones at the front door."

"Are the children for the trip in the morning all tagged, and do we have the necessary travel docs for them?" I ask.

"They're all ready, John. We're going to have to cram them into four vans since we're running out of drivers. Sister Joan wants to get Sister Nguyen and Sister Celeste out on that plane tomorrow. She also indicated that all of the Vietnamese volunteers will go on the next flight, whenever that is," she replies.

"What about the seriously ill children, Sister? Can we put them on the plane?"

"I'm not sure. An American doctor from our office in Saigon is due here today. He's going to help us get these badly ailing kids ready for the flights out."

"I hope he's a miracle worker. Some of the babies are on their last leg."

At that moment, Sister Joan, followed by two men, walks over to Sister Anne Marie and me. "Sister Anne Marie. John Ellis. I'd like you to meet Doctor Dave Lockman and Gerry Ryan from our office in Saigon. They're going to assist us with the evacuation of the rest of the children."

"Please call me Dave," Doctor Lockman interrupts.

Dave Lockman, a man about six-three, is dressed in cargo pants and a loose fitting short sleeve khaki shirt. He looks to be in his mid-fifties, has long salt and pepper hair and a black mustache. His John Lennon glasses give him a studious look. Gerry is short, has a crew cut, and is clean-shaven. He looks about thirtyish and is wearing Bermuda shorts and a multi colored short-sleeved shirt. After shaking hands with both of the men, I say, "Welcome aboard. We're certainly glad to have you here."

Sister Joan interjects, "Dave will be working with the critically ill children. Gerry is a social worker who'll be helping us prepare documents as well as helping us transport children to the airport."

She moves on and introduces the two men to the rest of the staff in the kitchen. Shortly, she is back at our table, looks over at me and begins reporting. "Gerry told me that Saigon has become more chaotic. People are scrambling to get out of the surrounding towns. Changes are occurring daily in the South Vietnamese government. They can't function efficiently anymore due to the near collapse of the military. Also, there are more ARVN convoys and checkpoints on the way to the airport. The four of us should be ready to drive the children and adults out of here at daybreak. John, make sure you have your weapon. Can you put some extra C-rations and water into the vans for the children?"

"We'll have everything ready before we turn in tonight, Sister. I'll drive the lead van in the morning. It would probably be best if you ride "shotgun" in order to handle any language problems at the checkpoints. Dave, Gerry and Sister Nguyen or Celeste can drive each of the other vans to the airport. Once we drop the sisters off, you can drive one van home."

Artillery and mortar explosions continue into the evening. Lying in bed and listening to the sounds of war again takes me back to 1970.

> Every night was crammed with the clatter of explosions and small arms fire as we crouched in our foxholes, not knowing when the Viet Cong might hit our perimeter. I scanned the black area to my front while taking my turn as sentinel in the crater we called 'home' each night. The shooting of weapons became so common that I was able to tune them out and listen only for human activity to my front—the swish of a branch or the clatter of one of the cans on our trip wires. I was tired, but the adrenalin kept me alert as my partner got his two hours of sleep. When I woke him up for his turn to protect us, I fell off to sleep like a baby, putting my life in his hands for the next couple of hours.

My eyes pop open and I look over at the clock. It's four-thirty in the morning. I slowly crawl out of bed and shut off the alarm button, which was set to ring at five o'clock. It's very quiet. A slight rain pats against the half-opened window. A breeze blows through the opening, which has a cooling effect in the room. After the typical morning routine, I arrive at the kitchen at five-fifteen, a half hour earlier than usual.

"Sister Joan. You're up early this morning. Big day today, eh?"

"Bad news, John. We lost three infants last night. Dave did everything he could, but they were in such bad shape that there was little hope of saving them," she responds, moving her head slowly back and forth.

"I'm sorry. Is there anything I can do?"

"No. Sister Nguyen will take care of getting the babies ready for burial before we leave. I don't know if I'll ever get used to seeing these innocent kids dying. It just doesn't seem fair," she says as she exhales and lowers her head.

Walking toward the table, Sister Anne Marie says, "The news stated that President Ford is trying to get a $700 million proposal through Congress to help the South Vietnam forces. Maybe there's hope for us to get all the children out of here. It also said that Americans can get out of the country just by showing up at the airport. All Vietnamese leaving the country need to have a passport and exit visa."

"Do we have passports and exit visas for our volunteers and Sisters Nguyen and Sister Celeste?" I ask.

"We do," Sister Joan answers. "But, the cost of passports and exit visas for any Vietnamese or non-American has risen as much as six-fold. People are desperate. They're selling their houses for discounts as much as seventy-five percent of value. Some Vietnamese are even advertising in the newspapers for sponsors to get them out of the country. American visas are definitely at a premium."

Others arrive for breakfast. After a nourishing meal of hot oatmeal, fruit, orange juice and milk, the children clear the tables, and exit to their rooms.

"Time to start loading up, everyone," Sister Joan announces. "John, can you get the drivers lined up and get everyone organized for the trip?"

"Sure thing. I'll get the vans ready and make sure we get all the children settled in the vehicles right away."

The rain stops, and the steam levitates from the ground. The air around us begins to warm quickly. Explosions pummel the background, as flickers of flames rise into the sky. The orange sun peeks over the horizon. The cumulus clouds hang over the orphanage, looking like floating balls of cotton. The atmosphere is moist, indicating that the day is going to be hot and sticky. Children whimper. Adults carry babies to the vans. The unremitting chattering of the singsong Vietnamese language creates an ambiance of anxiety.

I feel like a Marine Corps drill instructor as I direct the volunteers and nuns to load our vehicles quickly and orderly. Using my best command voice, I shout to Sister Nguyen, "We need to get this caravan moving! Put the babies and the younger children in my van. The older ones can go in the other three. Let's hurry!"

After about fifteen minutes, we're set to move out. Sister Joan jumps in the front seat, moves her feet around the two boxes holding babies, and says, "Are we ready?"

"All fifty of the children are loaded. Let's go," I answer as I start up the engine and lead the three other vehicles out of the gravel parking lot.

Once we get on the main road, the refugees again encircle us. It's a cauldron swimming with humans. Our vans move at less than ten miles per hour. More explosions detonate in the distance. I look in the rear view mirror. Fear seeps into the wide-open eyes of the children in the rear. They stare straight ahead, with stoic looks. Sister Joan bottle-feeds one of the babies. Some children in the back seat start crying. Several military trucks and armored personnel carriers dodge refugees as they make their way toward Saigon. More younger men in military uniforms walk among the refugees.

"Bang!" "Bang!" "Bang!"

On a barren strip of road on Highway One, gunfire erupts, and people begin running and screaming. Seeing a dirt road on our right up ahead, I pull off and signal, with my arm out the window, for the vans to follow me.

Small arms fire bursts behind us. We pull the vans behind a row of trees into a bushy area. "Everybody get down!" I yell. I frantically waive my left hand out the window in a downward motion at the other vans. Then I move my head below the dashboard.

Peeking toward the main road, I see a group of young men, wearing black pajamas and carrying AK-47s. They grab some of the men in South Vietnamese Army uniforms. They're shouting in Vietnamese, and the captured men are now on their knees pleading. Refugee women and children scatter, some leaving their carts and animals. I'm shaking. *Please don't see us or come our way.*

Finally, the ones in the black pajamas drag four of the South Vietnamese soldiers, with guns pointed at their heads, to a waiting truck, and drive away.

Other than slight whimpers from the back of the van, the children keep quiet. Sister Joan says nothing. We wait for about ten minutes. The refugees begin moving at their normal pace on the road. I slowly get out, and walk back to the other vehicles. Sister Nguyen and Sister Celeste look exhausted. Their faces are as white as a freshly painted wall.

I walk to Gerry's van. He apprehensively says, "Everything okay?"

"I think we can get back on the highway now. Looks like some Viet Cong unit grabbed some ARVN soldiers. It's probably a forward patrol for the North Vietnamese troops, who are moving closer to Saigon. We need to get to the airport," I say.

I give a thumbs-up to Dave, who is driving the last van. Trotting back to my vehicle, I jump in and we are again on our way. The rest of the trip to the airport is slow, with refugees trying to hand us their babies, knowing we're heading to Tan Son Nhat.

Women bang on the side of our van, begging us to take their children. Closer to the airport, the congestion is like gridlock. Arriving near the gate, we line up behind at least twenty vehicles. The heat of the day is in full force. Sister Joan passes a plastic jug of water and some apples to the children in the back. More of the young ones begin whimpering. I'm dripping with perspiration. We sit and wait. An hour passes before we finally get to the entrance. South Vietnamese soldiers, with their M-16's at the ready position, walk along the side of the vehicles, instructing drivers and passengers to stay seated.

Finally, an approaching Vietnamese soldier, with sweat stains under the sleeves of his wrinkled uniform, and a scowl on his face, walks over to Sister Joan. He looks as ruthless as a combat rifle. He asks to see the required visas and passports for the passengers. Surprisingly, when she opens her folder with the papers, he quickly signals us to move all of the vans to a waiting C-130.

The activity on the tarmac is frenzied. Buses, cars

and vans move in all directions toward waiting airplanes. South Vietnamese military vehicles roam the airport. Three military ambulances, with big red crosses on their sides, drive toward one of the aircraft. At least ten airplanes are on the runways, loading passengers of all ages. To our left a C-141 lands, and two C-130's wait to take off. When we approach our C-130, a Marine signals us to move to the rear of the plane.

Getting out of the van, I walk over to him and he says. "Sir, please get the passengers on immediately. This plane has to get out of here in fifteen minutes. Other aircraft are circling, waiting to land. Give me your visas and passports."

"The lady over there has all the papers," I reply as I point to Sister Joan.

Sister Joan quickly gets out of the van and hands the folder to the Marine. We off-load all of the children and begin taking them onto the airplane. There are many American volunteers in the cargo area of the C-130. I assume they are residents of Vietnam getting out before it's too late. Children sit in the jump seats along the bulkhead. Babies are in boxes, side-by-side, set on the deck, with cargo straps across each carton. An escort guides our children to an area in the front of the plane. Medical supplies, blankets and boxes of food are stacked nearby in this big 'gymnasium.' Sisters Celeste and Nguyen stay with our children and get them settled. Sister Joan, Gerry, Dave, and I assist.

An Air Force Sergeant yells to us, "Time for non-passengers to get off. We're closing these doors in two minutes."

"Have a safe trip!" I shout to Sister Nguyen and Sister Celeste as I walk toward the rear door.

"God bless you," they yell simultaneously over the clamor. The four of us then disembark the C-130. Looking back into the plane, I view a sea of children sitting and lying on the floor, in a disorderly manner. Many adult escorts tend to the children. *Sure looks unsafe to me. I hope they make it.*

We then jump into the vehicles. Our drive back to the main gate begins.

"Boom!"

The van wobbles from the shattering explosion. Off in the distance, some type of rocket hits an Air Force C-130, which just landed. The plane is on fire and completely stopped. Black smoke spirals from the plane toward the shifting white clouds moving through the blue sky. Emergency fire vehicles, with sirens blaring, head toward the airplane. Air Force personnel vacate the plane and run across the tarmac. Military vehicles quickly surround the crippled aircraft. Firefighters spray the flames with their water hoses. The smoke now engulfs the aircraft as the waterfalls cascade over it. The crew members manage to all get out.

"Let's go. Get the vans out of here!" shouts a Marine who signals for us to continue moving toward the main gate. I raise my hand out of the window and give a slight wave to acknowledge his command, and we proceed to exit the airport.

With the three vans following, we make our way onto Highway One, and continue our journey back to Binh

Trieu. Amazingly, we're not stopped at any checkpoints on the way to the orphanage.

Upon our arrival at Binh Trieu, the line of women and children in front of the orphanage is even longer than when we left.

After getting settled in the kitchen, Sister Anne Marie greets us and tells us that the main office in Saigon says we can get more children out in the next few days. "They indicated that there is bedlam in Saigon. The government is losing control of the refugee situation, and desertion among the South Vietnamese troops continues to increase," she says with a serious stare.

On April 21st, we're able to get thirty-five more children plus some Vietnamese volunteers, who have exit visas, to Tan Son Nhat. With only a couple of checkpoints to maneuver and payoffs to the soldiers, the trip is rather uneventful compared to other journeys to the airport. Explosions and gunfire still prevail on the journey.

That evening our Saigon office notifies us that President Thieu resigned. His remarks about America are rather harsh, suggesting that the Americans failed to support South Vietnam after the Paris Peace Accords. Vice President Tran Van Huong takes over the presidency. 'Radio Hanoi' indicates that the new regime is merely 'another puppet regime'.

The TV reports that Thieu's poor leadership up to this time was a main reason for the continued success of the North Vietnamese in their movement toward Saigon. The fall of Saigon to the communists is inevitable.

For the next five days, we continue to get our children

ready for evacuation. Two more children die. One is an infant who was dropped at the doorstep in the middle of the night, wrapped in newspaper and covered with afterbirth. The other is a toddler who had pneumonia and was very malnourished.

April 26th becomes a pivotal day for all of us at Binh Trieu orphanage. Sister Joan walks into the kitchen for breakfast and announces, "We've been ordered by the main office to vacate the orphanage immediately, and take as many kids with us as possible."

"Sister, we have forty-one children left here. All of them are processed. I understand that our agency reps in the U.S. will match our children's wristbands with their documentation and the papers we send with them. What time are we departing?" I quickly respond.

"John, I'm not leaving until we take care of all the children waiting out front with their mothers," Sister Joan answers. "Also, we have to get exit visas for the two remaining Vietnamese volunteers."

"I don't think we'll have time to continue taking in more children, Sister. Getting exit visas for the volunteers is out of the question now. The shelling around here from the North Vietnamese is going from random to targeting. This place is no longer a safe haven from artillery or mortars. We have to move before we lose everyone."

"Boom!"

An artillery shell lands a few hundred yards from our building. The orphanage vibrates. Children scramble to get under the tables. Babies scream. Looking out the window, I see smoke rising into the patchy white clouds, becoming visible through the orange rising sun. Green and white tracers rocket through the sky.

Sister Joan continues, "We'll continue to process the children outside. We can stay here a few more days."

Explosions again erupt close to the building. "No we can't," I respond firmly. "Those artillery rounds are getting too close. The main office knows we're in danger. We can't stay here. You've managed to get many children out of here so far. We just can't get them all out!"

"I'm not leaving yet," Sister Joan says, with tears swelling in her eyes. "Too many of those waiting in front will die or be persecuted by the North Vietnamese."

The building reverberates from the discharge of another shell, which detonates nearby. Rockets echo in the background. I quickly take command. "We're loading the children now, Sister," I blurt out. "We'll take three vans. Gerry, Dave and I will drive. Dave, put the sickest kids in your van. Sister Joan will be riding with me. We'll come back for these people after we drop off the children at the airport."

Dave stands up and moves toward the bedroom. "John, I have to check a couple of the infants. I'm not sure they'll survive the drive. Sister Anne Marie, can you please help me with the two children who have burns on their legs? Their dressings have to be changed. I need a little time to get the sickest ones ready for this trip."

"Okay, doctor. Let's shoot for departure in an hour. Those explosions are too close for comfort."

Surprisingly, Sister Joan says nothing. She moves out of the kitchen to help the others prepare for our evacuation. The stink of smoke from artillery explosions now surrounds our building. It smells like rotten eggs. Gerry loads his vehicle with boxes of C-rations and Sister Anne Marie gathers up the children and checks their wrist ID's. I make sure my Colt 45 is loaded and that we have enough Piasters and American dollars, if needed. Some of the children weep. The older ones help us pack up with some sort of order.

"Make sure the volunteers are dressed to look like children," I shout to Sister Anne Marie. "Have them get in the back of my van, and tell them to lie on the floor and cover themselves with a blanket and suitcases during our ride to the airport."

I continue, "The South Vietnamese government is getting upset about letting out Vietnamese adults without exit visas. We can't leave them behind. The guards at checkpoints aren't happy about people trying to get out of the country. Also, you'd better leave on this flight. The rest of us will get out on the next one."

An escape epidemic takes over the country. Radio announcements before we leave radiate with stories of North Vietnamese victories on their move to Saigon. The city is just days from being overrun. I know that if we can get into the airport, we'll get the children on a plane since U.S. Marines will be there to help us.

We begin another journey to Tan Son Nhat airport. It's nearly ten o'clock by the time we're ready to leave. Sister Joan sits next to me in the van. The blackness under her eyes has deepened, evidencing pure exhaustion. Two boxes holding four babies rest at her feet.

"Thanks for getting things going, John. I'm sick about departing, but I now realize we have no choice. God help those we have to leave behind."

"Don't worry. We'll come back for them after we drop off this load," I respond.

Due to the congestion on Highway One, I take a detour, which routes us through a bottleneck area of Saigon. The city streets are gridlocked. I weave the van in and out of bicycles, carts, water buffaloes and humans. One-way streets become anyway streets. Gerry and Dave follow me about fifty yards behind. People pound on the van, begging to ride with us. They are generally aware that we're heading to the airport, since we have vehicles full of kids.

A man on a bicycle, wearing a conical hat, grabs the handle of the van. I slap at his hand to try to break his hold. He screams, "I go. I go to airport!"

"No...No...No...," I rebuff his request, and whack his hand free as I step on the gas.

I'm disorientated from taking all the side streets. The roads are a heap of humanity. Many children lean against buildings with looks of pure gloom. A young boy, with two bandaged stumps cut off at the knees, dressed in shorts and a T-shirt full of holes, sits on the sidewalk and waves to us. Women with weathered faces, carrying children on their backs, look at us with desperation in their eyes. A young Amerasian girl, wearing a frayed dress, balances on two crutches due to the braces on her legs. No adult is nearby. She just stares at us as we creep by. *What will become of her when the North Vietnamese overrun Saigon?* I take a deep breath. People around us move like a herd of untended sheep, not sure where they're headed.

After another left turn onto a main boulevard, we are parallel to the Saigon River, moving past the Majestic Hotel. *Now I know where I am. Compose yourself, John. Relax. The airport is not too far away now.* We come to a halt. A motorbike pulls up next to the van. A young man dressed in army fatigues points a pistol at me and says, "I go to airport with you."

Slowly reaching into my right hand pocket, I feel my Colt 45. "No room in van!" I yell.

Not listening to me, he repeats, "I go to airport." He continues pointing the pistol at me. At that moment, I step on the gas and turn the van to the left, knocking him to the pavement. An opening in the human traffic ahead allows the vehicle to keep moving. I choose not to look back as we weave our way forward.

Pulling the Colt 45 out of my pocket and setting it on the dashboard, I look over at Sister Joan. Her face is white. Her eyes are watering.

"Whoa. This is getting serious, Sister. I'm going to try keeping this thing moving. These people will try anything to get out of here."

Exhaling with a blowing sound from her mouth, she says, "Thanks. That was quick thinking. I guess I'd better take out my pistol too. I didn't think I'd ever have to use a weapon here. I hope we don't have trouble getting into the gate at Tan Son Nhat."

Finally, the airport is in sight. I keep calm, but taste the salt from the sweat pouring off my face. "Sister, are you okay?" She nods her head up and down as she begins feeding a bottle to one of the infants.

"Let's have the children make a lot of noise as we approach the gate. I don't want those South Vietnamese soldiers searching our van. We need to distract them so they don't see our blankets and suitcases covering the volunteers," I say.

Sister Joan talks to the children in Vietnamese, and the volume of chatter in the back increases. I stop the van behind a small bus in front of us. Jumping out, I walk back to Gerry's van. "Follow me when we get up to the gate. Do exactly as I do. If we have to turn away from the gate due to problems, just follow me," I tell him. I approach Dave and repeat the same thing to him.

Back in the van, we move closer to the gate. Activity around the main entrance intensifies. The big turnaround area in front allows vehicles to leave the airport if they are refused entry. The gate area is crowded with many South Vietnamese soldiers, most with frowns on their faces. All are carrying rifles, some in the ready-to-fire position. The van inches forward. A guard, with meanness in his eyes, puts up his hand for us to stop. He points his rifle in our direction. I take a deep breath and try to look relaxed.

"Show me papers," he snaps.

Sister Joan hands me the folder, which I show to him. The children in the van become quiet, sensing some danger.

He slings the rifle over his shoulder and says, "I check bus. I get inside now."

I counter, "We have the necessary paperwork. Just count the children. We need to get on the plane."

"I check," the soldier repeats.

With that, I make a quick decision. With the engine still running, I step on the gas, make a sharp U-turn, and head away from the main gate toward the highway, hoping that the soldier doesn't shoot at us. Looking in the rear view mirror, I see the other vans follow. Two soldiers are yelling at us as they run behind the vehicles. Thank God, no shots are fired. Continuing onto Highway One, we head north for a few miles, and then pull off to the side of the road.

"Now what do we do?" Sister Joan asks.

"I know if we can get onto the airstrip, the Marines will be there to help us. We'll try again at dusk, when the guard changes at the gate. It means we'll have to spend the next five hours here. Good thing we brought some C-rations with us," I respond with a fake smile.

The two volunteers, soaking wet from the heat and the covered blankets, get out of the van. Their eyes can't conceal their fright. The rest of the children gather around the side of the vans as Sister Joan passes out the packages from the C-ration boxes.

At around five-thirty in the afternoon, the red sun begins its journey of falling out of the sky. The heat has been intense all afternoon. I'm bathing in a fog of my own body odor from being moist all day. Artillery and rocket explosions are continuous around Saigon. Belching smoke rises in all directions. Flashes of gunfire envelope the horizon.

"Everyone in the vans. We're heading back to the airport. Get the volunteers hidden under the blankets and suitcases," I state with authority.

"Sister, can you keep the children chattering and making a lot of noise as we approach the gate? Their quieting down when the guard approached us last time was not good. We need a lot of distraction."

"I'll make it happen this time, she replies."

As we approach Tan Son Nhat airport, the usual line of vehicles is in front of us. Pulling up, I notice a change of guard has taken place. The new group appears to have neater uniforms and they are laughing and chatting to each other at the gate. As we draw nearer, the children in the back make an unusual amount of noise and move around playing with each other. It's rather unruly in the van. The guard, with rifle hanging on his shoulder, and a cigarette hanging out of the corner of his mouth, approaches us slowly.

"Need papers," he says.

Handing him the folder, he looks in our van and then into the vans behind us. The laughing and talking sounds of the children in the vehicles increase. He looks again, shakes his head from side to side in disgust, and finally waves his hand for us to proceed through the gate. Once inside, a U.S. Marine directs us toward a C-130 Hercules. Cars, buses, trucks, armored vehicles, soldiers and civilians move all around the airport, heading toward various aircraft.

"Boom!" "Boom!"

The van trembles. A plume of smoke billows up at

the far end of the runway as a South Vietnamese A-37 "Dragonfly" passes over the airport and fires rockets at the tarmac. Armored personnel carriers on the ground attempt to shoot at the airplane, but their rounds are excessively slow for the jet plane. No airplanes on the ground are hit, but two large explosions nearby create a shower of concrete flying through the air.

"Oh my God. That's a South Vietnamese jet. Either it has been captured or some South Vietnamese Air Force pilot has turned on us. Let's get these kids on the plane," I shout.

The large back door of the C-130 awaits our arrival. Escorts, volunteers and Air Force personnel gesture for us to hurry onto the loading ramps of the big grey airplane. The Hercules, squatting close to the ground, looks like an overgrown fat guppy with wings. It's four turbojet engines idle, waiting to get everyone loaded. Handing off the cartons containing the babies and helping the younger children, we have everyone on board in just a few minutes. Sister Joan and I each give Sister Anne Marie a hug as she boards the plane. The red sun is disappearing and the sky is changing to dark grey. The lights of the C-130 blink on and off in the upcoming darkness, which is enveloping the concrete runways.

Sister Joan, Dave, Gerry and I jog back to the vans and start our trek to the main gate, and back to Binh Trieu. A mist engulfs the airport as we drive toward the main gate. The foggy wetness on the windshield distorts my view as a South Vietnamese soldier approaches my vehicle.

Raising his hand and then pointing a pistol toward Sister Joan, he shouts, "Out...out!" I put on the brakes. Sister Joan jumps out, and quickly walks up to the soldier and begins talking in Vietnamese as he lowers the gun. Her hands continuously move in various directions, and the singsong Vietnamese language reverberates from both of them. I put my pistol in my pocket, open the door, and get out. Standing to the side, I listen to the melodic tones. Both Sister Joan and the soldier exchange words with each other, both with looks of determination on their faces. With their M-16's at the ready position, two more soldiers approach us.

Abruptly turning away from the soldier, Sister Joan says, "He wants two of our vans. A South Vietnamese General has ordered him to get cars to pick up some of his relatives in Saigon. I told him that is not possible, but he said he would arrest us if we didn't comply. I told him we would give him some money, but he wasn't interested."

"You're kidding, Sister. We can't just give him our vans."

"I'm not kidding. He's very nervous, and I don't think we have a choice."

"Oh my God! This is insane," I answer back.

The two South Vietnamese soldiers with the rifles move closer to us. The glare in their eyes shows that they are serious. I put both of my hands up next to my face and move my head up and down, indicating that they can take our van. Backing up toward Gerry's van, I grab Sister Joan by the arm. One of the soldiers gets into my van, while the other one continues to aim his M-16 in our direction. The hiss of rain falling on my already soaking hair is all I hear now. Dave exits his vehicle and moves toward us. My van is now moving away. Sister Joan and I climb into Gerry's vehicle.

"Dave. Jump in Gerry's van with us!" I yell.

After we're all loaded into Gerry's vehicle, the armed soldier waves his hand and beckons us to move through the gate.

"Let's get out of here, Gerry. Don't ask me anything now."

Gerry drives slowly through the gate, in the direction of Highway One. Another rocket explosion at the airport jolts our van. A heavy spray of mist engulfs us. The heat of the afternoon changes into a torrential downpour. Gerry pulls the van to the side of the road to wait out the deluge.

"What happened back there?" Gerry hastily asks.

"Some general wanted some vehicles for his relatives. Everything seems to be up for grabs now. People are trying to get out of here anyway they can. I just hope we can get back to Binh Trieu."

"I wouldn't bet on it, John. Look at the masses of refugees and vehicles moving toward us. This monsoon doesn't even stop them."

Parked on the side of the road, I weigh our alternatives. *Can we really make it back to the orphanage, or do we need to get out of this country?*

CHAPTER

18

The monsoon stops as abruptly as it started. It's blinding black and quiet, except for the stream of car and truck lights passing by us on Highway One.

"We'd better get on the road, Gerry. Let's head back to Saigon and stop at the office before we drive to Binh Trieu. We need to check the status of things there first," I say.

"You okay with that?" I ask Sister Joan.

With her head bowed and frowning, she replies, "Okay. But I do want to get back to the orphanage."

Our trip to Saigon is slow due to the magnitude of refugees choking the road, and sloshing their way toward the city. Gunfire peppers the black sky, with red and white tracers creating a light show. Groups of children and adults, military trucks, bicycles, motor bikes, carts, and animals pack the streets of Saigon. Gunshots explode in the air. People yell and shuffle in all directions. We finally arrive at the administrative office around eleven o'clock in the evening.

We anxiously walk into the office Quonset hut. Father Raymond is listening to the radio. Sister Joan says, "What's happening?"

"We only have two FM stations broadcasting right now. The North Vietnamese have shut down most of the communications around the city. They're closing in on Saigon. We've been ordered to get out as soon as possible."

"But we've got to get back to Binh Trieu tomorrow to pick up some more children," Sister Joan states with concern.

"That's not possible. The roads are almost impassable around Saigon. We've only got a few days to get out of here ourselves," he answers firmly.

"We can't just leave them behind Father. They'll die or be killed!"

Shaking his head back and forth, he continues, "We have no choice. There's no hope left for the Vietnamese. The United States Embassy has ordered all of us to evacuate. We have a dozen Amerasian children who we're going to get to the airport tomorrow. They're being taken care of by the volunteers in the adjoining building. I'm not sure how much longer Tan Son Nhat will stay open. It's being bombed daily."

"Oh my God," she replies, lowering her head and rubbing her forehead.

Father Raymond moves toward me and says, "Would

you and Sister Joan be able to drive the children to the airport with us, John? I'm hoping to get you both on that flight, along with Dave and Gerry. We also have two Vietnamese volunteers to get out of here."

"Of course we can do that, Father."

"You can sleep on the cots in the room in the back of this building tonight. The bathroom is down the hall. There's a pot of pho on the stove in the kitchen. Help yourselves."

"Thanks, Father. See you in the morning."

We head toward the smell of spices and chicken emanating from the kitchen. Sitting down at the table, Sister Joan says, "I'm sick about those children at the orphanage that we left behind."

"I feel the same way. But, there's nothing we can do. You heard Father Raymond. It's hopeless. We have no choice but to get the rest of the kids from here to the airport. Then we have to get ourselves out. Let's try to get some sleep tonight. We're going to be busy all day tomorrow," I respond softly.

A half dozen cots rest in the middle of the room. Stacks of medical supplies and C-ration boxes surround the area. We make our way to the beds. I realize how tired I am when my head hits the small pillow. A strange calm overcomes me and within seconds, I'm deep in sleep.

The gentle nudge on my shoulder awakens me from the dead slumber. "Time to get up. It's six o'clock. There's coffee in the kitchen," says Father Raymond.

I stretch my arms, slide off the cot, and head to the bathroom. After a few minutes, I walk into the kitchen and see children eagerly eating bowls of rice. Sister Joan, Dave and Gerry are talking as I take a seat next to them.

"Morning John. Sleep okay?" Gerry asks.

"Yes. Didn't realize how tired I was."

"There's been a change of plans, John. We're taking two vans to the airport tomorrow. Dave and I are taking one and you and Sister Joan will take the other. A couple of the children are critically ill, and Dave needs to watch them carefully. We're not sure they're going to make it. We couldn't get on a flight today. Things have worsened at the airport."

Father Raymond walks over to me and says, "We've got to work with the children today. Some of them are in bad shape. All of us will be going out on a C-130 tomorrow as escorts. We'll be the last ones out of this office. All Americans have been ordered to evacuate immediately. The embassy is telling us they don't think the South Vietnamese can hold off the NVA through the end of the month. That's just a few days away."

We spend the rest of the day feeding babies, caring for burns on the arms and legs of children, changing dressings on wounds, caring for dehydrated and generally sick kids. Artillery and rocket explosions shake the building much of the day. The rat-tat-tat of small arms fire screams through the streets outside.

"Boom!"

A bomb strikes a building across the street. Our Quonset hut rocks like a boat hit by a big wave. Peeking through the curtain, I see the structure across the road fully engulfed in flames with a fountain of smoke spiraling upward. Sirens wail, and people on the street scream. A fire truck is at the scene, and a military vehicle unloads soldiers who run toward the fire. More explosions erupt in the distance.

There is a symphony of squeals inside our building. Babies cry, and adults lie on the floor and cover the brood with their arms. Tears and fear fill the eyes of most.

"Everyone stay down and away from the windows!" I shout. "Wait until the explosions stop before anyone gets up!"

After a few minutes, the blasts cease. Everyone slowly rises from the floor, and carefully moves around the area, getting back to the duties at hand. I look at the clock on the wall to see that it's four o'clock in the afternoon. *Damn, we do have to get out of here. This is definitely a dangerous situation.*

Father Raymond says, "Let's start packing the vans right now. All of those medical supplies in the back room have to go. Also, let's take a box of C-rations for each van. I've got a duffle bag full of Piasters and American paper money. I'll ride with you, John. I know you and Sister Joan each have a pistol. Make sure you bring it with you, but keep it concealed and use it only if necessary. Things on the street could get messy. The babies and seriously ill kids will be with Dave and Gerry. We'll take the older children. One Vietnamese volunteer can go in each van."

"Gerry, give me a hand with this stuff," I yell.

Within an hour, the vans are loaded and ready to go.

In the kitchen, Father Raymond briefs all of us on the trip to the airport in the morning. After helping to get the children ready for bed, I'm on my way to the luxury of another night on a cot. Lying on the sparse divan, I close my eyes and reminisce about the days sleeping in "luxury" in 1970.

> My squad of ten had just returned from six days of reconnaissance out in front of our defensive line. All of us were filthy and tired. Trudging back into the Battalion area was like arriving at a vacation destination. All the water we could drink was available. On patrol, we were limited to two canteens a day—hardly enough to feel satisfied in the intense heat and humidity. Outdoor showers were available and felt like water from heaven. We were given a hot meal at the mess hall. After six days of eating C-rations, it was like dining at a five-star restaurant. Then we got to sleep off the ground, on military cots. These cots felt like feather beds in a hotel compared to the rocks, rough ground, and foxholes we had lived in for six days. The Battalion area *was* our vacation. It would last only a couple of days until we would be sent back out into the "boonies". Oh, how I loved those two days of comfort!

My eyes pop open, and I realize I had better get some sleep since we will be up early tomorrow for our last trip to the airport.

The wake-up call from Father Raymond is right on schedule at five o'clock in the morning.

"Time to get up everyone. Breakfast will be ready in thirty minutes. We need to leave by sun up," he states in a command voice.

Sister Joan and Gerry are in the kitchen, preparing

hot oatmeal, coffee, and tea, and setting out a bowl of fruit as I arrive and sit next to Dave. "How are the sick ones doing, Dave?" I ask.

"Could be better, but I think they'll make it. Their condition is pretty lousy and the tools and medicine we have here are limited. The dehydration and over exposure is very stressful on these little ones. I'm hoping that the medical supplies on the plane are better."

Immediately after a quick breakfast, we're loading the children into the vans. Explosions persist in the distance. The crying is more subdued than before. *Perhaps everyone is getting use to rockets and artillery.* At about seven o'clock, we leave the main office. Father Raymond is the last to leave the building. He closes the front door and walks toward our van. His eyes are red and he blinks rapidly. He turns toward the empty buildings and gives a half salute.

Looking straight at Gerry, who is in the driver's seat of the lead vehicle, he hastily says, "Let's go," and then strides to our van and climbs into the back row.

I look over at Sister Joan, who is sitting quietly to my right. "Well, this is it. We're leaving Vietnam. I really didn't expect this quick departure."

"Me either. I thought I would be here much longer." With a misty reddish gaze, she continues, "I'm very frustrated. Those children we're leaving are really in trouble, especially the Amerasians. It just doesn't seem right."

"I know Sister, but we're doing the best we can."

Keeping Gerry in sight through the streets of Saigon is a harrowing experience. The orange sun is peeking over the horizon. The heat is growing more oppressive. I'm perspiring. Thousands of people roam the streets. Homeless children sit helplessly on the sidewalks and lean against dilapidated storefronts. Explosions continue to echo throughout the area. People loot the vacant stores. The children in the back of our van chatter in Vietnamese.

"Boom!"

An explosion makes the van sway. People scream outside. Some adults and children lie in the street. It's hard to tell whether they are dead or injured. Putrid smoke ascends into the air. Car and truck horns toot continuously. I try to slow the van to avoid hitting someone, but get bumped from behind by another vehicle. Refugees surround us. Some run haphazardly, trying to find shelter from the shower of artillery.

"When we get to the airport gate, have the children make a lot of noise. I want us to distract the sentries," I say.

"I'm not sure that's going to be a problem, John. From what I hear, it's pretty chaotic at the airfield," Father Raymond says.

"I hope you're right. We really need to get everyone in the vans on a plane out of here."

After about an hour, the airport is in sight. The sun casts a yellow haze over the entire area. The scream of artillery overhead is frightening. A rocket explosion on the landing strip, followed by a plume of smoke, scares the hell out of me. I'm stressed. *Man, this looks bad.*

"John, that Vietnamese soldier is waving his arm for

us to get up to the gate. He looks very anxious," Sister Joan shouts and then looks into the back seat and yells in Vietnamese to the children. She moves her hands up and down toward the kids. The chatter increases throughout the van.

Remarkably, Gerry's van is waved through the gate. I follow him to the rear of a C-130. The airplane engines are idling. A Marine, with an M16 over his shoulder, is beckoning with both arms and pointing to the huge rear door of the Hercules airplane. Gerry and Dave quickly exit their vehicle. Carrying babies and helping the sick children, they and the volunteer move to the airplane and enter the rear door. Cars, military trucks, limousines, fire engines, ambulances and people are all over the airfield. Three Air Force transport planes sit on the runway. The Marine holds up his arm, indicating for us to wait in our vehicle.

"Kaboom!" " Kaboom!" "Kaboom!"

Three A-37 "Dragonfly" aircraft fire rockets over Tan Son Nhat. The van shivers. The rockets hit and destroy some parked South Vietnamese Air Force F-5 jets off to our right. Another projectile hits a C-130 that has just landed. The children in our van wail and bawl.

"Get them on the plane. Quickly. This place is a mess. This aircraft is ready to go!" yells the Marine.

Sister Joan, Father Raymond, and I jump out of the van and instruct the children and the Vietnamese volunteer to run to the open grey cargo door of the C-130. Just as they enter the airplane, a black four-door sedan pulls up next to the plane, blocking the three of us. A

South Vietnamese officer and a woman carrying a child rush over to the Marine. They show him some papers. He signals for them to board the plane, as an Air Force Sergeant on the cargo ramp is waving his arms and yelling to the Marine.

"Boom!"

An artillery shell cascades on to the runway very close to our C-130. The large rear door of the "Hercules" starts to close. We move toward the plane, but the Marine stops us.

"Stop. You can't get on. The pilot has to get this plane out of here."

"We have to get on that plane. Our children are boarded!" I scream.

Three more A-37's thunder over the field, firing rockets which shake the earth. We all hit the ground. I close my eyes. The surface below me rumbles. Peeking up I see smoke and fire clouding the area. The C-130 moves as we helplessly watch. Sirens roar. People run. Vehicles wander all over the runways. Small arms tracers surge through the air. The Marine, crouched next to us, gestures with his hand to move and get into the van.

"Get out of here!" he yells.

The three of us quickly jump into the vehicle. I make a quick U-turn after starting up the engine, and we drive toward the gate. The Vietnamese soldier waves us through.

"Head back to the main office," Father Raymond says.

More explosions make the van pitch as we exit Tan

Son Nhat. My ears ring from the shell blasts of the rockets and artillery.

The trip back to the office takes about an hour and a half. We're now moving against the flow of refugees. People, animals, trucks, and bicycles make it feel like we are swimming upstream in mud. Humans choke the streets, wandering aimlessly. Some buildings burn from artillery hits. Rampant looting continues. Some children just sit against buildings with dejected looks on their faces.

Arriving at the two vacant Quonset huts, Father Raymond jumps out and jogs to the main entrance. Sister Joan and I follow as he unlocks the door and we quickly go into the building.

"I'm going to call the embassy to see what's happening. Turn on the radio," he directs.

I tune to the Armed Forces Radio channel. The radio station, full of static, announces that the final helicopter evacuation alert, "Operation Frequent Wind," is activated. The broadcast notes that Tan Son Nhat has been closed to fixed wing aircraft due to artillery fire and attacks from other airplanes.

"Father, the radio stated that 'Operation Frequent Wind' is in effect," I shout. Father Raymond puts the phone down and walks over to me.

"I couldn't get through to the embassy. Well, we know what to do now. The SAFE booklet from the embassy gives us instructions for getting out of here in an emergency."

"What's our plan, Father?" I ask.

"I've read the SAFE procedures, and its map shows

that we can get on a bus about three blocks from here. These buses will take us to the Defense Attaché Office compound adjacent to the airport. Too bad we just left there. We're not supposed to move now until we get the confidential signal on the radio."

"And what's that?" I ask.

Sister Joan responds quickly, "The station will announce that the temperature in Saigon is 112 degrees and rising. The playing of 'I'm Dreaming of a White Christmas' will follow."

At that moment, the radio announcement repeats the words of Sister Joan, and is followed by Bing Crosby's Christmas song.

Grabbing the duffle bag, Father Raymond states, "Let's go."

The three of us follow Father out the door and into the crowded street. We briskly scramble through the throng of humanity. My shirt sticks to my back as beads of sweat pour down the sides of my face. My adrenaline pumps. None of us talks. Three green military buses wait at the pick-up point. Two South Vietnamese soldiers, armed with M-16's, stand next to the door of each bus. Many people surround the vehicles. We wedge our way to an armed guard at the front door of one of the buses. Father Raymond speaks in Vietnamese to the soldier.

Completing his discussion, Father states, "We can board now. As soon as this one fills up, we'll be on our way to the DAO complex. They aren't going to waste any time. Evacuation choppers are already leaving the compound."

Sister Joan and I go to the middle of the bus and plop down on the grey leather seats. Quickly, the bus is full of Americans and Vietnamese civilians. The windows are all open to let the hot humid air circulate through the inside. The sight outside the bus is pure pandemonium. A line of people waits to board. Refugees beat on the bus, begging to get in. Cascades of artillery shriek overhead. Explosions discharge close to us.

The bus begins moving at a slow pace through the inundation of refugees, animals, bicycles, and other vehicles. People continue banging on the side of the bus. Women, with desperation in their eyes, hold up babies, and yell, "You take. You take!"

"Ka Boom!"

The thud of a mortar hits a building nearby. The bus shakes. People on the street scream and scatter. Black smoke fills the air above the building. Sister Joan and I keep our heads below the window. I'm shaking. Our bus moves slowly.

"Rat-tat-tat!"

Small arms fire reigns all around us. Gradually I look up and peek out of the window. No more refugees hit the side of the bus. Young adults and children loot the stores we pass, carrying a myriad of items as they run in all directions. Mangled bodies and injured civilians lie on the street in front of the ravaged buildings. Women with children run, trying to find shelter in any roof covered building or crevice between structures. Alarms and sirens blast throughout Saigon.

"Keep your head down," I yell to Sister Joan. "This

place is a powder keg. The VC and NVA must be right on the outskirts of town. I just hope to hell we can get out of here!"

Sister Joan says nothing. Her tightened jaw and straight-ahead stare reveal her feelings about leaving.

The next hour seems like an eternity, with mass confusion, and military armaments screaming through the air overhead. I think back to those days in 1970 when I wondered if I would make it out alive.

> The sounds of the mortars thumping into the ground all around terrified us. The foxhole would only protect us if there was not a direct hit. We were helpless, praying that this would not be the last day of our lives. It was a terrible feeling. Artillery shells rocketed overhead. Small arms and machine gun fire was ever present. It was bedlam. It was like being in the middle of the ocean without a life jacket, trying to survive by treading water.

The bus jerks to a stop at a roadblock. But, the South Vietnamese soldiers quickly let us through. They are totally distracted by the incoming artillery and gunfire.

"Rat-tat-tat!" "Rat-tat-tat!"

Machine gun fire rips through the air.

An American in the back of our bus yells, "They're hit. The bus behind us is stopped. Stop this vehicle!"

Our bus halts with a jolt. People from the damaged vehicle start boarding. Many breathe heavily, are sweating, and have looks of fear in their eyes. The aisles are now full.

"What happened," I ask a person standing next to me.

He nervously replies, "Some machine gun fire hit the back of our bus and also blew out a tire. I think we got caught in the cross fire of some skirmish between the VC and the ARVN."

Damn, I hope we survive this mess!

Our crowded bus proceeds. Shortly thereafter, we arrive at the Defense Attaché Office near the airport.

Father Raymond, who is sitting across from the driver, yells back to us, "Everyone out. There are helicopters waiting. Follow the directions of the guards outside."

Getting off the bus, I look around and see hundreds of people waiting in various lines. The sounds of chopper blades fill the sweltering air. Jets fly overhead. Military vehicles move in various directions. Sirens blare, as two ambulances move toward a helicopter.

A Marine signals to us, and shouts, "Twelve of you. Hurry over to that helicopter." He points to a camouflaged H-34 parked about a hundred yards away. Sister Joan, Father Raymond and I, along with nine others, run toward the aircraft.

A crew chief waits for us as we approach. "Get on and hold tight. We're not going to be on the ground much longer!" he screams above the noise of the chopper engine.

After the last passenger jumps on to the helicopter, the crew chief climbs aboard and sits next to the door, holding firmly onto his 50-caliber machine gun. He gives a thumbs-up to the pilot, and the chopper blades accelerate. The plane shakes vigorously. As the sound of the engine gets louder, the helicopter rises off the ground and turns into the wind.

"Bang!" "Bang!" "Bang!" "Bang!"

Small arms tracers of green and red dash through the air near our chopper. The H-34 continues to rise through the gunfire. Slowly, the building below becomes smaller and smaller as we head out to the South China Sea toward one of the waiting U.S. aircraft carriers.

I lean over to Sister Joan, and speak directly into her ear. "We made it, Sister." She looks at me with a blank stare. Little rivers of tears flow down her soiled face, "Yes we did, but so many won't."

EPILOGUE

On April 29, 1975, The North Vietnamese Army of 150,000 to 200,000 troops surrounds Saigon. Artillery bombardment pounds the city. Tan Son Nhat Airport closes to further evacuation by Americans due to the barrage of explosions and debris on the runways. Helicopters from the USS Princeton, USS Denver and USS Iwo Jima in the South China Sea continue to rescue U.S. embassy officials and the last of the citizens from Saigon. On April 30, 1975, the last Huey chopper leaves from the rooftop of a downtown building. This marks the end of the Vietnam War.

American civilians and military personnel, along with tens of thousands of South Vietnamese associated with the Southern Vietnam regime, escape. This is arguably the largest helicopter evacuation in history. Hysterical crowds evacuate as U.S. Marines help Ambassador Graham Martin aboard a chopper to fly to safety in the South China Sea.

On April 30, 1975, NVA troops enter Saigon and take over the city. The Viet Cong raise their flag at Independence Palace. Approximately twenty-five hundred orphans have been flown out of South Vietnam on "Operation Babylift." Twenty-six flights, consisting of C-141's, C-130's, 747's, DC-10's, 707's and 727's carried the children to safety. These orphans had adoptive parents waiting for them in many cities in the U.S. Agencies matched wristbands attached to the children with adoptive parents, many of whom had spent months or even years going through the adoption process of interviews, adoption papers, and waiting.

Sister Joan Mc Kenny – after her return to the United States, worked with families of Amerasian children for many years. She then moved to Ohio, and worked with former military personnel with mental problems.

John Ellis – spent the four years following his return from Vietnam in social work in California. Then, he taught Sociology at a Junior College in California.

Sister Anne Marie – was sent to inter-city Chicago and worked with underprivileged children.

Sister Celeste – went to Los Angeles, and worked with the Christian Adoption Services organization. She worked with refugees and their families who were able to enter the United States after the war.

Sister Nguyen – was transferred to a hospital in Ohio, which is run by her order of nuns. She became the Chief of Nurses at the hospital.

Doctor Lockman – returned to his hometown in New York, and set up a private practice.

Gerry Ryan – continued his work for Christian Adoption Services in San Francisco as a social worker.

Captain Becket and **Major Danak** – made it back to the United States and both worked for commercial airlines.

Father Tran – disappeared after the North Vietnamese took over South Vietnam. He, along with other Catholic priests, was never heard from again. The Communist government closed the Catholic churches after the capture of Saigon.

Xuan Yen – was welcomed by her family in California. She got married and had two children. She became a schoolteacher.

An – the boy who couldn't walk, was adopted by a family with six children in Salt Lake City. He graduated from Brigham Young University and worked as social worker with the city.

Chi – was adopted by a childless couple in Minneapolis. She received her law degree from the University of Minnesota, and became a practicing attorney.

Trun – the young man with a missing foot, was taken in by a family in Portland. He finished college and became a high school teacher.

Ba – one of the boys left at the doorstep at Binh Trieu, found his adoptive family in San Jose, California. He married and worked as an electrician.

Binh – the little boy with the "Failure to Thrive" condition, died on the flight to America.

The remaining children from Binh Trieu (approximately three hundred and eighty) all made it to adoptive homes in the United States. Of all the children who were rescued, it was reported that over fifty percent were less than two years old.

At the end of the Vietnam War, thousands of South Vietnam soldiers and government employees were sent to "re-education camps". Basically, these were prison encampments. Some died at these sites. Many were tortured and abused. Those who were released, after approximately one to three years, were allowed to have only certain menial jobs in South Vietnam.

The Amerasians left behind were treated very poorly by the North Vietnamese government. Many of them became "street people." They were considered outcasts by both the North Vietnamese and the South Vietnamese.

Finally, a quote by the Philosopher George Santayana is in order: "Those who cannot remember the past are condemned to repeat it."